BOHEMIA BEACH

by

Lucy Lakestone

VELVET PETAL PRESS

Florida

Published by Velvet Petal Press, Florida

Learn more about the author at LucyLakestone.com

Cover design and beach photography by Sky Diary Productions

Cover photo by Renzo79, iStock

Print ISBN: 978-0-9907836-3-3

First edition

"*W*ho is he?" I asked, trying to be heard above the party noise — the DJ, the chatter, the occasional drunken shriek echoing through the huge, high-ceilinged oceanfront condo. All I knew was that *he,* the mesmerizing man across the room, was our host and that I had never seen him before. Not that I'd seen anyone much, since I'd only been in town three days.

Damien, my ever cynical cousin Damien, in his tattoos, spiky black hair, eyeliner and mismatched earrings, laughed.

"He's the money," he said.

I didn't like my cousin's tone, especially when *he* — whoever *he* was — had completely captured my attention. Tall. Wavy, dark-honey hair growing just a bit past his ears. Strong jaw and sensuous lips. A faraway look in steel-gray eyes, aloof, scanning the crowd. He had to be more than what Damien implied.

I matched his mocking tone. "If he's the money, what are we? The moochers?"

"Oh, Sloane. Don't be such a country mouse. *We're* what

makes him interesting. We're the party orbiting around his dull axis. We're the art scene, baby."

Damien was already drifting, my one acquaintance from the art scene, having spied a choice young lad loitering by the sliding doors.

"You'll be OK, won't you?" he asked.

"Fine," I said. My cousin was getting on my nerves anyway. I was here to meet people. To get into the scene. I was nervous, but Damien, a multimedia artist, was such a big personality that I'd never meet anyone cowering in his shadow. And I was through cowering in shadows, always the girl on the edge of the party. It's why I'd moved here, to this small coastal city, to defy expectations, to learn my craft, to prove my worth as an artist, to take a risk on myself. On my future. I had clay under my fingernails and a restless desire in my heart. I wanted more of a life than I'd had in my quiet town in my northern landlocked state.

But I had to laugh at Damien's "country mouse" reference. Maybe I was one, but this wasn't exactly Metropolis. Still, it was the coast, in Florida, which for me was practically another country, with its palm trees, surfer boys and exotic accents. The coast was the edge where land and sea and imagination met. And I was on the edge, too, of seeing whether I could make a living out of my passion. I had enough money to fund six months of pure artistic devotion, and then I'd see. I was ready for adventure. Wasn't I?

As Damien headed for his quarry, I wondered where to dive in first. I delayed my decision by scanning *him*. Jeans, worn to sky blue, comfortable but clinging, suggesting ideas I shouldn't think about in public. A black leather belt. A white button-up shirt, loose at the neck, rolled up at the sleeves over strong arms. Casually elegant. My gaze slid up his body to his face to find his eyes drilling into mine.

Oh, fuck. Caught. And his eyes lit up, spectral, arresting, making me feel he knew exactly what I'd been thinking.

He started to walk toward me.

My bravery was gone. I was frozen to the spot. And, I realized with horror, Damien hadn't told me the man's name.

I looked around for an escape and didn't find one, just a glimpse of myself in an ultra-modern reflective vase on a nearby table that showed me distorted and strange, my head shrunken, my long, reddish-brown hair gone from straight to round, my blue-green eyes crazed, my lipstick-stained mouth twisted and red. A great moment for my self-esteem. I snapped my head back around, and he was halfway across the room, at least until a buxom blonde in a black miniskirt and see-through mesh shirt, sparkly black bra glinting underneath, stumbled drunkenly into him and started talking in his ear. He looked annoyed. And at the moment he looked at her, I took the opportunity to slip behind a pillar and make a beeline for the kitchen.

Two female caterers in black beanies and chef jackets were hogging the vast granite island, fixing up fresh trays to bring out to the crowd. To the moochers, I joked to myself. Our host must like the moochers, must find some pleasure in them, or he wouldn't spend so much on parties like this, right?

I grabbed a bacon-wrapped scallop and skulked in a corner beside a ridiculously large paneled refrigerator, next to a sleek, walk-in pantry of some kind with heavy, dark-wood doors. I'd seen one of the servers come out of there with wine, so I assumed there was at least a wine rack in there. And probably room for me. I could slip in there for a minute and collect my thoughts before beginning my campaign of social conquests.

The door made a tiny suction sound as I opened it and closed it behind me, and I found myself in much more than a pantry. It was a modest space, with a lower ceiling than in the main living area, but it filled my senses: windowless, unnaturally cool, lined with floor-to-ceiling wine racks in rich, dark wood. An antique chandelier and recessed lighting created subtle, glimmering reflections in the glass bottles. The walls were broken up by marble countertops and niches that displayed framed wine labels. There were a couple of ornate silver ice buckets on the counters, along with wine tools and decanters. Another niche held shallow shelves filled with delicate, clear glasses of varying shapes. In one corner rested a cello, subtly lit, a warm, russet glow under its varnish.

There was just enough room on the back wall for a small fireplace. Facing it was a plush red couch with a curvy, dark-wood coffee table in front of it. And above the wooden mantel was a colorful, modern painting of a cluster of wine bottles and, oddly, a pair of red gloves. The picture reminded me of stained glass. I couldn't take my eyes off it, off the lines of it, the brush strokes that made it seem fragmented even while the colors shimmered as one.

"Beautiful," I murmured to myself, just as I heard the door close behind me.

"That's just what I thought," came the resonant voice as I whirled to face the intruder.

Not an intruder. *Him.* If anyone was intruding, it was me.

"I — I didn't mean to —"

"I'm happy you appreciate it," he said, coming closer. Strangely, I felt no fear. My desire to flee had evaporated. I just wanted to hear him say something else. His voice, on the verge of deep, had a gentle trace of Southern.

I searched in vain for a response. "Some collection," I finally said. His eyes had struck me dumb. The stupid kind of dumb.

"You should see the library."

"You have as many books as you have bottles?"

"This is just the lot I like to keep on hand for drinking," he said, "and a few of the collectibles. The rest is in storage."

"You put your wine in storage?"

He laughed. "Not like one of those garages you rent when you don't have an attic. It's climate-controlled. Like this. Are you cold?"

I realized I was shivering. My thin, sleeveless green dress wasn't meant for climate-controlled wine dens. And I was already feeling drunk, but not from alcohol. *Hick seduced by suave wine collector,* the headline would read. But isn't that why I came to this place? To be seduced by it?

I smiled up at him. "I'm fine."

He almost imperceptibly scanned me, his gaze lingering for a microsecond where my chilled-to-attention breasts strained against the dress, and I felt the heat of his scrutiny curb my shivers.

"What's your name?" he asked. "I haven't seen you before."

"Sloane," I said. "Sloane Abbey."

I waited, hoping he would tell me his, but he only smiled. Oh. I hadn't seen him smile before. It was like watching the sun rise, but he held some of it behind the clouds, behind that reserve he so strongly projected.

"Sloane," he repeated. "Let me guess." He scanned me again, more obviously this time, and I felt a flush of warmth go through me. "You don't strike me as a painter. Musician? No — you're a poet. Right?"

It was my turn to laugh. "I haven't written poetry since high school, to the relief of pretty much everyone," I said. "Mostly, I'm a potter. A ceramic artist, if I'm trying to make it sound good."

"Hands in wet clay. Sexy," he joked.

"Not like that movie," I said, though I liked the way he said *sexy*. "That's always the first thing people think of. Ruining a pot I'm throwing would definitely be a turn-off."

"A crime against art," he said, humor in his tone. "Let me see." He gently grasped one of my hands, lightly stroking the palm, turning it over to see my short nails and the specks of clay I hadn't quite worked out. I watched his face and let the feel of his hand work its way into my skin. "I see nothing here that wet clay would improve," he said, finally lifting my hand to his lips and kissing it with sweet deliberation.

A sigh escaped me, and again I felt foolish. Any righteous annoyance I might have had melted into a pool of lust.

He released me and looked into my eyes, and I felt that pull again. "And how did you stumble into my private retreat? Or, should I ask, how could I be so lucky?"

Running away from you, I thought.

"I wanted to see the wine," I said. "Well, not just that. I — needed to escape the party."

"I often need to escape the party." A shadow crossed his face. "I suppose they've become a habit I can't break."

"But you're the host, aren't you?"

He smiled. "Yes, but that doesn't mean the guests want me here."

"I can't believe that."

"You're kind," he said drily. "Did you just move to Bohemia Beach?"

"Yes. I start classes at the art school next week. I wanted to get a fresh start, really work on my art."

He looked thoughtful. "Running away from something?"

"Running *to* something, I hope," I said, relaxing into the conversation.

There was a gleam in his eye. "I can't wait to find out what."

"Me either." I felt a new rush of heat. "I — I mean, I want to focus on my work. I've been out of college for two years, working two jobs. I just needed the time to really concentrate on art. To see where it takes me."

"And you chose this place," he said. "I think we have something in common."

I laughed out loud. "Sorry," I said, looking around, "but I don't see how that's possible."

He scooped up my hand again, took a step closer, and I was lost in those gray eyes.

"Maybe I'll surprise you," he said softly, kissing my palm, somehow a much more intimate gesture than kissing the back of my hand. I swallowed hard as he let go and looked into my eyes.

"I hope I see you again soon, Sloane Abbey," he said. He turned toward the door. "Grab any bottle you like. If you want to talk to me about it, or about anything, come find me." He paused in the doorway and looked back with just a hint of a smile, a smile that promised more. "Ask for Alex."

I AWOKE FEELING LIKE A FAILURE. For one, I'd lost my grasp of a beautiful dream in which I was lying on a beach, feeling Alex's hands run lightly over my skin, brushing fine sand into the wind. I woke just as he pulled down the strap of my bikini, and the sweet idyll fled from me, elusive and taunting.

Second, the real source of my sense of failure: I'd fled the party last night, fled the crowd, fled Alex, deflating my plan to jump into the social scene of this tightly closed art community.

I'd had so few friends at home in Ohio. I was always working. I had a rarely seen roommate who practically lived with her boyfriend, and I had a family that ignored me.

I'd been friendly with the others at the pottery co-op, but I was there by special arrangement, paying a half-fee in exchange for cleaning up the place every day. The others never treated me as one of them. There had been a couple of serious potters, several rich dilettantes and a smattering of hobbyists who never lasted more than three months. And me, throwing pots late into the night, monitoring the kilns until the wee hours, surviving on little sleep and less money.

I'd remembered Bohemia Beach fondly from trips my family made here when I was a girl, visiting my aunt and uncle. I'd slaved and saved to come here. I knew I might have to return to the starving artist life soon enough, but for six months, I had enough to survive, even to enjoy this potential paradise.

I was going to have fun, damn it. Learn a lot. And make wonderful, beautiful things.

But last night, I'd come up against myself, my own worst enemy. And now I had to admit I was unlikely to transform from an introvert into an extrovert overnight.

I groaned, turned over and surrendered to the brilliant light of an early autumn Florida morning. It poured in through a skylight in the high ceiling, on the other side of the room, softened by the shade of oaks above. And it sliced through the thin gaps in the Venetian blinds that covered the long, narrow windows at the front and back of my new space.

The light cast bright white stripes across my late grandma's quilt, a nautical design with navy-blue compass roses arrayed across a creamy background. The quilt covered my thrift-shop double bed with its weathered dark-wood posts and made it comforting, familiar. Surrounding the bed were a big, slightly used comfy chair in navy blue, a couple of dressers and an antique wardrobe my aunt and uncle had given me, since there were no closets in this place.

I wanted to make a screen to separate the sleeping and dressing space from the rest of the room. This studio was pleasant enough, but it was just one room and a bathroom that also housed a small up-and-down laundry unit. A screen would separate me from the shabby couch, the three bookcases, my clay play area and the minuscule kitchenette. Not to mention the handful of boxes I still hadn't unpacked.

The apartment occupied a former carriage house. It stood behind one of the old mansions in Bohemia, the city across the lagoon from Bohemia Beach.

The geography here was pretty easy to learn. If you went west of town, you hit the swamp and, eventually, Mickey Mouse. If you went east, you hit the lagoon — what most locals called the river — and then sister town Bohemia Beach. If you went north, you'd be back where I came from in a day or two, the land of ice and snow and dismal expectations. And if you went south far enough, you hit Miami and the tropical escape of the Keys.

I dearly hoped I could afford a trip to the Keys before I headed back north. *If* I headed back north, I corrected myself. Maybe I'd stay, even if I failed, though it was too soon to talk about giving up on my dream.

Ah, the dream. And Alex. Why had I run? Why hadn't I grabbed a wine bottle and taken it to him and asked to see his library? What was I afraid of? There was no one here to judge me. I was free.

But it's not like I needed any distractions. Not yet. It was Saturday. I had two days to get my space in order, and Monday I would throw myself into my classes and my work. Today — maybe today I would make that screen. Make this strange and exotic place a home.

I rolled out of bed in my sky-blue sleep shirt and tested the feel of the wood floor under my feet. It was nicer than the cold, hard tile I'd seen in some of the places I'd looked at, but it still could use a warm-up. Maybe I could get a small rug, too. I wasn't even sure where to shop for such things yet, but I'd noticed some cute stores and thrift shops around the art school in downtown Bohemia. And Damien had said something about a street fair happening there today.

I smiled. I could hear birds singing and the distant sound of a train. A shower and a yogurt and I'd be out the door.

On which there came a knock.

"Shit," I murmured. It might be Damien. I'd kind of ditched him last night, but he'd looked as if he wasn't going to have any trouble getting a ride home. Regardless, I wasn't answering the door in just my sleep shirt, which was loose and slipping off one shoulder or another. I found a pair of slightly worn jeans in the pile on the chair next to the bed and hastily pulled them on before padding across the floor in my bare feet. There was another knock just as I reached the door.

"Patience is a virtue," I said as I opened it.

But it was not Damien. On the doorstep was Alex, all that morning sun lighting up his dark blond hair like spun gold.

I immediately felt that magnetism again, that deep and irrational attraction I'd felt last night. He looked me over without the subtlety he'd used in his wine room, a smile playing around his mouth.

"Sleeping in?" Alex asked. "After leaving the party so early?"

It took me a few stunned seconds to realize a response was required. "It's Saturday. Isn't it a little early for *you*? A massive party like yours usually requires a decent period of recovery."

"It's already 10 a.m., and I'm not that decent. Besides, I never get drunk at my own parties. I'm going to take you to brunch, and then I'm going to show you around," Alex stated without any awareness that I might find his agenda objectionable.

I was pleased, and then annoyed that I was pleased. "I already have plans."

"Yes, you do. You're coming to the art fair with me."

"I —" Damn it. I couldn't object to the plan I already had. "I'm not ready."

"I'll wait. This is a charming place. The old Thomason mansion, right?" He nodded back over his shoulder at the main house, with its gingerbread and multiple porches and Victorian charm, the river sparkling across the road beyond it.

"A couple of doctors live there now. They rented this to me."

"I know," said Alex. "I'm on the museum board with Mrs. Doctor."

I chortled. "That's Dr. Doctor to you."

"Of course. Forgive me. She was the third person in the chain of phone calls that led me to you this morning."

"*Really*. How industrious."

While Alex had the acumen of a stalker and the looks of a demigod, I decided, he also had a geeky manner that suggested that, at heart, he was sincere. And he looked kind of delicious in a pair of worn-in jeans and a simple black T-shirt that clung to him nicely.

"Will you come?" he asked. At least this time, it was a question.

"OK," I said sternly. "But you'll have to wait outside. I don't have a parlor."

"So I see," he said, scanning the space behind me. "You'll find me colluding with the squirrels. Don't rush."

He turned back toward the shady yard and the gravel drive, where his gleaming black Mustang convertible sat next to my slightly banged-up silver Honda Civic. I closed the door and proceeded to rush like hell.

In thirteen minutes I'd showered, given my mop of hair a two-minute blowout, and put on my dark purple tights, a short purple and black tunic dress, teardrop purple glass earrings and black boots. A dab of dark red lipstick, and I was set. If I wasn't a wilting wallflower, at least I was me: almost fashionable, funky me. I grabbed my black leather bag and headed out the door.

Alex was leaning against his car, engrossed in a book. At least, I think it was a book, on an e-reader wrapped in a slim, black leather cover. He looked up as I approached and stared, his gray eyes widening. I smiled awkwardly, wondering if I was wearing too much purple. And then he smiled, tossed the reader into the front seat, walked up to me and kissed me softly on the cheek.

I let out a tiny breath and snagged his gaze, feeling the warmth of his lips linger on my skin. From hand to palm to cheek — insignificant little kisses, breathtaking kisses. I couldn't remember the last time I'd felt a physical attraction this intense. And then I did remember. Never.

"You look nice," Alex said, a catch in his voice. I knew he felt it, too.

"Thanks," I said, trying to shake it off, walking around him toward his car. "So where's brunch?"

"Oh," he said, his voice normal again. "In the trunk. We're going to the river."

"We're already at the river, practically."

"Not like this," he said. "Get in."

ALEX DROVE the convertible down the river road, winding under wizened oaks and palm trees, past late-19th-century houses much like the one I lived behind. This wasn't the Florida most people saw. It was a small pocket of history amid the new developments and trailer parks and strip malls, and it was lovely.

It was also warm. Up north, they'd be getting those clear, cool October days that made you get out your sweaters.

Here, the breezy ride had me basking in just the right, luxurious temperature, as the sun danced through the trees and heated my face and arms.

I glanced over at Alex. His expression was serene but far away.

"What are you thinking about?" I asked.

He looked at me as if he'd forgotten I was there, and then he smiled. "Sorry. I get wrapped up in my thoughts sometimes. The house where I grew up is near here. It brings me back."

"I'd love to see it," I said, my curiosity strong. I knew virtually nothing about him, except what I'd observed in his condo.

"It just so happens you will," he said, swiftly navigating an S-curve that sloped gently upward — a rare hill in this part of the world. The riverbank here extended several feet above the water. The houses shifted to the river side of the road, instead of the west side, so they overlooked the water directly.

We were passing a row of small houses and cottages, I guessed from the 1950s and '60s. They were built on generous lots, thick with vegetation, that overlooked the water. In the middle of them, a huge, out-of-proportion mansion was under construction, well on its way to completion. On another lot, fringed by orange fencing and warning signs, a cottage lay in a pile of debris. Its presumed destroyer, a bright yellow bulldozer, was still parked next to it.

"What a mess," I murmured.

"What a shame," Alex said darkly. "I hate that these places have become tear-downs. It's like I'm losing my childhood."

A moment later, he pulled into a driveway two lots down from the destruction site. The name on the old black mailbox said "ALWEND."

"This was yours?" I asked as he drove into the tropical jungle and pulled up to a 1960s-sleek mid-century home.

"Still is." He turned off the car and sat for a moment, looking it over as if it was his first time there, too.

So his full name was Alex Alwend. And he owned his childhood home. Had his parents retired somewhere else? Or were they gone? I was suddenly disturbed by how little I knew about him, how happy and heedless I'd been when I'd agreed to accompany him this morning. I made a vow to Google the hell out of him later.

The house was modest, white with turquoise trim. Its multi-level roofs were set at rakish angles, and the windows were tall and narrow. Palms, red and pink hibiscus and fuchsia bougainvillea surrounded it, along with a number of colorful plants I didn't recognize. Maybe I'd Google those, too.

"Is this where we're eating?" I asked.

"You'll see," he said, climbing out. "Come on." He went to the trunk of the car and lifted out a large cooler. "Can you get the bucket?"

"Sure," I said, grabbing the silver ice bucket, closing the trunk and following him. I licked my lips in anticipation. I was getting thirsty. Especially if champagne was involved.

Alex opened the front door with a key, and I followed him in.

"Wow," I said. "It's like a time capsule."

The interior could have come straight out of the 1960s, with its minimalist, space-age furniture. A low white couch in the middle of the room faced the front windows. In front of it was a wooden coffee table with angled legs, and under the windows was a matching credenza topped with framed photos and a retro lamp. Another lamp sprouted from the floor and swooped over the couch with an arching pole that ended in a large, white globe light. At the end of the room to my right, near a white-brick wall, was a vintage orange fireplace. Sitting in a square of dark river rocks, it was a metal, standalone thing that looked like a space capsule, with a chimney pipe extending straight up to the high, peaked ceiling.

Beyond, a few broad steps led to a lower level, where a '60s-modern dining room and glass sliding doors overlooked a deck and the river. That's where Alex headed, while I went in search of ice.

The fridge was the only modern thing in the kitchen, a gleaming, stainless-steel machine. I filled the bucket from the sluggish ice dispenser while marveling at the sea-foam-green cabinets, checkerboard floor and a gold pull-down light that hovered over the dinette like a miniature UFO.

"The cabinets may be a bit much," Alex said behind me.

I whirled, startled out of my imaginings. "It's pretty groovy."

He laughed. "My grandparents' taste. My mom's parents. She loved it and kept it that way, and after she and my dad were gone, I couldn't bear to change it. Except for the fridge. I don't use this place much, but it's nice to have working appliances."

Alex was a puzzle. He lived in a rich man's condo but kept a down-at-heel, although definitely cool, old house that he didn't use. And the way he said *gone* made me think his parents hadn't just left.

"Tell me about your parents," I said.

His face was impassive. "Food first."

I followed him out the other kitchen door and through the dining room to the sliding doors and the pretty wooden deck. It was large, dotted with pots filled with flowering plants and sheltered by a softly swaying colony of palms and oaks. Lounge chairs offered a spectacular view of the river.

Shaded by the trees was a round table he'd already set up with a light-blue-checked tablecloth, dishes, glasses and utensils. I was impressed with his thoughtfulness. And I had an immediate sense of peace here, of escape from the everyday world. It was Alex's world, and it was enchanting.

A wooden staircase led the rest of the way down the riverbank to a well-maintained dock and open boathouse, the water winking beyond it. I was almost surprised there wasn't a sailboat or some kind of massive vessel. There was only a small center-console boat that looked like it could be used for fishing, along with a couple of kayaks.

"The yacht's in the shop," he deadpanned, and I looked over to see him smiling.

"What, no cruise ship?"

"A boat is a hole in the water into which you throw money, so I keep it small. I don't have *that* much."

"Well, that's a relief," I said. "I really prefer to date poor artists."

Whoops. I hadn't meant to call this a date.

His smile just got bigger. "I'm happy to be the exception," he said. "Sit down. Relax. I just brought a few things."

Alex's idea of a few things was enough to feed a small army with wide and possibly demented tastes. He sat next to me, pulled the already cold champagne out of the cooler and popped it into the ice bucket on the table, a towel around its neck. I picked up the bottle, noting the label but having no idea what it was — Krug Brut Grand Cuvee — and began the process of removing the golden foil as he loaded the table with food. From the cooler, he extracted an array of cheeses and a cutting board, a baguette, cinnamon pecan rolls on a small tray, a crab salad, a fruit salad, a pair of roasted quail, a dozen deviled eggs ("not fancy, but the Silver Palm Deli's are so addictive," he explained), and a platter of prettily cut and arrayed sushi rolls.

"Something for everyone," I said, unwinding the wire of

the thing that held the cork in place. "In fact, I think there's enough for anyone you'd care to invite."

"Only you," he said. "I wasn't sure what you'd like, so I bought a bit of everything."

"A bit," I said drily. "What do you call this?" I held up the wired metal cap, figuring he would know.

"The muselet."

"I'll try to remember that." I wrapped the towel around the top of the bottle and pulled on the cork with difficulty as he watched, amused. Finally, it gave with a *pop!*

Alex sighed. "One of the best sounds in the world."

I echoed his smile and filled the glasses before returning the bottle to its icy bath. "I suppose you should educate me about the champagne, too."

He held up his glass to the light, so the bubbles sparkled amid blue and green reflections, sky and jungle and sun. His eyes were dreamy. "Three champagne grapes and fifty wines of worthy vintages, complex, creamy, perfect."

"Intimidating," I said, holding up my glass, too.

"That's just it. It's easy." He looked me in the eye and took a deep sip.

I did the same. And it *was* easy. Refreshing. As light as his eyes, as deep as the sea.

"You are so right," I said, savoring the bubbles and taste. "Is it just as good with sushi?"

"Better."

We ate with relish, more relaxed with each other now. The food was all excellent, obtained from the deli he mentioned, its sister bakery and his favorite sushi bar downtown, whose owners hadn't been thrilled to be called in early until, according to Alex, he'd made it worth their while.

"I could have cooked, but then I would've had to wait until dinner to track you down," he said, polishing off a quail.

I swallowed the last of my second deviled egg. He was right. They were addictive.

"I'm glad you didn't wait," I said. "I'd probably be eating a sad little bagel right now."

"I know where to get great bagels, too."

I laughed. "Maybe if we ever have breakfast."

"I do hope we do," he said, his tone teasing, suggestive.

I felt a warmth rush through me, more heat than could be explained by the sun or the champagne. "So you grew up here?"

A shadow flitted across his features.

"Yes," he said. "Nice, right? When my grandparents bought the land, it went for a song. Not anymore. They left it to my mom. My parents lived here for a while with my grandmother before she died. I barely remember my grandfather; I was very young when he passed."

I took another sip of the champagne, feeling slightly buzzed and bold enough to ask what I really wanted to know.

"And your parents?" I inquired softly.

Alex turned away from me and looked toward the water. His wavy, golden-brown hair lifted lightly in the breeze. He didn't move as he spoke.

"They died in a car crash when I was nineteen, the spring of my first year in college. They'd just landed in Paris. They'd never been out of the country. Mom had always wanted to go."

Oh, no. "I'm so sorry."

"That was eight years ago. I'm — OK now," he said. "I'll never really be over it, but I'm OK."

"And they left you this house."

"Well, that's where the story gets interesting," he said, turning back to me. "They left me a lot more than this house."

"What do you mean?"

"You ever see one of those news stories about an old guy who lives in a shabby little house with piles of newspapers and eighteen cats and a freezer full of frozen dinners, and it turns out he was a millionaire from scrimping and saving his entire life?"

"That was your *parents?*"

"Almost. I mean, they had good jobs. He was an attorney. She was an English teacher. But they didn't make that much money. From what I could gather from their papers and their lawyer, they'd played the lottery on a whim when I was in the eighth grade and won — well, let's just say it was enough to make their wildest dreams come true."

"And you never knew?" I shook my head. "You had no idea?"

"They didn't spend it, at least not so anyone would notice," Alex said. "And they cashed the ticket through the law firm. There was no publicity. Nobody was knocking on our door asking for donations. I had no clue. When I thought about it, I recalled we had a few more improvements around the house, really just fixing stuff, nothing spectacular. As you can see, they weren't much for redecorating." His small smile made me feel better about my question. "They joked some-times, 'When we win the lottery —' And every time, they acted like that was about the funniest thing either of them had ever said. I guess it was."

"Why didn't they travel when they won? Or, I don't know, buy you a Camaro or something?"

A wistful expression crossed his face. "I think they wanted

me to have a normal childhood. A normal life. And then I guess it just became a habit. It must have been like a happy secret they had, something that made them feel secure, knowing it was there if they needed it. And they probably thought they'd have a long life and plenty of time to tell me about it. The irony is, when they finally decided to spend a little money on their dream trip..."

"Oh, God, I shouldn't have asked," I said, feeling bad again. "I'm so sorry."

"It's OK." Alex reached over and took my hand. "They were good people. I want to talk about them, remember them. They believed in hard work, and that's what they did. The other irony is that now I hardly do any work at all. I've made good investments. I have a nice place, but mostly, I spend conservatively — except on wine." He nodded at the bottle. "And I pursue my own small dreams and try to figure out what it all means."

I looked down at where his hand held mine. I used both my hands to grasp his with a reassuring squeeze and looked up at him.

"Dreams are good," I said. "You know mine. What's yours?"

"Oh, I write. Only I'm blocked. Or maybe I'm just bad." He mocked himself with his laugh. "I don't have that connection to other people that I think writers need. I have parties. I work in the community. But I feel set apart from society, somehow. I don't have enough source material. I was always into writing and the arts in school, never knowing I'd have the means to pursue the creative life full time. But I write hollow poetry. I write stories that go nowhere. I end up reading a lot more than I write. Maybe I need a muse."

He gave me a long, searching look, his gray eyes lighter

now, less sad. I was glad. But I felt a little overwhelmed with all this information.

"I'm a potter, remember?" I released his hands and sipped my champagne. "I'm not a muse. I could use one, too. Though I think I need a lesser muse than might be required by a writer or painter. My work is more earthly."

He grinned, and the tension dissolved. "Earthly or earthy?"

"Both," I said.

"Writing can be earthy. Dirty, even," he teased.

"Now you're getting silly."

"That's my problem. My writing needs gravitas. Substance. Something I can't get from my life."

"You mean, your life filled with tragedy?"

"I can't write about that," he said, looking back toward the water. "I just can't."

I let the quiet day soothe the eddies of emotion between us. I heard the distant whine of a boat engine and smelled the brackish scent of the river mixed with the fresh breeze as it wafted through the plants all around us.

"That was delicious," I said. "Thank you for brunch."

He turned back to me, his gaze soft and intense. "Thank you, Sloane." Then he smiled. "Hey, we have an art fair to go to, don't we?"

"Sure do. Maybe I'll get some ideas. I want to make a divider for my room, a screen."

"Oh, good, a mission. That makes two I have today." And there was that flirtatious tone again as he gave me what I could only describe as a lascivious glance. One that I didn't mind at all. What a crazy conversation this had been.

From there, our chatter was light and friendly as we cleaned up the meal and stowed the leftovers in the refrigerator. He led me back to the convertible. The sun sprinkled us with dappled light under the trees.

I paused and took a deep breath of the fresh air. A second later, he swept me against the car and pressed himself against me. Before I could even think, his mouth was on mine, heated and hungry. I didn't have time to resist. I didn't want to. I felt his lean, muscled form against me and slipped my arms around his waist, opening my mouth to his, feeling a rush of response in my lips, my body, between my legs. He tasted like champagne and smelled like the wind. He released me almost as fast as he'd kissed me and opened the door. With my head spinning, I dropped into the seat. He closed my door with a smoky stare.

And then we were rolling toward downtown, a satellite radio rock station cranked up on the stereo, toward an afternoon that seemed electric with uncertainty. With possibility.

"I THINK that's the third booth we've seen with paintings of palm trees," Alex said as we strolled down the crowded, sunny street lined with square, white canopies, each an outpost for an artist.

"Fifth," I said. "Some of them are good."

"I knew you were kind the moment I saw you," he quipped as we stepped into a booth filled with drawings of cartoonish women wearing bikinis made from beer bottle caps.

"Now *this* is art," I whispered.

"Now you have a standard to live up to," he said, matching my playful tone. We moved on, his hand lightly touching the small of my back. He'd been touching me all day, subtle touches that could have been interpreted as friendly if not for the erotic charge that passed between us each time. I'd never felt anything like it.

"I have a lot to learn from the artists here," I said, trying not to lose myself in his fingers stroking my spine through my dress. "There's a lot of amazing pottery." And there was. I'd seen gorgeous raku work in glistening, metallic glazes and crackled white finishes; sculptural pieces with dazzling structures; and intricately carved and built pots that were half as tall as I was. There were fine, practical pieces, too, the kind I liked to make when I wasn't feeling daring. I loved the feel of a solid stoneware bowl in my hand, a smooth glaze of blues and greens and whites, warm under my fingers, fresh out of the kiln. I saw a lot of great technique here. I knew I had a lot more to learn.

The Bohemia arts district was an extension of a downtown centered around a cluster of medium-rise office buildings. The district wasn't large, but it was charming, with restaurants and antique shops all bustling amid the fair. A band played country music on a stage down the street. Hand in hand with their parents, children walked by, grinning behind fresh face paint that turned them into kittens and tigers and butterfly princesses.

At one end of the main street, anchoring the fair, the three-story Bohemia School of Art and Design filled a city block and spilled over into buildings beyond. In front of the school's large gallery windows, where pictures and pots and sculptures caught the eyes of passersby, a roomy demonstration tent was filled with kids wanting to get their hands into paint and pastels and clay. I remembered that exhilaration, the first time I'd made something at an event like this, and how much I'd wanted to do more.

Among the demonstrators, a tall young man with a shock of unruly brown curls was throwing a towering, slender pot with amazing dexterity, stretching its walls and shaping its narrow neck into a graceful vase. Three children were gathered around him, watching him as if he were a magician, and he smiled and chatted with them as he worked. His hands were huge, I noticed, and that probably helped. He must have felt me watching him; he looked up and gave me a friendly nod. I wondered if I'd see him in the studio.

I looked around for signs of Montrose King, the legendary potter-in-residence who would be teaching one of my classes, but I didn't see anyone who looked like his web photo. I'd be facing his intimidating reputation soon enough. The enormity of what I was about to do filled me with momentary anxiety, and I let out a long breath.

"Hot?" Alex asked. "Want a lemonade?"

"Um. Yeah, sure," I said. "Just feeling a little overwhelmed."

"Staring down the barrel of the future?"

"Something like that."

"That's good. It's good to have a future." But his voice seemed tinged with sadness.

The fresh-squeezed lemonade helped. We sipped on our straws and wandered back down the other side of the street, learning we had similar tastes in art, a similar feel for what was good and what was mechanical or contrived or weak.

We were both mesmerized by an artist's booth that displayed just three six-foot-square pieces. Each popped out of its frame in three dimensions, incorporating all sorts of found objects, antiques mostly, in tones of cream and brown and black, along with old sepia-tone portraits of families, in a juxtaposition that suggested all the bits and pieces that made up a life.

"They look grim," Alex noted of one family of five surrounded by seed packets, gardening implements, keys, a hollow-eyed doll's head and all the trivial objects that might be found in an early-twentieth-century junk drawer.

"Family life will do that to you," I replied.

"Not good?" Alex asked, turning his attention to me.

"Oh, no complaints of any merit," I said. "But let's just say my folks were much more interested in my two brothers' football careers than in the little art contests and exhibits that got me excited. It was all respectable enough, but sometimes I felt invisible."

"Where are your brothers now?"

"One got injured playing college ball and is coaching at our old high school back in Ohio. The other washed out of the pros and bought a car dealership. Both older than me."

"Sisters?"

"No," I said. "I always wanted a sister. I'm hoping I'll get some time to hang out with my cousin Calista, Damien's sister. You know him, right?"

"Everybody knows Damien," Alex said.

"You're right." I chuckled. "He makes it impossible not to know him. He's a force of nature."

"Is Calista an artist?"

"I think she's a photographer with the local paper. So — in a way. But I don't think she hangs out with the art crowd much. You'd know more than I would."

"I know nothing," Alex said, humor in his tone, as we worked our way back into the crowd, aiming to complete our circuit of the fair.

Just before the end of the street, I spotted a booth that brought me up short.

"Those are so cool," I said, marveling at the repurposed pieces there, wonderful shelves and tables and privacy screens made from bits of architectural salvage — doors, windows, shutters, posts. "Look at this one!" Five long, wooden panels with arched tops, inset with stained-glass windows, were hinged together to make a perfect folding screen.

"Why don't you get it?" Alex asked.

"I don't know," I said, blanching at the $1,200 price tag. "This one is great, too." Three eight-foot-tall, narrow accordion doors in a beautiful red lacquered finish were hinged together; at the top of each panel was a square carved with intricate geometries that one could see through, if one were at least six feet tall. It would also work well in my big space. Except . . . "Yikes," I said, looking at the tag: $1,500.

"Looks like it came straight from a Chinese restaurant," Alex joked.

"If it comes with dim sum, it might be worth the price."

"Hmm, the price," Alex said, as if he never had to worry about such a thing. Which he didn't. "Why don't you let me buy you one?"

"I couldn't," I said quickly. "I barely — it wouldn't be appropriate."

"Were you going to say you barely know me? You already know me a lot better than almost anyone."

I looked at him and tried to hide what I felt: wonder. A little pity. A desire to know him, really know him, understand him. If what he said was true, he was more alone than I thought. But why did he come to me?

"You're too generous," I said. "And it's not like it's Christmas or anything."

"Not yet." He smiled.

"Come on." I tugged at his arm, and he seemed happy to enfold mine in his. I stole one last, longing glance at the screens and settled into the pleasurable feeling of being close to this intriguing, magnetic man. I felt the melancholy of a perfect day nearing its end when he spoke.

"You never did see my library," he said.

I laughed. He didn't want the day to end, either. He was dangling the apple in front of me. I wanted to take a bite.

"They don't have etchings anymore, do they?" I asked.

"I don't," Alex said. "Just some very good paintings. Anyway, I don't think 'Come up and see my library' is really the most effective pickup line these days."

"Only for the right kind of girl," I said in a mischievous tone he couldn't fail to interpret.

Alex shot me a surprised glance, a spark of heat in his eyes. He pulled me closer as we walked. I felt the waning day accelerate toward a delicious and dangerous denouement as he quickened our pace toward the parking lot, his car and Bohemia Beach.

ALEX CALLED and ordered a pizza on the way to his place, and we found the delivery guy leaning on the buzzer as we drove up to the building, one of many in a long row of beachfront towers. Alex jumped out, paid him and got back into the car, handing me the awkwardly large pizza box as he drove around the corner and into the garage under the building.

"You don't mind, do you?" he asked. "Being guardian of the pizza?"

"You keep feeding me. How could I mind?"

He stopped the car, and we got out. "I'll take it now."

"No, you won't," I said, pushing my purse back on my shoulder so I could get a better grip on the box. "And next time, I'm buying."

"Oh," he said, wearing a droll smile as we walked toward the lobby door, "is there going to be a next time?"

His teasing rumpled my assurance. "If there's a next time, of course," I said faintly.

"Oh, I do hope there is," Alex said as he held the door for me and the giant pizza box.

I caught a whiff of garlic and sauce and his subtle scent as I walked past him and almost drowned in sensory overload. He joined me at the elevator and pressed the up button. Inside, he inserted his key in the panel so the elevator would climb to his floor: eight — at the top — the *whole* floor, like all the other condos in this building. He stared at the numbers as we rose, and I wondered if he felt any of the nervousness I was starting to feel.

The door slid open to the foyer, with its rustic wooden bench, antique hall tree and ultra-modern curvy mirror framed in anodized aluminum. An antique half-moon table in front of it held a contemporary glass sculpture whose twists and swirls echoed the mirror's curves. Like Alex, this space was a microcosm of contrasts: bold and shy, modern and old-fashioned, urbane and artless. I caught a glimpse of myself in the mirror — cheeks pink from the sun, my hair a tangle from the wind and the convertible.

"OK, you can take it now," I said, handing him the box as we walked through the double doors into that big living space I remembered from the party — only now, all traces of the party were gone (professional work, I had no doubt), and it looked even bigger, empty of all but furniture, a couple of potted palms and one very large television, with a few huge paintings adding color to the walls. "I'll join you in a minute."

Before he could answer, I ducked into the powder room, flipped on the light and closed the door. I closed my eyes and breathed deeply, wondering if this was what I had in mind when I decided to live my new, audacious artist's life. Was that just a cliché? Most of the artists I'd met were quiet folks, though the good ones always had a streak of creativity in everything they did, whether it was in the way they wore their clothes or arranged their garden or chose their friends.

I needed friends. I needed to embrace my creativity. And I needed to be just a little bit audacious.

I opened my eyes, used the toilet, washed my hands and face, then rummaged in my purse for a comb. I restored my hair to glossy calm. All that sun had brought out its red highlights. I found my lipstick and added a bit of color to my mouth, remembering Alex's heated kiss only hours ago. And meeting him less than twenty-four hours ago. The folks back in Ohio wouldn't approve of this behavior at all. I scrunched up my face and gave them a scowl. Exactly.

I found Alex in the kitchen, the pizza box open on the huge island. He'd already taken off his shoes and socks, and he was uncorking a bottle of red wine.

"Cabernet," he said at my curious glance, his eyes roaming to my hair, my lips, as I set my purse on one of the counters. I thought he suppressed a smile. "Not as extravagant as the champagne."

"That's OK. I have a feeling you know what you're doing."

"Some of the time," he said, that wry tone back in his

voice, as he pulled out the cork and picked up a small, funnel-shaped device. He poured the wine through it and into two glasses. It gurgled hilariously, and I grinned. "Excuse me," he joked, finishing the operation.

"And that does what?"

"Aerates the wine quickly. Enhances the flavor. Not everyone is convinced it works, but I like to believe in magic. And muses." He handed me a glass and lifted his. "To art," he said.

"To life," I answered, taking a sip. I had never had much in the way of good wine, but I immediately knew that this was wonderful. He must have seen it in my eyes.

"I know, right?" He smiled. "Want a slice?"

"Sure," I said.

He pulled a couple of square white plates from a cabinet and handed me one. It was obvious just one of the huge slices would be plenty, with tomatoes, fresh mozzarella, pesto and mushrooms. It barely fit on the plate, the pointy end threatening to sag away. I bit off the point as Alex watched with unnerving interest. He looked hungry.

"This way," he said, that catch in his voice again, and he led me into the living area and across the big floor to the sliding doors that led to the balcony. I could hear the ocean, a sound that the noise of the party had obliterated the night before. It was entrancing.

Alex left the doors open and led me to a square, glass-topped table. But I wasn't interested in food just yet. I put down the plate and the wine and walked to the railing, feeling as if I were on the deck of a ship, and looked out over the Atlantic.

The ocean was deep blue, and the sky above it held the last hints of sunset in a deepening twilight, though the sun set in the opposite direction. To the east, dark rays radiated from the horizon. The burst of wide spokes of deep orange and purple echoed the western sunset. It was an effect I'd seen rarely, and never over the sea.

"Oh, Alex," I murmured, all of my wonder at this beautiful place, his presence and his charmed watchtower rolled up inside my two little words.

He came up behind me and put his arms around me. "Do you like it?" he whispered, kissing my neck.

I felt a shiver pass through me. I rested my hands over his, on my belly, as I drank in the horizon and the feel of him against my back. Well below us, shallow waves rolled up onto the beach, where a lone walker quick-stepped north, elbows gyrating, her earbuds keeping her ignorant of the sounds of nature all around us.

"I like," I whispered back, turning to face him. I leaned closer, looking into his eyes, and he took my invitation.

This kiss was not like his earlier burst of fire. It was as cool as the ocean below, light at first, then more demanding, and I opened my mouth to his, letting his tongue touch mine. I moaned slightly as he pressed his body against me, wrapping his arms around my waist. I felt his need through his jeans. I felt my own in my core. I, too, needed this. I needed him. It had been so long. And I had been so timid.

I ran my fingers through that irresistible honey hair as I drank in his kiss and heard him make a noise of his own, male, ravenous. I felt dizzy, suddenly, and I pulled back, my breathing shallow and fast. I looked at him, wondering if I should stop this. If I could.

"I want you," he whispered in my ear, kissing me there, my neck again, my lips.

I had known him for one day. A day that felt like a lifetime. More than that, I was aching and ready to give in to whatever this was, this crazy attraction unlike anything I'd ever felt. So what if it had been just a day?

"I want you, too," I murmured.

He paused in his kisses, looked into my eyes, caressed my cheek. "I want you *now*."

"What about the pizza?"

"Fuck the pizza," he said, and he pulled me by the hand through the open doors and into the condo.

He was moving fast, hauling me along, and I almost stumbled after him, a train that had jumped the tracks. He turned right, taking me into a short hallway and then, a dark bedroom. He flipped a switch, and one dimly glowing floor lamp came on in the corner — a tall lamp, all one twisting square column, that looked like big green leaves stitched together. The whole room was in greens and dark woods with white accents, I realized, as if it had grown out of the jungle.

I didn't have much time to observe as he turned to me again. He paused in his frenetic motion — with difficulty, I thought — held both my hands and searched my eyes.

"Are you sure?" he asked.

"Yes." I was nervous, but I knew I would not be satisfied until I held him in my arms.

He started to pull me close, but I resisted and nodded toward the sliding glass doors that led to the balcony. "Would you — would you open the doors? I want to hear the ocean."

He smiled and nodded, walked over to the doors and pulled them open. The cool evening breeze wafted in, with the fresh sea air and a rolling, hypnotic roar. I felt the primal sound in my bones, releasing something in me that had been held too long.

Alex turned back to me, walking slowly, stopping in front

of me, looking me over from head to toe with frank appreciation. With desire.

"Sloane," he said in a low, inexorable voice, reaching up
to hold my face in his hands. "You *will* be my muse."

He pulled me into him, his mouth hard on mine, and I
felt my knees buckle. He pushed me toward the vast bed,
pushed me down on the mattress, pushed one knee between
my legs, devouring me with his kiss — he was pushing, pushing, but I wanted him to; I opened my mouth to him, my legs.

"Yes, Alex," I murmured between kisses. *"Yes."* I would be
his muse; I would be anything, as delirious as I was from his
touch.

He ran his hands down my legs, over the crazy purple
tights, and unzipped my boots. He tossed them behind him,
then touched me at a more leisurely pace, his fingers
gliding back up my hose-clad legs as I sat up on my elbows,
out of breath, watching him. He caught my gaze as his
hands traveled higher, caressing my knees, the insides of my
thighs. There, he kissed me, just above the line of my short
tunic dress, and I shivered in anticipation as his hands
roamed. He stared me down as he cupped my mound
through the thin fabric, lightly at first, then with an
increasing pressure. I let my head fall back, and a low sigh
escaped me.

"You *are* an inspiration," Alex said, his voice still low, and
more powerful by being so. He slipped his fingers under the
elastic waistband of the tights and pulled them off me, slipping them down, down, until he'd peeled them off and
thrown them into the shadows with the shoes. Then his
hands were traveling up again, and I lifted my head to watch,
licking my lips, feeling a rush of desire that no man until now
had touched. Not that there had been more than a couple for

comparison. I had lived life far too quietly, I thought, as Alex's hands swept under the dress.

"I like what's under the tights," he said, this time a small smile playing around his lips.

"You're easy to please," I said. "That took no work at all."

"Sometimes nothing is everything," he said, cupping my naked bottom with one hand and grazing my pussy with the other.

"Oh, God." I lay back on the bed, on the soft, deep blanket, as he touched my bud ever so lightly. My legs still dangled over the edge, and I felt limp under his touch, exhilarated in surrender.

"I like this, too," he said, brushing the neat patch of soft hair there. I liked that he accepted me as me. And somehow that made me even more wet, a fact that became all too obvious as he pushed a finger inside me.

"Thank you," I breathed, and not just for his sweetness. For his desire. For his possession of me.

"So polite," he teased, probing me with one, then two fingers. I closed my eyes and clutched the blanket as he teased me, stroking me senseless. After a few moments of delicious torture, he withdrew.

"More," I whispered.

"Oh, there's more." He got down on his knees and dipped his face between my legs.

His tongue was a devilish thing, a delightful dancer upon my sex. My clit was at attention, was on fire, as an aching pleasure radiated from where his mouth played upon me, radiated into every cell and muscle, until I was straining and bucking against his lips. His hands had crept up under the dress, holding my bottom, restraining me against him. I was trapped, a willing prisoner under his exquisite command, feeling him lap my wet slit, my throbbing nub until I came with a cry.

When I opened my eyes, I saw Alex standing in front of me, leaning over me. He'd taken off his shirt, and in the half-light, his musculature reminded me of a life drawing class I'd taken, when one model's body was so stunning I found myself wishing I'd had a pile of clay to sculpt him in three dimensions rather than sketching him in the flat gray and white of two. Alex's body was like that, not some caricature from a gym ad, just strong. Solid. Real. Completely captivating. His eyes glimmered, and his lips were still wet.

"You're beautiful," he said.

I sat up, holding his gaze. "I was just going to say the same thing." I pulled my dress off over my head, leaving me in only my bra, a black lace number I was really glad I'd donned in my morning haste. Especially when I saw the desire in his eyes.

I reached out and hooked him by the waistband, pulling him closer. I unbuckled his belt, unbuttoned his jeans. My hands shook a little. *Country mouse,* I told myself as I unzipped them and tugged them down. He stepped out of them, and I saw the strain in his blue briefs. I wanted to touch him. I looked up. That amused look was back in his eyes.

"Allow me," he said, pulling the briefs down and off.

His cock sprang free, hard, generous. He watched as I reached out my hand. I thought I felt him shiver as I clasped his thick and lengthening shaft, feeling the velvety softness and the firmness beneath the skin. Using my thumb, I gently rubbed the slit at the end, feeling the moisture there. And then I sank to my knees in front of him, ran my tongue along his erection and took him in my mouth.

He gasped. I was lost in a haze of desire, tasting him. I had no idea I could be this hungry for a man, but the pleasure he had given me needed an answer, and to stroke him with my tongue, to suck on the hard length of him gave me a thrill in return. I reached up and cupped his sac, rolling it in my hand as I sucked. He moaned, and I enjoyed knowing I could enrapture him, too. I felt so free, so high as I focused on his pleasure, and I felt an ache grow again between my legs as I tasted him.

"Sloane," he whispered, grasping me by the shoulders, pulling me up. "Lie on the bed," he commanded, almost lifting me as he pushed me backward until my whole body, still not quite naked, lay before him, my head propped up on the pillows.

"I love your lips around me," he murmured, on his hands and knees over me. He stroked my cheek, ran a finger over my lips. I took it into my mouth, sucking. "I want to fuck your mouth," he whispered. "May I?"

This was strange, dirty talk. Nothing like what my brief boyfriendesque experiences had provided in the past. I liked it.

"Yes, please," I whispered back, waiting for him, wanting him.

He straddled me so that his knees squeezed the sides of my breasts, which were still restrained by the bra. Guiding his cock with his hand, he dipped it toward my mouth, and I accepted it with a tremor of arousal.

He lowered over me, moving slowly, getting me used to the feel of him. He felt even bigger this way, but he was gentle, and I started to enjoy the wanton feeling of sucking him deeply, of having him fuck my lips. He pushed more insistently but let me control how deep I wanted to take him, and I lifted my head, signaling more, until we both relaxed into his deliberate rhythm.

I grasped the base of his shaft with my hand, rubbing him, guiding him as my mouth wrapped around his pulsing need. He made a low, rumbling sound, and I reveled in his satisfaction as his tip hit the back of my throat. I took his fullness with an aching desire, the thrill of submitting to him, of simultaneously having this power over him as he pumped his cock against my tongue.

He pulled out; he hadn't come, I knew that, but I'd tasted him. He was breathing heavily, and I knew he must be aching for release. I felt lusciously used. I stretched my jaw, felt my mouth relax. My pussy ached. I wanted completion.

"I want you inside me, Alex," I whispered. I liked saying the words. I felt so free with him. Maybe because he was almost a stranger.

He cupped my face and leaned down, kissing me with delicate, surprising tenderness. "I've wanted you since I saw you last night. I can't believe I'm so lucky."

"Now."

He moved aside and opened the nightstand, where he grabbed a condom from the drawer. He ripped open the packet and rolled it on, watching me with something between lust and reverence.

"You want me?" he asked, his tone teasing but somehow uncertain.

"Now," I groaned, and he grasped me under the knees, pulling me up to him, pushing my legs open.

His hard length thrusting inside me had me instantly on the verge of climax. But he took me even higher with his cadence, staring me down, his face strained by passion, fierce and magnetic, and I moved with him, meeting him with my own yearning. I clenched around him, cried out as he penetrated deep inside me, pressing me to the bed, grasping one breast, kissing the other through the lace.

I moaned again, wrapping my legs around him as I shuddered, my lingering climax rippling through my body. And then I felt him come, a burst that triggered a new spasm of pleasure, wracking me until I felt the tension melt away from me. I collapsed against the bed.

Breathing hard, he withdrew slowly, tossed the condom and lowered himself beside me, naked and hot and moist, kissing my neck, my lips, my shoulders — he worked his hand behind my back to unclasp the bra and pull it off — and he sucked on my nipples, still hard with desire.

"So lovely," he said, circling them with his fingers.

I turned to my side and caressed him in return, kissing his arms and his chest, touching his wet shaft, causing him to shiver. Our mouths joined again and our kisses lengthened, dreamy and intense, the ocean's sweet roar our soundtrack as our tongues intertwined. We tasted one another as if it was still that first kiss. As if we hadn't done everything we just did.

Finally, we came to rest. I breathed against him, resting my cheek against his chest, nestling in his arms.

"Alex?" I felt some of my uncertainty return.

"Sloane," he murmured, kissing my hair.

"I —" Oh, hell. I was about to blow all of my cool. "I want you to know this is not my usual M.O."

He laughed softly. "Divine temptress?"

I couldn't suppress a smile.

"That might be my fantasy, but usually I'm more like Cinderella. Running away when the clock strikes twelve, or when I see a man carrying a shoe with intent."

"Hmm," he said, his voice soothing. "I think you knew I had intent."

"I think I did."

"So what's different?"

"I don't know," I said. "It might be me. Or it might be you."

"I hope it's both of us," he said, kissing me again, and I forgot my qualms in the soft persuasion of his lips. "Come on," he said when he released me. "I'm hungry. And I refuse to waste that wine."

ALEX PULLED on his T-shirt and jeans — no briefs — giving me an eyeful of his sculpted torso, waist and hips as he did so. I found his careless attire as sexy as he seemed to find me when I pulled on just the dress for our short stroll onto the balcony and down its length to the table. He lay a hand on the curve of my bottom, under the fabric, as we walked into the balmy wind.

The pizza was cold, but I didn't care. It was still delicious, and I was suddenly ravenous. The wine was wonderful, too.

"It's breathed so much, it's out of breath by now," Alex quipped.

A waxing moon had risen over the ocean. It set the waves glistening like snow, winking and moving in the night. The moon cast shadows; it ferreted out the mysterious places between palm fronds, between blades of sea grass, and cast them in sharp relief on the sand. It bathed Alex's face in a cool glow, and I saw he looked content, relaxed. I wondered if I really would see him again after tonight. I felt a little wave of anxiety and pushed it back down. This wasn't how an adventurous woman thought. She had her way with a man and decided later if he was worth her time.

I wasn't sure I was her, yet. The adventurous woman. But I was happy to be with Alex, here, now.

"It's dark out here. I like it," I said.

"It's not just for atmosphere. We do it for the turtles, so the hatchlings don't get confused and go the wrong way."

"Oh, I hope I see them sometime," I said, looking out toward the sea.

"Nesting season is almost over, but you might get lucky and see a turtle laying eggs if we go for a late walk some night." He poured us more wine, emptying the bottle. That had gone quickly. "There's more where that came from," he said.

"Oh, really? You have more wine somewhere around here?" I teased.

"One or two bottles."

"I hope it's enough."

He looked at me with a sexy half-smile. "I don't know if I'll ever get enough."

I didn't have a witty comeback. I was too busy feeling the heat grow inside me again. I was tipsy, now, and I found him as intoxicating as the wine. He gave me the full smile, the one full of light, and I longed to devour it with my mouth. Instead, I sat very, very still, admiring him, enjoying my buzz.

"You never did see my library," Alex said. "Want to?"

"Sounds good," I said. "I'm a little chilly out here."

I stood. He got up and walked over to me. In slow motion, he reached down and pulled up my dress just enough to expose me.

"That's what happens when you go around half-naked," he said.

I breathed in sharply. "I — I hear some guys like that."

He reached between my legs and ran a finger along my folds, and I could see he felt how wet I was, how wet already.

"I wonder if we should get some practicalities out of the way," he said, withdrawing his hand, much to my regret. But I knew what he meant.

"I suppose we should have thought of that a couple of hours ago," I said. "But I'm on the pill. And I just had my physical before I came down here. I'm good."

"Yes, you are," he said, his eyes twinkling in the moonlight. "But I'm glad to hear it. So am I. Do you think it would be OK if we —?"

"Yes," I said quickly, wondering if I was rushing this; but what was to rush after what we'd just done? And I instinctively trusted him. I knew he was not like other men, though I wasn't sure if that was good or bad. He seemed strange, or sad, or both. But I trusted him. He'd let me inside his life today. I liked the way he wanted me. I liked our instant connection. He'd unlocked something I'd held close for a long, long time.

His eyes were hooded, shadowed with blue fire in the semi-darkness. He pushed his hand under my hem again and slipped two fingers inside me.

I gripped the back of the chair and subtly opened my legs, an invitation, watching his wicked smile grow. *The mild-mannered lothario,* came my fleeting thought.

I reached up, grasped his shoulders as he probed me, and I kissed his neck.

"Fuck me." The whisper slipped out of my mouth before ever skating through my brain.

He withdrew his fingers, twirled me roughly in one motion and pushed me toward the railing.

"Hang on," he whispered as I grasped it, feeling him behind me, pulling up my dress. He was yanking down his jeans as he pressed up against me. I moaned, and he put a hand over my mouth.

"Shhhh," he whispered into my ear before taking his hand away and grasping my hips.

I became acutely aware, then, of my surroundings. We were lit dimly by moonlight, but no one was watching. Not yet. Far below, a couple walked along the beach, caught up in each other; if I lost control, I might give us away. I had never been so wet. I felt his cock touching me, exploring, until he found my cleft. Alex guided it home, and I shuddered to feel his fullness plow hard into me. I bent over, gripping the railing, pushing back against him as he grasped my hair, kissed my neck, held me tight. I felt pinned, penetrated, wild, free. I bit my lip, fighting the urge to scream with pleasure. It took almost no time for my body to reach its release; I quaked around him as I came. This was faster than last time, more fierce, and the waves of sensation rocked me from my center as he came inside me, panting in my ear. He held me hard against him as he pumped against me one last time, then slowly withdrew, gently pulling my dress down. I felt his wetness against my inner thigh as I stood up, watching him pull up his jeans. I felt boneless, drained, high as a kite.

"I need to sit," I whispered, swaying.

He caught me with one arm and guided me into the house. I leaned against him. He smelled of man and wine and sex. I closed my eyes, not noticing where he was taking me until he lowered me onto a leather couch. I opened my eyes and found myself surrounded by books.

"Relax," he said. "I'll be right back."

I curled up in a corner of the couch against a couple of

throw pillows, slowly coming back to my senses. I felt comfortable in here with stories all around me, stories no doubt more dramatic than mine. My eyes roamed the rows and rows of books, fresh paperbacks, old leather, cloth bindings, picture books, atlases, all on floor-to-ceiling shelves in an oblong room. A rolling ladder granted access to the top shelves.

In front of me was a fireplace — a lot like the wine room, I thought, wondering how odd it might be for a Florida home to have not one but two fireplaces, with the air conditioning running. This one was surrounded by a carved, white stone mantel that seemed to be embedded with the impression of shells. Fossils? There was art; there were interesting objects; I didn't have the energy to absorb it all just yet. I closed my eyes.

I awoke from my brief doze when Alex came back into the room, holding our half-full wine glasses and another bottle.

"I'm already drunk," I said with a sleepy grin.

"Good," he said, a smile playing around the corners of his mouth as he set everything down on a nearby table that was half-covered with books. He handed me my glass, and I sipped it, enjoying the last few mouthfuls of the delicious cabernet. I wondered what else he had in store. In more ways than one.

He grabbed his glass and sat next to me, casually draping an arm around my shoulders. I leaned into him. He sat up abruptly.

"Wait. What am I thinking?" he exclaimed, reaching for the end table and coming up with a remote control panel. He touched the screen, and the gas fireplace flared to life. He hit another combination, and the lamp that had been lit behind me turned off, while charming stained-glass sconces now emitted a dim glow on either side of the fireplace. Another few touches of his fingers, and a stereo came on, playing jazz.

"Boys and their toys," I said wryly.

"I like toys," he said, returning the remote to its perch and lifting an eyebrow at me. I wasn't sure what he meant, but I decided to take his comment as a simple joke. For now, I just wanted to curl up against him and process this delicious fatigue.

He didn't seem to mind. He handed me my glass, held me close and sipped his wine as the music softened the air around us. I wasn't sure what to say. We'd collided like two fireballs, but we still had a lot to learn about each other. And I was in foreign territory, a little scared of myself, of how much I'd opened myself to him.

"What kind of stone is that?" I asked. A safe question.

"The fireplace?"

I nodded.

"Coral rock. That whole piece was recovered from a 1930s house in Miami that a developer tore down to build some monstrosity. He had no idea what he had."

"It's gorgeous," I said, enjoying the light of the fire, the music, everything. "You seem to like preserving — old things. You have antiques here and there. And this. And the river house."

"And myself, of course."

"Oh, you're not old." I finished my wine, and he took the glass and got up to pour from the other bottle.

"Older than you by, what, four years?"

"About." I'd figured from what he told me earlier he was around twenty-seven, and I was twenty-three. Close enough.

He filled the glasses with the new wine, another red, and brought them back to the couch.

I took a sip. "Oh, my God."

"You have a palate," he said approvingly as he took a healthy swallow.

"I don't know about that, but this is ambrosia."

"It's an estate blend from California. I won't bore you with the details, but yes, it's very special."

"Thanks," I said.

"What for?"

"For giving me the special."

He looked puzzled for a moment, then leaned in and kissed me, a sweet, possessive kiss this time. "I don't think you realize that you are special, that this is special."

"Oh," I said, trying to put my country mouse back in its barn, "I'm not totally naïve. I mean, Alex, you're handsome. You have — all this. Which, by the way, is not why I'm here. But I can see how it could turn a girl's head."

"No, no," he said, more serious now. "You don't get it. You don't think I do this every weekend, do you?"

I was getting uncomfortable, wishing I hadn't said anything. I took another sip of the heavenly wine. "Maybe every other weekend?"

"Little fool." He smiled, but the smile was brittle.

"What is it?" Now I leaned into him, kissing his cheek, his lips. "It doesn't matter. I'm happy."

"This is a rare event for me, Sloane," he said, letting me kiss him on the chin, the neck, with barely a reaction.

"Then other women are stupid," I whispered, flicking his ear with my tongue.

Alex chuckled. "I went through a time, of course, when I first got the money and sowed a lifetime's worth of wild oats in the span of about three years. A lot of travel and drinking. The women were — pleasant. Good training for a geek."

I'll say, I thought, pulling away at the mention of other women. I didn't want to imagine them. I watched him for a moment as the fire played on his stony features.

"What happened?" I asked.

"They weren't what I was looking for. I mean, I date occasionally. Dinner or a concert. I don't live like a monk. But it never lasts, and I never fit into a crowd. Over time, I got this crippling fear of being in uncontrolled social situations. Of course, I was never good with other people. I've tried, but . . . Sloane, don't treat this like a one-night stand."

His decree annoyed me. "I told you this is not my usual mode of operation," I said. "I have never had a one-night stand, unless this is it. For Christ's sake, I only met you yesterday."

Alex looked alarmed as I sat up and put a pillow between us.

"I'm sorry. I didn't mean to piss you off," he said. "That's not what this is. This is — this is incredible. It's you. Look, it's irrational, OK? You can call it raw attraction, or lust at first sight, but I pretend I'm a writer, so let me call it a waking dream. A thunderbolt. That's what this is. It's all wrapped up in you. I'm not going to profess undying love. You're right. We just met. But whatever this is, it's powerful. I'm thunderstruck."

He threw the pillow aside and reached for me, gently wrapped me in his arms. Somehow he'd put down his wine glass; I clutched mine as I awkwardly returned his hug.

It wasn't sexual, exactly, but in my buzzed, arousal-hangover state, I still felt his physical pull. And something else, a deep need in his embrace. Not physical. Emotional. I gave in to it, to him, and held him close. Screw thinking. This was The Moment, as in, Living In It. In his arms was the warmth of the tropics, and I was caught in his waking dream.

"You're kinda crazy," I whispered, half-teasing.

"You don't know the half of it," he replied, releasing me, and I laughed. "Or maybe," he added, "I'm just a little drunk."

"Not just a little," I said. Not just drunk. Not just crazy, I thought. Easily both. A combination that was weirdly attractive right now, as I shredded my inhibitions. "I should go home."

"No, you shouldn't."

"No, I shouldn't," I said, drunk, too. I sipped my wine and looked into those gray eyes, warmed to gold by the flames.

He studied me. "I can't drive you right now, anyway, and cabs take forever to show up here."

"So much for the big city," I said.

"Who told you Bohemia Beach was a big city?" He laughed.

"Compared with where I came from, it's close enough."

Alex wrapped one arm around me, and I leaned my head against his shoulder.

"I don't want you ever to leave," he said, "but muses have their magic to weave."

"Muses. Artists. Writers."

He fingered my hair.

"I'm sleepy," I murmured into his shoulder.

"Too sleepy?"

"For what?"

"Sloane," he whispered, stroking my shoulder, taking my glass.

I looked up into his face, so handsome in this perfect light, as he bent down to kiss me, an aching, endless kiss that had me floating in a dark sky, deep in Alex's cloud of stardust.

He let go, slipped his jeans and shirt off, pulled my dress over my head. It felt so good to be naked with him, and I realized I was wet again, and he was hard, his shaft at attention. He was gentle; perhaps he didn't wish to startle me out of my dream. Our dream. He pulled me up so I straddled him on the couch, and he guided me on top of him.

I sighed as he slid inside me, as I took him to the hilt, deeper than before, a divine pressure upon my sweet spot as he started to rock me, rock-a-bye, a thrilling lullaby. I closed my eyes, lost in our powerful cadence, then opened them to look down into Alex's gray gaze. It was fire-lit and full of emotion. I almost lost myself in it. And then he lifted me, shifted, penetrating even deeper, and I gasped, my climax rising, expanding in rippling waves. He detonated inside me. I clutched him tightly, moaning as I felt his release, and he groaned, too, at my response, lost in my body. I had never held anyone so close.

WE FELL ASLEEP THERE, on the couch, wrapped up together. Sometime in the night, Alex got up and led me to his bed. He secured me under the covers next to him, our naked bodies touching, and I slept again. I internalized the ocean's pulsing roll of sound, falling through it in my dreams, like falling through the air and never hitting the ground. Even when Alex closed the sliding doors, I heard it, a never-ending constant that, as dawn broke, mixed with the cries of birds and the distant hint of traffic and life beyond this sheltered space.

I woke sober in the light of day and alone in the bed, trying to figure out what had possessed me the day before. I rolled over and looked out the sliders toward the golden morning sky and the turquoise ocean, muted to pastels through the sheer curtains, and wondered what had happened. What had turned me from circumspect little Sloane into the whore of Bohemia Beach?

I knew I wasn't being fair to myself. This is the sort of thing normal people did all the time, I thought wryly. It's just that I'd only ever had a couple of short-term boyfriends who'd been as inexperienced as I was, and I hadn't had time for much more, given all my classes and jobs and studio time. I'd been a long-simmering pot poised to bubble over. Now I was blowing steam.

So why was my surrender so hard for me to accept? Catholic guilt? I'd abandoned the church while still in college, settling on a more free and easy spirituality. My mother's lectures? Maybe. She'd been pregnant with my oldest brother when she got married, a calculation I'd figured out when I was in high school. But she'd always seemed reasonably content with her secretarial jobs and crafting and, of course, fundraising for the football team and going to my brothers' games. Maybe she really had wanted more for me. She hadn't made much effort to say so.

Well, this was more. My stay in Bohemia Beach was starting in a most unexpected way. I felt wide awake. I stretched, feeling pleasantly sore muscles, and smiled at what I'd done with Alex.

Alex? Where was he?

I slipped out of bed. Oh, that's right. I was still naked. I walked to the balcony doors, hiding behind the gauzy curtains, and contemplated the morning. What day was it? Sunday. I would have to get home, maybe impose more order on my space, get psyched up for class tomorrow. As much as I loved pottery, class seemed like a dull prospect when compared with the past twenty-four hours.

I poked my head out of the master bedroom door, and then into the main living space. I hadn't seen the other rooms yet. I wondered if he wrote in one of them; I had yet to see the trappings of a writer, a desk that bespoke the life of the mind. I wasn't ready to go exploring. All was quiet. He must be out.

I returned to the bedroom and wandered through the door I thought led to the master bathroom, and there it was.

The toilet was ordinary, hidden behind a pocket door. But the shower, with two shower heads and two doorways, was big enough to hold half a dozen very friendly people. There was a bench on one end and multiple niches stocked with high-end shampoos and conditioner and body wash.

The walls and floor of the room and shower were tiled in a gorgeous, gray and brown, heavily veined polished marble. There was a huge spa tub on one end of the room. Double sinks, of course. And a linen closet. This bathroom was easily ten times the size of mine.

What was it about being rich that made people need so much space to live? No matter. I used the toilet, then figured out the hot and cold and turned on one of the shower heads. I stepped under the square head, lit by blue LEDs. It dropped a wide column of water like rain, softly. It was nice enough, but after I soaped my hair with some lovely lavender shampoo, I picked up the hand-shower, attached to a silver hose, and rinsed my hair thoroughly under its more practical pressure.

Or not so practical. Was it the fact that my body was still humming from last night that made me turn the water elsewhere?

I twisted the dial to get a more pulsing flow and relaxed

into the warm, intense stream as I ran it over my shoulders and gave my breasts special attention. And they came to attention, too, as I remembered Alex's fingers, his mouth from last night. I slowly moved the head lower, closing my eyes as I felt the stream of water hit my thighs, washing away the carnal evidence of my affair; and then I directed it between my legs.

My sigh was long and resonant in the tiled shower as I felt the stirrings of arousal again, along with a sense of renewal as the stream washed me, awakened me, and, directed with deliberation, brought my clit into a thrumming, ecstatic state that echoed through my body. I held it just long enough to feel one deep spasm of pleasure, making a small cry only I could hear, and opened my eyes.

I *thought* only I could hear my cry. Alex was standing in the doorway of the shower in khakis and a blue button-up shirt, watching me. I froze.

His face was impassive, except for what I thought was a slight flush in his cheeks. He'd been caught watching me. I'd been caught masturbating in his shower. I was pretty sure I should have been more offended, but I was still high on my sweet little orgasm, and I was drowning in his gray eyes.

Barefoot, he stepped into the shower, clothes and all, and moved slowly toward me, as if I might flee. I dropped the hand-shower, and the artificial rain gushed over my head. He stepped into the flowing water with me, grabbed my long hair at the nape of my neck, pulled my head back and kissed me hard.

OK. I definitely wasn't offended. I was on fire.

I reached to his soaking shirt and fumbled with the buttons, finally able to yank it off his shoulders, dropping it sopping on the floor. He pushed me up against the wall, still kissing me, his hand already slipping between my legs, into my cleft, his finger deep inside me. My orgasm had made it easy for him; I was wet in more ways than one, and I quivered at his skillful touch.

I grabbed at his waistband, wanting him now with a furious desire. He pulled his finger out of me and wrestled his wet, clinging pants off. His rock-hard cock sprung free, and he pushed it against me.

"Hold on to my neck," he said harshly as he reached behind my thighs and lifted me against him, thrusting inside me in one motion.

"Oh, God," I cried out, feeling another orgasm ready to overtake me.

"Wait," he grunted.

"What?"

"Wait," he repeated as he began to fuck me relentlessly, holding me up against the wall. "Don't come. Not yet."

"Yes," was all I could mutter into his ear as I hung on to his neck, wrapping my legs around him, fighting the craving to explode as he built his cadence of passion. "Please," I gasped into his ear. "Soon."

Alex said nothing, but he filled me with his hard need, pounding me as the water flowed over our heated skin. I felt the cold tile at my back, his strong body enfolding me, lifting me, hammering me with ecstasy. And then he came; I could feel it with sensitivity honed by deprivation.

"Please," I gasped into his ear.

"Yes. Come." And I did, my cry sounding a note some-where between pain and exhilaration as I shuddered against him.

He held me for another moment, and then he let me down, sliding out of me. I stood before him, spent, feeling vulnerable in my nakedness. The blue lights of the shower head glimmered on his wet skin. I touched his chest. A storm brewed in his gray eyes, and after only a moment, he turned and walked back out of the room.

For that moment, when my hands were on him, I could have sworn that he was trembling.

I took my time drying off, wondering what Alex was thinking. If he'd been thinking. I certainly hadn't been. I was the wanton little art student who'd taken advantage of Alex's shower hose.

I laughed quietly at myself, but under the humor, I felt a frisson of worry. Was he about to throw me out? Or worse, calmly drive me home and never talk to me again? I stepped with trepidation back into the bedroom and found my clothes from yesterday neatly folded on a chair. It wasn't ideal, putting on my old clothes, but, ironically, I decided going through Alex's closet might be a kind of intimacy neither of us was ready for. I put on the bra and pulled on the dress. I got the purple tights back on, and then my boots. And then I was almost ready to face him.

He wasn't in the living area or the kitchen, though I saw a paper bag there next to his keys. His morning errand? I walked back through the condo and spotted him outside, at the balcony railing, looking at the ocean. Full circle, I thought. I pulled myself together and walked up to the doors, opened them and stepped out.

He was wearing different clothes, now — jeans and a gray Bohemia Beach T-shirt. His wavy hair was still wet, and therefore dark. I liked him this way, less put together, informal, if not entirely relaxed. It made him look younger, like a college kid on spring break.

I waited for a moment to see if he would speak, and then I walked up to him and touched his arm.

"Alex, I'm sorry if I —"

I faltered as he turned to me with a strange look on his face that expanded into incredulity. "You're sorry? *I'm* sorry. I should have never — I was watching you. And then to take you like that — I don't know what came over me. Jesus, Sloane, I'm the one who should be sorry." He turned back to the ocean. "I didn't want to fuck this up. For once."

His confidence had vanished again. Inside, he was fighting some war that I knew about only because of the distant cannon fire — these outbursts, these doubts. I took his arm and leaned my head against his shoulder.

"Don't be silly," I said. "You weren't exactly expected. But I think it was obvious that I didn't exactly mind."

He let out a long, low breath and then turned to me and took me in his arms, a strong and comforting embrace. I closed my eyes, breathing in his masculine scent mixed with the salty ocean air. I would have stayed that way forever, but after a minute, he released me and gave me a small smile.

"I was out getting breakfast while you were plotting my ruin," Alex joked.

I suddenly felt shy. "You did say you hoped we'd have breakfast sometime."

"It's those bagels I told you about. Stay here. I'll get it."

I took a deep breath as he left me there to gaze out on the ocean. In the distance, a couple of large ships on the horizon made their way south. Below on the beach, a runner passed a pair of walkers heading in the opposite direction. Far to the south, I saw a larger cluster of beachgoers, probably around the boardwalk area I'd heard about. A line of condos extended on both sides of me, set back slightly from the dunes and the vegetation there. To the north, I could see a surf fisherman and, in the distance, more walkers and runners, with plenty of space to enjoy this lightly used beach. Paradise, indeed.

"Here we are," said Alex. I turned. On the table, he set a tray loaded with bagels, a small bowl of cream cheese, knives, napkins, glasses and a pitcher of orange juice. "This is fresh squeezed at the local grove," he said, pouring the juice. "Fantastic stuff."

"What, no mimosas?" I teased.

"I don't have any champagne lowly enough to be mixed with orange juice, no matter how good the juice." He sat at the table and gestured for me to do the same.

"Snob."

"I know. It's really terrible," he said, and I laughed.

The shower wasn't mentioned again. We consumed the juice and the bagels — excellent, as he'd promised — and enjoyed the cool morning as I told him what I'd heard about the school and Montrose King. Alex listened closely, barely looking at the ocean, but I couldn't keep my eyes away from the sparkling waves. He was used to it, I guess. As a lifetime landlubber, I couldn't get enough of the play of light on the water, the shifting clouds in the sky.

"I should probably go home," I said after our conversation and breakfast reached a natural lull. I still felt the pleasant tingle of the fresh juice in my mouth.

"I suppose you should," Alex said, but his voice was filled with regret. Selfishly, I was glad. I wanted him to miss me, to want me again. This had been the most intense day and night of my life, and I didn't know if I could walk away from it thinking I might never come back.

Alex looked me over, his face unreadable. "I had a good time."

"Me, too." I could hear how small my voice sounded as I uttered this almost ridiculous understatement. The truth was, he'd changed me. Even if I never saw him again. The idea made my stomach hurt.

We put away the breakfast remains, I grabbed my purse, and we headed to the garage and the convertible. In short time, Alex was driving us down the beach highway, past condos, beach emporiums and large, modern homes, before turning west on the causeway toward Bohemia and my place.

When we pulled into the driveway, I noticed an old black Jeep parked next to my Honda and someone sitting on my front step. Damien.

"He looks pissed," I said under my breath.

"He always looks pissed," Alex joked as he stopped the car far enough from Damien so he couldn't hear us. "I wouldn't worry about it."

I ignored my cousin's puzzling presence and turned to Alex, reluctant to get out, to let this end.

"Come here," Alex said softly, reaching for me, placing a hand behind my neck as I leaned toward him for a sweet, lingering kiss. When he released me, his eyes were cloudy. "I want to see you again."

"I hoped you would say that."

"I guess tonight is too soon."

I laughed. "I need a good night's sleep before my first day at classes, and I have a feeling you might make that difficult."

"Damn straight," Alex said, a grin taking over his face. "I'll call you tomorrow. If you give me your number."

I gave him the number, which he entered into his phone, while in the back of my mind I recalled my phone dying sometime yesterday afternoon. I'd been too distracted to recharge it, and besides, no one ever called me. At least until now.

I opened the car door and got out, precluding any door-opening gallantry on his part. And I smiled at him, this enigmatic, handsome man who had begun to consume me.

He gave me a very warm look and backed the car into the street. And then he was gone.

I walked toward the carriage house, where Damien, clad in his usual black, his hair a spiky, inky mop, stood on the front step. Bafflement was written all over his face. Bafflement and something like disgust.

"What in the hell are you doing with that creep?" he demanded.

"What in the hell business is it of yours?" I snapped, an equal and opposite reaction to his obnoxious question. "And he's not a creep."

Damien looked me over shrewdly. "You spent the *night* with him?"

I swallowed a denial. There was no need for a denial. "Why are you here, Damien? Oh, and I'm sorry I ditched you Friday."

"Were you with him then, too?"

"Shut up," I said, stepping past him to unlock my door. I went inside, leaving the door open. He followed me.

"Were you?"

"No," I said, then paused, dropping my purse on the heavy work table in my clay play area. "Not Friday."

"So you spent last night with him." Damien sat on the rough mauve velvet of the thrift-store couch and started laughing. "Damn, cousin, I didn't know you had it in you. Or should I say, I didn't know he had it —"

"You shouldn't say," I said, getting really ticked off. "If you don't have anything nice to say, get out."

"Whoa, it's cool, Sloane. I just got sent on this mercy mission to find my innocent little cousin, and here she is, shagging the richest, weirdest guy I know."

"You make it sound so refined." I scowled at him, heading to the kitchen and the fridge, looking for a ginger ale. I popped a can open and took a long sip, letting the sweet bubbles soothe away my unsettled fury.

"I'll take one of those," he said.

"I'm sure you will," I said, grabbing a can and tossing it to him.

He caught it with a smile and popped the top. "Thanks."

"What do you mean you were sent to find me? Who sent you?"

"In case you don't remember, your annoying mom is sister to my annoying mom, and I guess your annoying mom was wondering how you were doing and couldn't reach you by phone. She was worried and called my mom."

"And you said you would check up on me?" I looked at him skeptically. "What's in it for you?"

Damien smiled. "A little subsidy. My November rent. It's OK. Mom can afford it. My dad got a promotion, and he can't shut up about how awesome his shitty little raise is."

"Maybe he has lower standards than you do," I said drily, sitting on the couch next to him.

He shook his head at me. "At least one of us is getting some, but really, you could have done better. I had at least three guys at the party ask who you were. *Straight* guys," he said to my doubtful glance.

"Again, not really your business," I said, looking out one of the front windows toward the leafy green day, thinking about the ocean. And Alex.

"Aw, come on, girl. We might as well be friends. And Cali can't wait to see you again."

I softened at the thought of his sister, my more lovable cousin. "How is Calista?"

"Desperate to leave the dying newspaper, but still loving it too much to make her move. She said something about going to the school Tuesday to shoot photos for a story. Something about some big-deal potter on the staff."

"Montrose King," I said. "He's here for a year, and he just started teaching last session. As soon as I heard he was here, I sped up my move so I could take his classes. His work is incredible."

"Pottery's not my thing, but I'll take your word for it."

We sat there for a minute, not talking, until I couldn't stand it anymore.

"Why are you so hostile about Alex?"

"*Alex,*" he said, mocking the way I said it until he saw the smoke coming out of my ears. "Sorry. Look, I went to school with the guy. He had problems."

"Such as?"

"Such as, everybody hated him." Damien finished his ginger ale and put the can on the floor, given the lack of a coffee table.

"That shouldn't be an unfamiliar sentiment to someone like you," I said pointedly.

"Touché. He was the kind of guy who doodled spaceships and scribbled stories in his notebooks in the back of every class and never said anything. Who hung out in the

Dungeons & Dragons club. Who got beaten up in the locker room after gym."

"That's awful!"

"Yeah, I hate Dungeons & Dragons," Damien said, and I scowled at him again. He grinned, and then became more sober. "No, you're right. It was awful. I guess when he was having the shit kicked out of him, I was just glad that day it wasn't me or some other art kid I knew. There was plenty of hate to go around."

"Fucking school," I said, remembering my own experiences with the bitchy clique that enjoyed screwing with the lives of people like me.

"Fuckin' A," Damien agreed.

Still, I wasn't beaten up in the locker room. Poor Alex. "Why do you still hate him?"

"I don't," Damien said. "I never did. But he was always kind of strange, and then when he came back to town after college, he had all this money all of a sudden. There were all kinds of rumors. You know, maybe he killed somebody, or sold drugs, or had a rich uncle die on him."

"It wasn't an uncle," I said, not elaborating.

"OK," Damien said. "OK, maybe I'm not being fair. I know he's changed. I've never known him that well. Some of the crowd is getting together tomorrow night at a bar downtown for a few drinks. Why don't you come? Bring him along."

"I'll have to ask him."

"Whatever. Oberon's. That's the bar. Anytime after nine." He eyed me as if inviting his cousin and a dubious would-be boyfriend to a bar wasn't such a good idea. "Are you OK? I mean, I'm not going to tell my mom this shit, but I have to tell her something."

"Just tell her my phone died and I'm fine. I just forgot to charge it. I can't believe they're that interested."

"Are you kidding? You rocked their world back in Ohio when you said you were ditching all their bullshit and moving down here."

I couldn't help but laugh. "I didn't exactly put it like that."

"You didn't need to. They could read between the lines." Damien got up and turned to me. "Sloane, I'm not in a position to tell you what to do, and I really don't want to. But I've been around this scene for a while, and I'd like to give you a little advice."

I lifted an eyebrow, waiting.

"Go slow. That's my advice. These people are fun. They're creative. They're bizarre. In some cases, they're deeply fucked up. You'll have plenty of time to get in all the beds you want to. Don't rush it."

"You really are full of shit," I said.

"I know, but do as I say, not as I do, OK?" He grinned again.

"Right," I said, finishing off the pop. "And I don't have all that much time, just for the record. I've saved enough to study and live here for six months."

"Oh, don't worry about going broke," Damien said with a smile as he went out the door. "If you're not broke, you're not doing it right."

THE BOHEMIA SCHOOL of Art and Design was not a college. It was not a trade school or a place where you got a graduate degree. It was a school built out of love for the arts, founded by a few smart, ambitious people who'd had the sense to bring in talented artists and managers that in turn attracted students not just from Florida, but from all over the country.

They, like me, came to take their work to the next level. There were still plenty of locals who just wanted to explore their artistic side, but the school had a reputation for bringing out the best in those who studied here. And it had grown to the point where coming here opened doors for artists to go elsewhere, to get into exclusive exhibitions, to win fellowships that let them develop their work even further.

The school itself offered a handful of those fellowships, and in the back of my mind was a fantasy that if I worked hard enough, maybe I'd have a shot at one someday.

In two or three years, probably. And I didn't know if I'd last that long.

I showed up in jeans and a T-shirt with my toolbox and satchel, dealt with the paperwork of the first day, was assigned a locker and made my way to Pottery Studio B. There were five pottery studios, with a mix of wheels and equipment to suit whatever classes were offered at the time. Studio B was filled with two long rows of electric throwing wheels, perhaps twenty of them, along with a handful of taller work tables, a slab roller, and shelves lining the walls, labeled with names.

I picked a seat behind what I hoped was a lucky wheel and settled in. I pulled an apron from my bag — a thrift-store find, black with a glow-in-the-dark skeleton outline on it — and pulled it over my head, tying it around the waist. I already had a heavy bag of clay I'd bought from the supply store; my materials fees would cover glazes and gear, but I would pay for clay as I went.

Other students — ranging from a couple of years

younger than me to their seventies — were pulling plastic bags off their half-finished projects or cutting pieces from blocks of clay and packing them on the wheel. They were obviously continuing students, unlike me.

It was a few minutes past 10 a.m., the official start time, and our instructor hadn't appeared. I supposed Montrose King could set his own hours. I would have this class on Mondays, Tuesdays and Thursdays; I hoped he showed up for some of them.

The tall, curly-haired young man I'd seen demonstrating throwing at the art fair walked into the room and grabbed a bag of clay from a shelf. The shelf and the bag were labeled with masking tape on which the name "GORSKI" was lettered in black marker.

He looked around and picked the empty seat next to me. He didn't have much choice. It was the only one left.

Without speaking, he dropped the twenty-five-pound bagged block of clay onto the wheel with a *thunk*, then went around the room getting an apron and a water bucket.

He called out as he sat next to me.

"OK, everybody. Montrose will be a few minutes late, but he asked that you get started on whatever you're working on. And I want any new students to talk to me."

The others were chatting, barely acknowledging him. Someone turned on a clay-spattered boom box in the back, tuning the radio to a pop-rock station.

My neighbor looked around. "No new students?"

"Um, me," I said, and he turned around and smiled at me, his brown eyes twinkling.

"I thought so," he said. "I just wanted to see if you were paying attention. I noticed you at the art fair. I'm Gary."

"Gorski," I said, returning his smile. You could cut a diamond on his dimples.

He saw me nodding toward the clay bag with its label.

He laughed. "Yeah, Gorski. Gary Gorski. Either name will work. I help out around here, when I'm not doing real work. And, of course, that gives me a lot more studio time."

"I'm Sloane," I said. "I had a similar arrangement where I came from."

"Really? If you don't mind working, we could use another part-time assistant. I mean, if you have time when you're not going to class. You know, if you need a job."

"That would be perfect!" I might have money saved up, but the more I worked, the longer I could stay.

"Great," Gary said. "Of course, this assumes you are not a rank amateur and know your way around a studio and a kiln. We have electric kilns here with computers, which make it easier. Except for the raku. My specialty. I have a thing for fire." He grinned.

"So you were going to tell me something? About being a new student?"

"What? Oh, yeah. You're supposed to throw a vessel. Whatever you want. Montrose wants to get your temperature. See your level. This class is about creative projects, so you can get as crazy as you want."

"Um, OK," I said, unsure about this wide-open format. Still, it was exciting to get in front of a wheel again. It had been almost two weeks since I'd thrown anything in clay, with the move and everything. "I guess I just help myself?"

He started pointing around the room. "Buckets. Sink. Extra tools. Toys in the drawers — the funky stuff people use as tools, even if they aren't — stamps, cookie cutters, all that. Plastic bags. Slab rollers. Heat guns. Glazes and brushes.

Tape — you'll need that when you claim a shelf. Let me know if you need anything."

By the time I'd gathered everything and found a shelf, Gary was halfway toward pulling another towering vase like the one I'd seen him making at the art fair. Intimidating. I was pretty good at throwing, but height had never been one of my strong suits. He'd already balanced the mound of clay and was drawing the floor of his piece while pulling upward in a perfect balance of pressure with those huge hands of his. Those hands and long, skinny arms easily let him reach deep inside the vase he was pulling and draw up again, applying equal pressure inside and outside the walls, extending the height as it spun. He shot me a quick grin while he was in the middle of the process but never faltered. In moments, a cylinder well over a foot high was in place, and he was about to stretch it again.

I tried to ignore his prowess and used a wire to cut a fair chunk of white clay from my block — really, it was light gray, but it would be white after drying and its first firing. I pounded down the corners of the square and packed it into a ball with my hands before slapping it onto the middle of the wheel. Power on. Pedal down. I dribbled some water onto the spinning lump of clay and, with wet hands, began the process of centering it. I locked my left elbow to my body to stabilize my arm and hand against the clay and used my right hand to apply pressure.

It felt good to feel my strength meet the spinning force of the wheel as the clay responded to my touch. In a few moments, the lump had become a rounded ball, a nascent cylinder, with a slight dip and nipple in the middle.

I tried not to think about the nipple shape, but it triggered a tumble of images in my mind's eye that I'd been trying to suppress, moments from my lost weekend with Alex.

I pulled my hands away, released a little sigh and watched the clay spin. As long as I'd been doing this, I still felt a certain satisfaction when I got the clay centered. That first step was one of the hardest things to master when I started, and it was critical to anything a potter did to the clay later on.

"Half the battle, right?" Gary said at my side, giving me another smile as he ran his fingers up the walls of his work-in-progress. His vase was now a good twenty inches high, and he'd begun to shape it into something tulip-like, but long and sinuous.

"Big hands," I murmured as I paused to watch him.

He laughed. "That's what she said."

"Ugh," I groaned.

"Sorry. Only joke I know," Gary said. "And hey, don't look now, but our fearless leader has entered the building."

I peeked over my shoulder and saw him, Montrose King, though in person he looked more waspish and severe than he did in the smiling photo on the website. He was pale, with a full head of black-and-silver hair and a dark goatee threaded with gray. He wore a light denim shirt with rolled-up sleeves, loose over dark jeans, not a speck of clay on him.

"Attention, everyone," he called out, moving to the front of the room. "I see a lot of familiar faces, so you know the rules: In this class, there are no rules. But there is a goal. The Bohemia Art Museum's juried exhibition of regional art will open January eighth. Submissions are due at the end of November, the day before Thanksgiving. I see no reason why a few of you might not be selected for this well-respected show. To reach that level, you can't just be good with clay. You have to have intent. I ask you, then, to answer this question: What is your intent?"

I looked around. Half the students looked as anxious as I was.

"All right, then," Montrose King said. "To work."

I decided it might be better if I had more than a round ball — or, let's face it, a breast — to show him and started digging into my clay.

In a few minutes, I'd pulled and compressed the floor of my piece and pulled up the sides into a fair cylinder, though not half as high as Gary's. I'd been playing with the idea of rippling, vortex shapes recently, so I shaped this cylinder in that way, pulling up again on the walls and pushing out so they flared. I pressed a finger into the clay near the bottom and drew it up the side as the piece spun, creating a spiraling groove. I paused, liking the look, wondering how I'd finish it, when I felt a presence at my shoulder.

"Very pretty, Ms. Abbey, but I don't want you to do pretty."

I snapped my head around to see Montrose King standing over me. He was just a bit taller than I was, but since I was sitting, he seemed more than a little intimidating. Especially because he was *Montrose King,* the man whose clay creations were featured in some of the biggest botanical gardens in North America.

"I'm here to learn, Mr. King," I said, wondering how he knew my name.

"Your portfolio was impressive technically," he said. So that's how he knew my name. "My mission is to make you abandon the technical. Keep your technique, but abandon the technical. Abandon yourself, if you will. Though it is very pretty."

He took the tool out of my hand, and before I could figure

out what marvelous technique he was going to show me, he stabbed the spinning vase in the middle. The clay immediately peeled apart, as the wheel's rapid rotation forced the clay to shred itself around the shaft of the tool.

He handed the tool back to me with a wolfish smile. "And you may call me Montrose. By the way, just because you have a friend who is a patron of this school, don't expect any special treatment. In fact, you may expect exactly the opposite. Try again."

He walked away, and I was left feeling as torn up as the clay. And what was that about having a friend who was a patron? I didn't know any patrons, unless he meant Alex. What had he done?

"He knows I'll kill him if he does that to one of my pieces," Gary said when Montrose was out of earshot, and then he chuckled at my shocked expression. "Don't worry about it. He did that to almost every student at the beginning of the last session. Though without as much gusto, I have to admit."

Gary's words were comforting, and it was nice to have someone with that much confidence sitting next to me. Maybe it would rub off.

"It's going to be a long fall," I said. I stopped the wheel, picked up the pieces of clay and began pounding them back into a ball.

THE LONG FALL had started with a long day. I had the unsatisfactory first class with Montrose King, then a strangely freeform hand-building class with a sweet hippie sexagenarian named Rose, followed by an unsatisfying sandwich wrap at the school's cafe. In the afternoon, I had studio time, in which I unsuccessfully tried to make something that wasn't pretty. Actually, whatever I made wasn't pretty, but it wasn't art, either, and I think that's what my scary teacher had been getting at.

I washed up, stowed my projects and left about 4 p.m., ready to relax. I checked my phone, something I didn't do when I was making pottery, because I didn't want it covered in smears of clay. There was a voice message from my mother, saying she was glad I was safe, and would I please keep my phone charged at all times in case I was mugged? As if a mugger would pause to let me make a phone call.

And there was another message, a text from Alex.

"Tonight?" was all it said.

He'd sent it barely a half-hour before, making me wonder just how well he knew my schedule. I guess I was still a little puzzled by Montrose King's comment that morning, about the patron. I stowed my toolbox and bag in my car and leaned against the hood to call him back, enjoying the golden late-afternoon light and warm breeze. Even here, it carried a whiff of the sea.

Alex answered after just one ring.

"Sloane," he said.

"I think you're confused. I'm Sloane."

"Oh, I know you're Sloane. If you weren't, I'd start to think the weekend was just a dream."

"Maybe it was a dream," I said, his voice triggering an emotional response I wasn't expecting.

"I want to see you."

I nodded at a couple of the other pottery students who were heading to their cars in the crowded parking lot. "I think that can be arranged. But I need to ask you something first."

"Yes?" His voice was more guarded.

"Did you — are you what the school would consider a patron?"

"Sometimes," he said.

"Recently?"

"Occasionally. And recently."

"Did you do something I need to know about?" I asked, trying to be as casual as I could.

He paused. "I just donated some money to the ceramics program," he said. "Not much. Enough to fund every student's clay this session."

"That's a lot of clay!" I said, stunned.

"I didn't think you'd let me buy just yours," Alex said, "so I made it a broader donation."

"Why on earth?"

"I'm a patron of the arts!" he said in a joking tone.

"Hmm. I'm not sure how I should feel about this."

"Happy," he said. "I want you to feel happy."

"And you didn't mention me, by chance, did you?"

"Oh," he said. "Well, I did mention something to Mrs. Doctor about knowing you."

"You mean Dr. Doctor."

"Right, Dr. Doctor," Alex said.

"Well, Montrose King gave me shit about it this morning in my first class."

"Oh," he said, pausing. "I'm sorry. I guess gossip travels fast."

"Gossip? What did you *tell* her?"

"Nothing!" he protested. "Just that we were friends. And you inspired me to learn more about pottery."

I saw Gary heading out the door and getting into an old, white work van. He gave me a wave.

"See you tomorrow, Gary!" I said.

"What?" Alex asked.

"Just saying goodbye to my first pottery friend. He helped me survive my first class."

"Your first friend," Alex said. Did I detect a note of jealousy in his tone? "So I'm buying clay for him, too."

"You're buying clay for, I don't know, a hundred or more students, I think. It was nice of you, but I'm not sure whether to thank you or be mad at you."

"Sloane," he said in a coaxing voice, "why don't I pick you up, and you can thank me in person? Or take your revenge," he said, more flirtatious.

I felt a little flutter.

"I'm heading home now," I said. "Want to pick me up at six?"

"I'll be there."

I REALIZED on the drive to my place that I hadn't asked Alex what we were doing. Dinner? Some other outing? Or would we go out at all? On a practical point, I hoped dinner was included. I was starving after eating so little. Though it didn't generally involve running or heavy lifting, pottery was physical work. I could feel it in my arms, shoulders and back. I hadn't had that much concentrated pottery time in a while.

I pulled into the drive that wound behind the old Thomason house — now owned by the Pullmans, or the Doctors, as we kept calling them — and up to the parking area by the carriage house. The waning sun still dappled the white brick walls, and I felt lucky to have found such a pretty place to live. And puzzled that yet another vehicle was waiting for me in the driveway, a pickup truck rigged with a ladder and tool box.

As I got out of the car, a sun-creased, gray-blond man in painter's pants and a spattered white T-shirt got out of the truck. I stopped where I was, wondering if I should be worried about him.

"Miss Abbey?" he asked in a Southern accent.

"Yes?"

"Oh, good. I've been waiting for ten minutes. He said you'd be home about now."

"What? Who?"

"Oh, I've got something for you, miss. Don't you worry about it. But you might want to open your door."

"I'm not going to open my door. I have no idea who you are."

"Oh, I'm sorry," he said, seeming friendly enough. "I'm Jimmy. Mr. Alwend sent me. Got a present for you."

Alex. Again. What was it this time? I was torn between curiosity and a feeling that this was too much, too fast.

I walked cautiously toward the door, getting my keys out of my bag, watching Jimmy as he wrestled a large, flat object, wrapped in heavy brown paper and tied with string, out of the bed of the truck. He lifted it onto his back with a grunt and started toward the door.

"Go on, if you don't mind," he said. "I'll carry it inside for you."

I decided that he was legit, and even if he wasn't, he was unlikely to batter me with a weapon the size of a thick door and at least as unwieldy. I unlocked my door, allowing him to go in ahead of me.

Inside, he set the object on one end, pulled out a pocket knife and cut the strings. He stowed the knife, then ripped the paper off. I realized why it looked so much like a door. It *was* a door. Or doors — folding doors — seven-foot-tall panels with arched tops in weathered white paint and stained glass. The screen I'd so admired at the art fair.

Jimmy unfolded one section, revealing the beautiful patina and winking glass colors of the five-paneled screen.

"Wow." It was gorgeous. And it looked a hell of a lot bigger inside than it did outside.

"Where do you want it?" he asked with a grin, apparently pleased at my reaction.

"Over here," I said, directing him to where I imagined my bedroom wall would be. He set up the screen and unfolded it fully. It was an effective and attractive divider between the sleeping area, with its adjacent bathroom, and the rest of the space. I loved it. But now I felt almost uncomfortably in Alex's debt.

I realized Jimmy was looking at me.

"Um, thank you," I said. Then I wondered if he wanted a tip. "Oh, I guess I should —" I opened my bag to rummage for whatever dollar or two I might find when he held up a hand.

"Oh, I don't need anything, miss. Just wanted to let Mr. Alwend know how you liked it. Now, you enjoy that. I'm sure I'll see you again." He gave me another friendly grin, gathered up the paper wrapping and headed out the door, which I closed and locked behind him.

What the hell? Alex had a handyman elf spy delivering gifts to my apartment? I was thrilled to get it, of course, but where I came from, one didn't get gifts without giving something in return. At least without knowing the person really well. And I barely knew Alex.

But that wasn't right, either. I knew him more intimately

than I'd ever known a man — and yet I didn't know him at all. Shit. And he was coming to pick me up in an hour.

I showered and decided that I was happy enough with the prospect of seeing him again to find some frisky underwear amid my collection of mostly comfortable cotton. It was a matching satin set in light blue-green, a color I thought set off my eyes. The panties were cut high; the bra was cut low. In the mirror on the inside of the wardrobe door, I looked almost voluptuous. But I knew I was fast running out of cute underwear. If this crazy affair was going to continue, I might want to remedy that situation. Or make him deal with me in cotton.

Next: clothes. I didn't have much in the dressy department. And I had no idea what we were doing, anyway, except maybe going to drinks later at that bar Damien had mentioned, not that I'd told Alex about it.

I'd been told Florida was more casual than what I was used to up north, and from everything I'd seen, it was true. Beach culture had its benefits.

So: a short, black denim skirt that showed off my legs. Black leather sandals with a low heel, because it was October in Florida and still pleasantly warm. A light green tank top, almost the color of the underwear, and a floaty, sheer top over it with flaring sleeves, the same shade of green, only with black, swirling flourishes printed lightly over the fabric. I put my hair into a loose braid tied with a sheer black and green scarf.

I used eyeliner and mascara this time. The smoky look picked up the black in my outfit. My favorite dark red lipstick completed the look. I actually had a *look*. I pouted comically at the mirror. I should take the time to do this more often.

Then the knock came at the door, and I felt myself going all to pieces.

Buck up, Abbey, I told myself. *It's just a guy.*

No. *It's Alex.*

I took a deep breath, walked to the door and opened it.

I thought I must have guessed right about what to wear. He had on black pants and a button-up, long-sleeved, dark-gray shirt with turned-up patterned cuffs and trim. Kind of hip. And his stoic face was overtaken by a look of pure desire when he saw me.

"Come in," I said, smiling at his reaction.

He closed the door behind him, still not smiling. There was something so intense in his eyes, it was almost scary. And completely enthralling. He walked up to me, slowly, and put one hand lightly on my waist as he looked into my eyes. Then he leaned forward and kissed me in slow-motion, opening his mouth against mine, touching my tongue with his, until I felt a wave of molten heat work its way through my body from my lips to my toes.

He stepped back after this fathomless kiss and, finally, smiled, completely in possession of himself, just when I was stirred to my core. I let out a shaky sigh and tried to return his smile, but I knew my face betrayed everything.

"Have you forgiven me for the clay? Or would you like to punish me?" he teased.

I found my voice again and pointed at the screen. "Maybe we should talk about that, instead."

"It looks really nice in here," he said, walking toward the screen and strolling around it, making a pass through my newly defined bedroom space. I felt as if he'd run a hand over my naked body just by doing so. He came around the other side and looked at me, a trace of uncertainty entering his voice. "Do you like it?"

"It's beautiful, Alex, but I can't keep accepting gifts from you like this."

"Why not?"

"Because — I can't give you anything like it in return. And I don't want to feel like . . ."

"Feel like what?" he asked, walking up to me again, not touching me, except with his eyes.

"Look, I don't want to feel like I'm being paid for my services or something." I knew it sounded paranoid, or schoolgirlish, but it was what I was thinking.

He grinned. "If I were paying you for your services, as you call them, I couldn't afford you. Sloane, I don't think you realize that I enjoy being with you. If I give you things, it's because I want to make you happy. That's all."

I sat on the couch and looked up at him. "It just seemed like a lot. Today was kind of overwhelming."

Alex sat next to me and put a hand on my knee, circling it with his fingers. I could feel them wanting to travel, was tense with wanting it.

He looked up at me. "Just take this as it comes. As it goes. Because it's going somewhere nice." He kissed my cheek. "And it's very nice already." He kissed my neck. "More than nice." My chin. "This is — you are — everything I want right now." My lips, lightly. "Forget everything else. It's just me and you."

And he devoured my mouth with his, as that roving hand roamed up the inside of my thigh to my carefully chosen underwear, stroking me through the fabric, which grew more damp by the second. I moaned and almost involuntarily opened my mouth, hungry for him, sucking on his tongue as it penetrated my lips. He answered with "Mmmm," and that roving hand pushed the crotch of my panties aside. Now he was touching my clit, playing with it with his thumb before pushing one very deft finger inside me as he continued to kiss me. His other hand was at the small of my back, reaching up under the shirt, holding me lightly there; it was as if all of his powers were reaching me through his mouth, his thumb and that one finger, which probed me expertly, finding and stroking my sweet spot until I fairly vibrated under his touch. And then I came, groaning as he kissed me even harder, owning me in that moment. I was ready to give him anything.

But as my paroxysm quieted, his kiss became more gentle, and he withdrew his hand. He ended the kiss and touched my lips with his wet finger, pushing it inside my mouth. A strange sensation, tasting myself on his skin. Still in a haze of desire, I sucked on his finger until he withdrew it and looked at me.

"It's good, isn't it?" he whispered. "You and me."

"Yes." He made me want to say yes.

"Do you want more?"

"Yes, Alex." I leaned into him, nuzzling my head against his neck.

He stroked my hair and kissed my forehead. It didn't matter what had come before. What came next. Except —

"Alex?"

"Yes?"

"I hope we're going to dinner, because I'm ravenous."

He laughed. "Yes, we are. I'm ravenous, too. And not just for dinner." I looked up to see his eyes full of mischief. He took me by the hand, and I stood unsteadily. I took a deep breath and grabbed my purse, and we headed out into the cooling darkness of early evening.

BOHEMIA HAD a small harbor stuffed full of gorgeous boats that had easy access to the river — that is, the lagoon — and those boats had access to the ocean farther south and north at channels in the barrier islands. But mostly, I think, the boats enjoyed their pretty little home. The pretty people who lived in the condos that overlooked the pretty harbor had a short walk to the pretty riverfront restaurant where Alex now took me. Pretty, pretty, *pretty*. I felt as if I had moved into a postcard.

It had started to rain lightly. He used valet parking and escorted me in, on his arm. It all seemed so old-fashioned and sweet and strange. This wasn't the world I'd grown up in, even believed existed. But there we were, sitting at a candlelit table, eating shrimp cocktail with a delicious glass of sauvignon blanc, looking out through the glass at the waves crashing against this fragile spit of land. It was dark already, thanks to the rain, but the lights around the building caught the onslaught of water.

"That's pretty rough for the river," Alex commented. "Cold front coming through."

"Cold front," I giggled.

"What?"

"Florida's idea of a cold front. What, it's supposed to be sixty-two tomorrow?"

"That's cold for here! You watch," he said. "Everybody will be wearing sweaters tomorrow."

"Not me."

"If I'm lucky, you won't be wearing anything," he said innocently, sipping his wine as the waiter cleared the first course.

"I have class tomorrow. Trust me. I'll be wearing something."

"Hmm," he said. "I can imagine a few things."

"And I can't throw pottery in a garter belt and stockings," I joked.

"Ah, now we're talking." His eyes flared with interest.

"You just keep leading me down the garden path." I felt my face getting hot.

"And you keep following," he teased again, reaching across the table for my hand. "What's that about?"

"Good question."

I wasn't really sure. I'd never been a follower in my life. But there was something about Alex that made me want to do anything for him. Especially when he made me feel so — what was it? — *wanted*. Physically, I felt as if every cell in my being was alight when he was around. Surely this couldn't last. But honestly, for once in my life, I just didn't care. His hand was warm in mine; my hand was warm in his.

"Here you go," the waiter said, interrupting my reverie. We both withdrew our hands, the link broken, as the young man put a steak in front of Alex and a plate of pasta and scallops in front of me.

The meal was delicious. Alex told me stories about fishing with his parents when he was a kid, first casting lines into the surf, and then angling from small boats in the river. Once, when he was a slight six-year-old, they'd been fishing in kayaks and he'd hooked a huge redfish that fought him for ten minutes before he lost his little pole overboard.

"I cried," he said. "It was really embarrassing."

"Because you lost the fish?"

"Because I lost the pole!" he said. "My dad laughed his ass off. I loved that fishing pole. It was red. After that, he got me better gear, and I learned to feel more like a grown-up. But I never caught a fish that big again."

"Or maybe it seemed that big because you were so small."

"It could've swallowed me," he said, lifting the corner of his mouth.

"Fish stories. Just what I would expect from a writer," I said as his eyes danced.

The waiter arrived again to clear our plates and asked us if we wanted dessert.

"The Chocolate Bombe, two spoons," Alex said, "and two glasses of the Graham's Vintage Port."

The waiter's eyes grew big, as if he smelled a large tip. "Yes, sir."

"Are you being extravagant again?" I asked as he disappeared.

"Only a little. I told you. Wine doesn't count."

I looked Alex over, thinking about him as a little kid with his fishing pole, and then as the student Damien told me about who got beaten up all the time.

"Where'd you go to high school?" I asked, though I already knew.

"Bohemia High." His voice was flat, and he looked out the window into the darkness.

"Did you know then that you wanted to be a writer?"

"I used to write then, if that's what you mean," he said, turning back to me. "A lot of fantasy and science fiction. I loved it. Geek all the way. I haven't touched that stuff in years."

"Why not?"

"My college literature professors beat it out of me," he said drily.

"Professors, huh?"

"Mostly," he said lightly. "High school wasn't that great for me, either. Let's just say I was glad to get out of there."

"High school sucked for me, too," I said.

"Were you an artist then?" He seemed glad to be talking about me and not him.

"I was always into it, but I wasn't that good. I just had a love for it. So I put in the hours and got better. And it was a way to avoid other activities with other kids."

"Hell is other people, as the saying goes," Alex said.

"I don't think that's true. I actually started to like other people once I got to college and found my tribe."

"I want to like them, but they've proven disappointing so far. Although there are notable exceptions. Like you."

"I can't believe you had no friends at college." The idea worried me a little.

"Oh, I had a few," he conceded with a wry smile. "I tend to exaggerate. But remember, my time was seriously disrupted when — anyway, I took a year off, then went back, but I was less engaged in everything then. I just did enough to get by. I took a lot of classes at night or online. And my fellow writing students, who were so supportive in our early classes, became cutthroat competitors in later ones. It was really interesting to see. Their criticism gained an edge when they knew they had careers and MFAs to think about. By the time I graduated, I'd had it with the academic world. I traveled for a while, as I told you. But I really didn't have any other world I wanted to go to, except Bohemia Beach."

The waiter brought the glasses of port, long spoons and the dessert, a mound of mystery coated in a dusting of fine chocolate, accompanied by a scoop of ice cream and dark cherries.

"I think you're too hard on people. And on yourself," I

said, taking a sip of the port. The flavor was deep and dark and sweet. "Oh, my God, you did it again."

"You really do have a palate." He grinned. "And I don't think I'm too hard on people. I just choose not to put myself in a position where they'll let me down."

"That's life, you know," I said, picking up my spoon and looking for a way to attack the dessert. "You have to go through a lot of disappointments to get to the good stuff. That's the story of success, too. Which is why I'm willing to put up with my scary new teacher and do the work it's going to take to get really good."

"This is why you should be my muse," Alex said, taking his spoon and whacking the bombe with the edge. The shell cracked, revealing a coating of dark chocolate under the powder and over a layer of chocolate mousse. "You're brave. You're going after what you want. I want you to tell me about it. Your struggles. Your feelings. The people you meet." He dug out a spoonful of the mousse and held it out to me.

"Alex Alwend, investigative journalist," I joked as he held out a loaded spoon.

"Novelist, maybe," he said, waving the spoon in little circles, a spark in his eyes.

I opened my mouth, and he slowly inserted the bowl of the spoon. I closed my lips over the delicious burst of chocolate as he withdrew the spoon, watching me with his own kind of hunger.

"That's delicious," I said after it dissolved on my tongue.

"Now the ice cream," he said, offering me a spoonful.

I looked at him skeptically, but I was enjoying this little game. I opened my mouth, and he pushed the spoonful of heaven inside — caramel and — what was it?

"Caramel bourbon," he said, answering my unspoken

question as it melted rapturously in my mouth. He took a spoonful himself. "Mmm."

I dipped into the mousse and came up with not just chocolate, but deep red fruit.

"You've busted its cherry," Alex said innocently as I closed my lips around the spoon.

I smothered a laugh and got the bite down. "Don't do that, or you'll find *bombe* exploded all over you."

Alex just smiled and ate more of the ice cream.

"You don't need a muse," I prodded. "You need more people in your life."

He shook his head and finished his bite, topping it with a long sip of the port. "I want you to be my muse. Tell me your stories."

"You're silly," I said, taking another spoonful of the mousse and washing it down with the port. I could do no more. I groaned, overwhelmed by delicious food. "I'm so full now. We need to take a walk."

"It's raining," Alex said, waving at the waiter for the check.

"Do you have an umbrella?"

"Are you just trying to avoid being alone with me?"

"On the contrary," I said. "We have an invitation to drinks, and I want you to come."

A shadow flitted over his features, but only for a moment.

"With whom?"

"Damien said a bunch of the crowd is getting together at Oberon's. We could go have a drink, don't you think?"

"I'd rather take you home — I mean, not to end the evening, but — "

"Why, Alex," I said, surprised, "are you actually flustered?"

"Of course not," he said. "But why would I want to go out and have drinks when I can be alone with you?"

"Because I want to meet more people. I'm sure it's all people you know. And Damien invited you especially."

"He did?" Alex asked with suspicion. "He didn't look all that thrilled to see me with you the other day."

"Nonetheless."

I had to admit it: Alex looked uncomfortable. Unhappy, even. But I'd rather him be with me, among friends — potential friends — than be his imaginary muse, his lifeline to the world. And there would be plenty of time to be with him later, time I wanted very much. I gave him the most seductive look I could muster.

"One drink," I murmured. "And then I'm all yours."

"All mine," he mused, looking more interested. "All right. We can try it. But I'm going to drive. That's five blocks in the rain, and trust me, it won't seem that fun when you're soaking wet. At least not that kind of wet."

The twinkle had returned to his eyes, and he was back: the flirtatious, confident Alex I knew. He paid the check, silencing my objections with a wave, and we went outside to retrieve the car.

A few minutes later, we'd parked just a block from Oberon and began our walk under the umbrella.

There were more people on the street than I would have expected for a Monday night in the rain, but the bars here were lively oases of light and music. I could feel the pounding beats in my bones as we passed one dance club. It wasn't really my scene, but the energy transmitted itself into my body, and I leaned into Alex and smiled up at him. He smiled, too, but his mouth was thin and tense.

I thought little of it until we reached the open, black iron gate that marked the entrance to the indoor-outdoor bar. "OBERON" was spelled out on the ivy-covered brick wall outside, the metallic letters backlit by blue neon.

A hypnotic club groove spilled out onto the street, at a more friendly volume than the other place we'd passed, and I heard a cheer go up inside, followed by laughter. I stepped into the courtyard as Alex folded up the umbrella and saw Damien standing on a chair at the head of a packed table in the indoor area, knocking back a shot. Another cheer followed, and he held up the glass in triumph before catching my eye. He waved it at me, pointing at the glass, and I walked toward him with a grin.

Almost immediately, I realized I walked alone. I held up a finger to Damien, denoting patience. His brow wrinkled, but he quickly turned back to gabbing at his friends and admirers.

I turned around to find my date.

Alex was outside, leaning against the umbrella as if it were a cane, breathing hard as the rain hit his face.

I touched his shoulder, and he flinched.

"Alex! Are you all right?"

He looked up at me with a pale, hunted look before realigning his features. In a moment, he wore the blank face I'd noticed first at his party, the look of self-control.

"I'm fine," he said. "Maybe too much wine. Let's go to my place, OK? You can drive."

I knew in my heart that Alex had not had too much wine. Although I didn't understand why, he was afraid.

"Sure," I said softly, taking him by the arm, trying to cheer him with a smile, wondering what had made him so ill. "As long as you don't mind me driving that pretty convertible."

"As long as you don't put the top down," he said, a half-hearted joke. He opened the umbrella and walked slowly with me back toward his car. By the time we got there, he seemed like himself again. The spring was back in his step, and his face had regained some of its color. But he let me drive.

I HAD to ask a couple of times to make sure I was heading in the right direction, but I was mastering the geography pretty quickly, and the thrumming car was fun to drive. Alex guided me to his building and the garage beneath, and I parked the car.

"I wonder if I can afford a chauffeur," he said as I turned off the engine. "You'd look sexy in the hat."

I glanced at him. He sounded OK, flirtatious as always, but I thought he still looked a little wan.

"You can't afford me, remember?" I said as we got out. I pointed to a door at the back of the garage. "Hey, does that go to the beach? Maybe we can get some air."

"You are a fiend for the outdoors this evening."

"Alex," I said, walking over to him and grabbing his hand. "It'll be good for you."

"For me?" He laughed, but his eyes held a trace of vulnerability. "If you say so. At least the rain's stopped."

Walking through the door from the stuffy, cement-walled garage into the windy night was a revelation. The rain *had* stopped, and scudding, moonlit clouds raced overhead. I could hear the waves but couldn't see them, yet; we had to use the wooden steps to walk up and over the dunes, through a cluster of palm trees and sea grapes. As we descended to the sand, I took in a great lungful of air.

"This is fantastic!" I let go of his hand and kicked off my sandals. And then, with arms outstretched, feeling a joyful freedom I hadn't known since I was a child, I ran in a big circle on the beach, through the moonlit waves, over the rough bits of shell in the sand, and back into Alex's arms.

He kissed me briefly, then enfolded me in a long embrace. I could feel a current between us, felt him drawing strength from me. At least that's what it seemed like. He released me and touched my cheek.

"Let's walk," he said.

He took my hand, and we walked along the shore. Still in his shoes, he stayed just out of the water's reach. I let the foamy edge of the biggest waves catch my toes. The wind and waves caressed my skin. The moon played hide-and-seek with the clouds, creating a high contrast between the alternating darkness and bursts of cool white light, which threw our shadows onto the sand.

"What's that?" I stopped suddenly, sensing more than seeing a large, dark shape before us on the edge of the water.

Alex stopped, too, looking. Then he whispered: "I think it's a turtle. Let's just sit here and watch."

He lowered himself to the sand and held out a hand. I let him pull me to his lap. I could just make out his smile as he wrapped his arms around me.

"Stay still," he murmured into my ear.

We watched the hulking, rounded shape move slowly out of the water, not ten feet in front of us. She paused often as she eased up the sand, almost to the dune line, with the moon picking out the symmetrical tracks made by her flippers. And then, after some consideration, she started to dig.

I could see bursts of sand shooting out from under her body as she carved out a well big enough to hold her eggs.

She turned, completing the circle, and settled into place as she began to drop the white, round eggs into the hole. I felt caught up in her trance, in a ritual that had been repeated for thousands of years, and shivered against Alex's body. He held me more tightly, in silence, as we watched the turtle complete her sacred rite. And then she began digging again, covering the eggs with her rear flippers, filling in and scattering sand with her front flippers to disguise the nest.

When at last she moved back toward the ocean, I was stiff from holding the same position for so long. I moved slightly, and the turtle lifted her head toward me. I caught her wide eye, startled, clear, and then she made her way into the waves and was gone.

I rolled off Alex and lay flat on my back against the sand.

"That was incredible," I sighed to him, to the night.

"Primal," he whispered, lying next to me, putting a hand on my stomach under the gauzy shirt, the tank top.

He lowered his head to mine and kissed me deeply, his mouth pure heat in the cool darkness as he drew my lower lip between his teeth, nipping me, as he matched his lips to mine, opening, probing with his tongue. I trembled as a delicious flame warmed me from the inside out, as my senses sang in this beautiful and wild place, touched by this new friend, lover, almost stranger.

He ran a hand up one of my bare legs.

"You have goose bumps," he said with surprise. "I'm taking you inside."

"You can take me here."

"Oh, I'll take you," he said, his voice more rough. "But in comfort, and without the world watching. I want you to myself tonight." I became aware of the rows of faceless condo buildings behind us for the first time; with Alex, I forgot everything.

He pulled me up, and we walked back to his building. I found my sandals, and we got into the elevator, brushing off the sand, exchanging almost sheepish smiles.

"We might need to wash off some of that sand," he observed.

"You're fine," I said as we got out of the elevator and entered his condo. I headed for the powder room and called over my shoulder. "I'm the one with the sandy limbs."

"Exactly," he grinned. "I'll get some wine. Meet me in my bathroom."

I paused in the doorway. "You're bossy."

"You like it."

I felt myself blush and closed the door behind me. Damn him, but he was right. I'd always lacked confidence; I wasn't a first-move kind of girl. And no one had ever called me beautiful before. It was heady and freeing to put myself into his hands. Now was not the time to analyze why.

I used the toilet and looked at myself in the mirror. My hair was half out of its braid, a wind-strewn riot. My cheeks looked pink from the wind and arousal. My eye makeup looked just as dramatic as it had earlier, but my lipstick was gone. He liked my lipstick, I thought. I applied the deep red color and took the scarf out of my hair, running my fingers through it until it was just this side of wild. I glanced down at my sandy legs and feet and arms.

There was one move I could make.

I pulled off all my clothes and picked out just the gauzy top, pulling it back over my head. It skimmed the very tops of my thighs. Through its sheer colors, it revealed everything.

Perhaps I could drive him just a little bit as wild as he drove me.

I took a deep breath and walked out into the living space. It seemed so empty and modern, filled with comfortable, chic furniture as it was. I heard water running and followed the sound toward the master bathroom, home of the infamous shower. Was that what he had in mind?

I knocked lightly on the bathroom door.

"Come in," he said, and I pushed it open.

Shirtless, shoeless and gorgeous, Alex was just turning off the faucets for the huge tub at the end of the room. He had the lights dimmed, but candles were lit on the ledges around the tub. Bubbles foamed up from the water. I could hear jets gushing. He'd already poured two glasses of champagne. I felt a tumble of emotions, from arousal to amusement; it looked like a commercial. But it also looked wonderfully inviting.

Alex looked up at me. His mouth dropped open — ever so slightly — and I saw him swallow.

"Sloane," he said with difficulty. "Once again I am reminded how lucky I am."

His response pleased me, and I smiled. "Are you going to offer me some champagne?"

He picked up a full glass and held it out, and I walked over to him. I took a long sip. I set it down on one of the ledges by the tub and just stood, watching him as he looked me over, his eyes bold and possessive. He reached out one finger and traced a nipple through the fabric. I closed my eyes, feeling it tighten, harden under his touch, sensitivity growing by the second. In a moment, both of his hands were on my breasts, which were more than a handful as he squeezed them. And then he was touching my waist, moving down to the tops of my thighs, where he brushed away some of the sand that still clung to my skin.

"Oh, you are dirty, aren't you?" he whispered.

"Yes, Alex." I opened my eyes. He was unbuttoning his pants, which he dropped to the floor, along with his dark blue briefs. Just like that, he was naked, powerful, a sexual force that made me almost forget his earlier fears. What conflict must rage in his soul? There was none here, as he scooped me up and set me in the tub, gauzy top and all. It clung to my breasts and swirled in the jets of water.

I felt myself breathe harder as I watched Alex climb in with me, but he didn't lower himself completely into the water. His cock was at full attention, and he held it with one hand as he gently reached toward me, grasping me under the chin, commanding me with his eyes.

I moved to my knees and ran my wet hands down his tapering waist, the inviting hips. First, I reached to my champagne and took another long sip, looking into his eyes, reading his hunger. And then I took him in my mouth, deeply, with pleasure, sucking his sweet hardness with a curious thrill. There was power in making him want me so, and I wanted him even more in return. I ran my tongue up and down his rigid length, giving special attention to the moist tip, where I tasted the dew of his desire. Then I took him deeper, feeling a tremor go through his body as I moved back and forth, lost in his taste, his bliss. He withdrew with a grunt; I could tell he had more in mind.

He sank into the water and pulled the wet sheath of clothing over my head, casting it into the shadows. He grasped me around the waist.

"Lean back," he said, and I did so, against one of the jets of the tub, feeling a drowsy satisfaction as the stream massaged my back and he gently massaged my bud. I let out a stuttering sigh as he lifted one of my legs to his shoulder and pushed himself inside me.

I clenched around him almost immediately, feeling his heat transition from my clitoris to my core as he built his rhythm, angling deep inside my tight cleft. The jet pounded my back; he pounded my sex. The water was a warm embrace, and I floated on a wave of pleasure and sensation until a tsunami of orgasms crashed through me, one after the other.

He came hard, spurting inside me, and I cried out, wrapping my legs around him as he repositioned and pulled me onto his lap, deeper, for an even more wrenching climax. He nibbled on my neck, his body slippery and hot beneath my hands as the water whirled around us, sloshing over the sides. I heard myself moan into his shoulder with something between anguish and pleasure.

Alex kissed my shoulder, my neck, my ear and then my lips with languid, exquisite tenderness. He filled me completely. Did he feel the same?

We came off our high slowly. Eventually, he withdrew from me, and I missed him; he leaned back and turned me, pulling me close so I leaned back against him, and we drank our champagne.

"Oh, Alex." I loved the feel of his name in my mouth, as I loved the feel of him nestled against me, one arm around my waist as the water gurgled around us.

"We fit together," he murmured, kissing my shoulder, echoing my earlier thoughts. "You'll be my muse, won't you, Sloane?"

He was back to this odd subject, but here, in his arms, completely under his spell, I couldn't refuse.

"I'll try," I said. It wasn't exactly yes. But I wondered if I could ever tell him no.

ALEX DROPPED me off at my place in the morning. Though I'd slept like a rock in his bed, with the sound of the ocean lulling me, I hadn't slept for long enough. I was exhausted. I dragged myself to school in jeans and a T-shirt, enjoying the mild weather, noticing how many people were wearing sweatshirts around me. Cold front, I remembered with a smile.

"Sloane Abbey?" asked the older woman working at the front desk as I walked in. Great memory; she'd only seen me my first day.

"Yes?"

"Your application's been approved. Can you start today?"

I was confused for a moment until I took the piece of paper she was holding. A work schedule. I was the newest ceramics assistant, which meant a small paycheck to supplement my new starving artist lifestyle.

"Great!" I said. "Sure!"

"Talk to Gary to find out what needs to be done," she said, turning away from me to answer the ringing phone.

I found Gary in the same place I'd met him the day before, with a large leather-hard vase on the wheel, this one more round than the one he'd thrown yesterday. It was held in place with clamps; he had a trimming tool in his hand, about the size of a pencil, with a wooden handle and an open metal triangle on the end.

"Welcome, minion!" he said cheerfully as I sat next to him with my gear, clay and water bucket.

I grinned. He was funny. And cute. "So you heard."

"Thank God. I was getting tired of doing everything myself. Plus I have a real job, you know."

"What do you do?" I asked, preparing my clay.

"Plasterwork. Foam carving. Fancy stuff. You know, all those mansions that have elaborate trimmings that look like stone?"

"Really? You do that?" I cut my slab of clay and dropped it on the still wheel.

"When there's work. Which is sporadic." Gary lowered his voice. "I've started doing a few art shows, too, and a couple of galleries have picked up my work. But I don't like to advertise that in class."

"Prodigy," I teased.

"Maybe it's the big hands." He held them out and smiled, reminding me of my observation the day before. Hands were a fairly innocuous physical trait to note, but his tone had a touch of flirtatiousness. Or was I imagining it?

"So you have work for me today?"

"Yeah." He applied the trimming tool, and a thin snake of clay peeled away from the vase, creating a neat foot. "I'm trying to schedule you around your classes. I'm going to have you help Rose with a kids' class she's doing after lunch. And then, around five o'clock, we'll empty a couple of the kilns that are firing this morning."

"Who does the night shift?" I asked, pounding the corners of my chunk of clay.

"Night shift?

"Cleanup, monitoring firings, that sort of thing. That's what I did at the studio in Ohio."

Gary chuckled. "We get our firings done during the day, but I always believe in having someone around when a kiln is going. Did you ever hear the story about Montrose's first kiln?"

"Was this before he did the really big pieces in the garage-size kiln?"

"Yeah, way before," Gary said, touching his tool lightly to the side of the spinning vase, carving concentric circular grooves in succession. "When he was still married to Vanessa Wylie."

"Oh, I love her work!" I said, recalling the delicate sculpted porcelain pieces she was known for.

"Well, they had a kiln in a shed outside their house in Colorado, and one day they were doing a Cone 10 firing." Cone 10; I rummaged in my brain for the number. Almost 2400 degrees. "And both of them thought the other one had turned it off. It fired *all night* at Cone 10."

"Holy shit."

He laughed. "Exactly. When they figured it out over breakfast and went out to check, the walls of the shed were glowing red hot."

"Damn!"

"They had to use a rake to reach in and flip the breaker. Hours later, when they finally could get in there, half the kiln had melted, and everything in the shed was well and truly singed."

"Scary," I said. "Between the heat and the chemicals, this is really dangerous work."

"And don't forget the personalities," Gary said in a low voice, nodding at the door, where Montrose had arrived late again.

He hadn't arrived alone. Behind him trailed a man with longish, graying hair, worn khakis and a golf shirt, carrying an audio recorder. With him was a young woman my age, with long blond hair pinned up roughly on her head, pieces sticking out in a way that added to her attractive energy. She carried an overstuffed bag and an impressive camera. It took a moment for me to realize it was my cousin, Calista.

I waited for her to scan the room and caught her eye with a little wave and a smile. She shot me a big, toothy grin and mouthed, "I'll talk to you later."

The journalists followed Montrose around the room as he talked; Calista shot photos of him whenever he paused to interact with a student. I wondered if he was interacting with the students just because the newspaper people were there. He sure seemed nicer than yesterday.

I decided I'd better get something going before he got to me. I still didn't know what would make my teacher happy, but my projects from the day before seemed unworthy. I closed my eyes and thought about what I wanted to see, to feel with my hands. The image of the great sea turtle came to me, burying her future in the sand, and I imagined her long voyage through the ocean each year to lay eggs on the same beach. I imagined the life she must see in her underwater world, and I began to center and shape my clay.

I already had two quirky tubes stuck to pieces of board by the time Montrose came around, and I was working on a third. I glanced up at him and his entourage. His brow creased, but he said nothing to me.

Calista made a little face that told me she wasn't all that impressed with her subject, but she snapped a photo of me and smiled.

"Now this is one of our finest students," Montrose said, stopping by Gary, whose vase had taken on striking texture under his deft fingers.

"What are you learning from your teacher, here?" the reporter asked.

Gary didn't answer for a moment, as he concentrated on a subtle pattern he was creating with his tools. Calista snapped a few fast photos as he worked. Then he looked up with a thoughtful gaze.

"I'm learning to develop a vision for my work," Gary said. "Montrose is a man of vision, and he's good at helping us think a project through."

The reporter smiled, happy with his quote, and he and Calista jotted down Gary's name before moving on after the nodding Montrose.

As she passed by, Calista squeezed my shoulder and whispered in my ear. "Lunch? We'll be done here by noon."

"Sounds good," I replied, "unless Gary has some work for me?"

"Not till 2," he said, happily manipulating his stout vase.

"Meet you in the lobby gallery," I said to Cali, and she nodded, catching up to Montrose and the reporter as they left the room.

I glanced at Gary as I pulled up on my spinning clay with my fingers, extending the height of my third cylinder. "Vision? Nice one."

"I think he helps students with that," Gary said. "Maybe not me, but some people." He shot me an wide-eyed, innocent look under his mop of curly hair that made me laugh.

"Anyway," he said, "the school will love it. And any good press that helps the school helps us. Did you hear somebody donated money for all our clay this session?"

"I heard," I said drily, thinking of Alex and his generous impulses.

"I'm going to throw twice my usual pieces in the next two

months!" Gary said with enthusiasm, and I laughed again, turning back to my clay and my vision of the sea.

"So I HEAR you're dating Alex Alwend," were Calista's first words when she got me outside on the sidewalk.

"God damn Damien. Who else has he told?"

"Not sure," Cali admitted. "But probably just me. He wants me to talk you out of it."

"Do *you* want to talk me out of it?" I asked with more uncertainty as we walked through the door of Picasso's, a bakery-café a block away from the school. "You know him, too, right?"

Cali smiled kindly as she plopped her photographer's luggage next to a corner booth and took a seat. I joined her.

"I was a few years behind them in school," she said, "but I knew Alex a little. He seemed OK. He had some trouble with other kids, but I think it got better in his last couple of years. You know, when the other kids grew up a little. But he always seemed kind of shy."

"If you say so," I said, giving the menu more attention than it deserved. I snuck a glance at Cali, who was looking at me with amusement, her wide blue eyes twinkling.

"So," she said, "he's not shy?"

"Not with me," I said, and she laughed.

"You never struck me as someone who would jump feet-first into a torrid affair. Assuming it's a torrid affair," Cali said, her idle tone failing to hide her interest. She did a quick scan of the menu as a young waitress with blue and pink hair arrived. "I'll have the quiche special. Sloane?"

"Um, the BLT looks good. With un-sweet iced tea."

"I'll have some of that, too," Cali said.

"That was easy," the waitress said with a smile, heading off behind the counter.

"You're right," I said. "I've — surprised myself with this thing with Alex. I mean, I guess I need a reality check. Am I crazy?"

Cali looked me over, and a grin slowly took over her face. Though she was more fair than Damien, I could see some of his angles in her cheekbones, her eyebrows.

"You've got it bad," she said. "But that's OK. Reality is overrated."

"Maybe." I sipped my newly arrived tea.

"Besides, he's loaded," she said flippantly. "Not that it matters."

"Of course not." I grinned back at her. "Actually, his — environment is kind of intimidating. But the beach is so beautiful."

"That it is," Cali said. "But the best things in life are free, and that includes the beach."

"It's not about the beach," I said, feeling a little defensive. "It's definitely not about the money. I just — can't help myself."

Cali laughed. "Oh, my God, you *have* changed, haven't you? I remember you from years ago — the straight-A student, super-serious, working your ass off."

"I'm not that different," I said, "though I decided it was time to do what I wanted instead of worrying about what everyone else wanted for me. That's why I came here."

"And Alex was something you wanted, too?"

"Not until he made it clear to me," I said, not wanting to get into details.

"Really? How interesting." She arched one eyebrow. "So how's the school?"

"I'm only two days in, but it's good. And I got a part-time job there, too, so that gives me a little wiggle room, budget-wise."

"If you're not on the Alwend scholarship," my cousin teased as the waitress arrived with our food. I gave Cali a dark look and took a bite of my sandwich: delicious tomato, cool lettuce and crispy bacon with a nice spread of seasoned mayo on wheat toast. And hot, salty fries to boot. Much better than the school's snack stand.

"That guy Gary is cute," Cali said.

"I know," I said lightly. "So how are you? How's the job?"

She rolled her eyes. "I love the job, but the job I love is disappearing. There's a new round of layoffs coming up. They're making everybody reapply for their jobs. The company is killing its newspapers to save them. Well, really, to make stockholders happy until it all goes to hell."

"And it's going to hell?"

"Definitely," she said. "I'm working on Plan B."

"You going to stick with photography?"

"As long as I can." Her smile betrayed a tinge of anxiety.

"So who's your latest beau?" I asked. Cali had always had a boyfriend in school. Or serial boyfriends. They couldn't resist her bright energy and blond good looks.

"Ugh," she said, swirling her tea. "Damn reporter who broke my heart. I'm on hiatus."

"Not that guy who was with you at the school?" I asked, thinking of her tired-looking companion.

"Oh, hell, no," she said. "A cutie who went to New Jersey for another job."

"That sucks."

"Yeah, I know. I'm trying to ignore men and spend time with my friends. Hey, why don't you come out with me tonight? I'm going to see my friend Esme's band. Ez and the Emeralds. You'll dig it. You can invite Alex, if you want."

I hesitated, not wanting to tell Cali about Alex's spell outside Oberon the night before.

"I can come," I said. "I think he might have something else."

She looked at me with a mix of curiosity and concern. "It's a few blocks down the street at the Junction Box, by the railroad tracks. Meet me there at 8, OK?"

"Do they really go on that early? Because I have to get in at a reasonable time tonight, or I'm gonna die."

Cali nodded, her expression pure mischief. "I take it you're not burning the midnight kiln."

"Shut up," I said, eating a fry with a mock frown.

She laughed again. "I've missed you, cousin. You're the sister I never had."

I offered Cali a fry, which she took with a wink. It felt good to know I had someone on my side. Even if she did love giving me crap.

On my way back to the school, I checked my phone and saw a message from Alex, the same one he'd sent the day before: "Tonight?"

I stopped outside the main building and leaned against the wall, where a few other students were smoking and chatting and checking their phones.

"Meeting cousin Cali at Junction Box at 8 to hear a band," I texted back. "Want to come?"

While I waited to see if he'd respond, I clicked through email and social media, finding nothing of interest. I'd really shut myself off from the world in the past several months, or at least the online world. I'd been too busy trying to get where I was going.

My phone chimed with a new text. "Can't. See you later?"

Can't. What did that mean? He'd been available to meet me when I wasn't going to the club. He just didn't want to go to the club.

"Not sure," I typed back. "Need my beauty sleep."

"No you don't. If you get any more beautiful my heart will stop."

I felt my knees go rubbery and looked around, wondering if anyone noticed the wave of heat that surely must be emanating from me in the cool afternoon.

"If you haven't heard from me by" — I pondered how late I was willing to stay up — "10, can't do it."

That would almost certainly ensure I wouldn't see him, but I had to be careful not to burn out. And maybe it was healthy to stay away from him for a night, even if my body and soul wanted to feel him next to me more than anything. It was almost like saying no.

His response came back quickly. "A shame to waste such an early bedtime."

Damn his teasing, his pointed distractions. "Going back into school. Talk to you later."

"We don't have to talk," came his reply. "Though I need a muse report, too."

"So demanding," I couldn't resist replying.

"I thought you were going back to school." I could see the smile in the words.

I decided not to respond with words. I took a selfie of just my lips — after a quick application of lipstick — and sent him a picture of a provocative pucker. Then I headed inside.

His response came just as I was about to turn off my

phone and stow my purse in my locker. It was a photo of his torso. Shirtless. With one hand tucked just inside the waist-line of his jeans, not so far as to be more than suggestive, but oh, how suggestive it was. I turned off the phone, tried to ignore the ache between my legs and focused on innocent thoughts as I made my way to help Rose with her afternoon class, filled with eager preschool kids and their mothers, ready to play with clay.

I HAD some free time after Rose's class, so I returned to the wheel in the now-empty Studio B and worked on shaping the wet tubes I'd thrown that morning. I transformed them into imaginary pieces of coral reef, textured and organic, and threw another cylinder, tall and skinny. I wasn't sure what it would be yet, but I had started to envision a larger sculpture, perhaps even a water feature — a fountain with a broad bowl or base, a rippling ocean floor. Suddenly, I was excited at the work, at how much I had to get done and how inspired I was to do it.

As I was extending the new cylinder, I heard a noise behind me and turned. It was Montrose, observing me from just inside the doorway. He gave me the barest suggestion of a smile and walked toward me.

"Ms. Abbey, good to see you working."

"Sloane, please," I said, pausing, letting the piece spin, wondering if he'd stab it to death. "I can't really call you Montrose if you keep calling me Ms. Abbey. Since you're the teacher. It doesn't seem right. And especially because — I'm such an admirer of your work. I really appreciate the chance to take this class with you."

He looked pleased, and his devilish face relaxed into a more approachable mien. He sat on the stool where Gary usually sat. "Thank you. So what are you working on?"

"I had an idea about sea life. About what a turtle sees as she moves through the ocean. So that's what I'm working on. I thought it might be a good assemblage. Even a fountain."

Montrose stroked his goatee and looked me over with what I discerned might be more than a professional interest, but his tone was as sharp as ever.

"So-called 'art' about the ocean is about as common around here as flip-flops and burrito shops," he said dismissively. "What are you trying to *say?*"

I felt my brow wrinkle. "I'm trying to evoke a feeling —"

"Feelings aren't enough. A feeling doesn't make great art. It might be nice, but at least in my class, I don't want my students to be *nice.* Their work should not be *nice.* Are you too nice for my class — Sloane?"

"I'm not too nice." I thought I saw a flicker in his eyes, of mischief, as if he'd forced me to say something I didn't want to say. In fact, I was nice. I'd always been too nice. But maybe I wasn't, given the past few days. Maybe I shouldn't be.

"That's good," he said. "Nice girls are so dull. Think about your work." He stood, laying a hand on my shoulder. "Think about what you're trying to say. And we'll talk again."

At his touch, I was instantly sorry I had told him not to call me Ms. Abbey. I wanted that formality, more distance between me and this man, who offered me another of his unpleasant smiles before turning and leaving the room.

On the other hand, when I turned back to my cylinder, I knew what it was going to be. It was a tentacle, menacing, reaching up from the dark depths to take what it could, a wrenching disturbance in the world of what was peaceful and good, dull and nice.

At the end of the day, I found Gary in his clay-spattered T-shirt and jeans in the firing room, which held an impressive collection of kilns. The large cylinders of fire brick, wrapped in metal skins, were arrayed around the square room, each equipped with a computer panel for programming each firing. Two of the ten were operating, and they emanated deep heat.

"Just a couple of bisque firings," Gary said. "I don't like working in here during glaze firings. Those chemicals make me nervous, even with the venting."

"Wow," I said, still marveling at the large work space and number of kilns. "This is awesome."

"Yeah, it is. I've just gotten started on this one. If you'll get the pieces out of the one next to me and put them on those shelves?" He pointed to empty shelves that lined the walls. There was a table in the middle, too, which had several greenware pieces on it — delicate pots, dry but not yet fired. "And then we'll load it up with those. I'll crank them up in the morning."

"No problem." I lifted the lid of the kiln until it stood upright and carefully started to remove the freshly glazed pots. They still held a hint of warmth. "Whose work is this?"

"It's a mix," he said. "Mostly night classes. Some of it's really good, but most of it is kind of, shall we say, by artists-in-progress."

"Aren't we all."

Gary must have caught my sardonic tone. He set a broad, pretty green bowl on a shelf and looked up at me. "What is it?"

"Montrose found me working earlier."

"And?" Gary's gaze was unusually dark.

"He basically told me what I was doing was crap. But I suppose that's why I'm here."

"Oh," Gary said, his face lightening a bit. "Did he destroy your piece?"

"No, but I think he took a little bit of my soul," I said.

Gary let out a laugh that wasn't all merry. "I think he collects them," he said, then more seriously, "Be careful."

"What do you mean?" I was admiring a handful of tiles I was pulling out of the kiln. They were decorated with the impressions of shells and glazed in a buttery gold and light blue.

"I just think he's fonder of some students than others."

"With me, I'm pretty sure it's the opposite," I said wryly, but I wondered, remembering his touch on my shoulder. I looked up at Gary, who gazed at me with concern. "Don't worry." I was trying to convince myself as much as him. "I can handle myself."

He nodded, and we got back to work, lifting out the pieces and the shelves, excavating the layers of pots. We chatted about the other teachers and departments in the school, and eventually about restaurants, after I told him about the great BLT I'd had for lunch.

"Why don't we grab a burrito after this?" he asked as he helped me load the last of the greenware into the kilns. "I know a great place."

"Ha! Our teacher mentioned the abundance of burritos around here."

"Did he? I doubt he ever eats them. He's missing out," Gary said with a smile.

"That would be nice," I said. Nice. That word again. "I'm

meeting my cousin in a little while at the Junction Box to hear a band, but I have time for a bite."

"Ez and the Emeralds!" he said. "They're really cool. I was thinking about going to that."

And there it was, the makings of a date, though I quickly told myself it wasn't. Gary was a friendly sort, and I was happy to be making friends here, especially one who watched my back.

The burritos were delicious, full of wholesome, tasty ingredients, and mine was so big I had to eat it with a fork. And Gary was easy to talk to. We found we both had a love for old movies, and our conversation made the short walk to the Junction Box fun.

Inside, we found Cali, Damien and a lot of the people I'd seen at Alex's party loitering around the bar, waiting for the band while canned rock music filled the space. Gary saw some friends and called out as he headed across the room to exchange high-fives with them and order beer.

Damien gave me a crafty look over his gin and tonic. "You do switch tracks quickly, don't you, coz?"

"What? No! That's Gary. I work with him at the art school."

"I know who he is," Damien said. "Good guy. You could do worse. In fact, you may already have."

"Shut it, Damien," Cali said, coming up behind him and holding out a drink to me. "You just skated in at the end of happy hour. You can have my other Old-Fashioned. These are awesome. You like whiskey?"

"I think so," I said doubtfully.

"She's a journalist," Damien said, aiming a thumb at his sister. "She has to like whiskey."

I took a sip of the drink and found I liked it very much. I

lifted my head with an "ah" and a smile. Damien nodded with approval as Cali shouted, "Ez!"

I looked over my shoulder to see a pretty brunette with a mod haircut, bangs swooping low over one eye, heading toward Cali. They exchanged a big hug. "Ez, I want you to meet my cousin, Sloane. She just moved here. She's a ceramic artist."

"Trying," I said with a smile, reaching out to shake her hand.

"Cool," Ez said. "I sing."

"More than sing. She's the main attraction," Damien said. "When do you go on?"

"Five minutes," she said. "I'm so glad this place has a real piano. The guys are already set up. They're just, uh, taking a break in the back." She turned to me and whispered: "Not my scene. I prefer drinking to smoking any day." She called out to the bartender. "Neil! One of those!" She pointed at my glass.

"Two for you, Ez. It's happy hour," said Neil, who sported a full head of rusty hair, a handlebar mustache and suspenders over his button-up white shirt. "For about thirty more seconds."

"He likes me," Ez said simply. "Watch. They'll be doubles. Where'd you come from?"

I took another sip. "Ohio."

"The land of ice and snow," Cali said. "Suckers."

Ez laughed, taking her very full drinks from Neil. She downed one of them in one long draft.

"Fuck, that's good," she said, the lights of the bar sparkling in her brown eyes. "Here, you have this one." She shoved the other glass into my hand and walked off toward the stage.

"She's kind of keyed up when she performs," Cali explained.

I just nodded, not sure what to think. The rest of Ez's band mates — the Emeralds — came out from their hiding places. There was a drummer, a banjo player, a bass player and a guitarist, all guys. In addition to what they carried, I saw a few funky percussion instruments, a flute and a recorder set up on one of the speakers.

Ez sat at the baby grand, a nice accessory for a place like this, I thought. The bar was attractive, with a lot of dark wood trim and Victorian touches, but this was no piano lounge, that's for sure. The buzz around me dimmed with anticipation as the musicians hit their first couple of notes, tuning, getting into the zone. And then Ez started playing.

Her music was surprising after our frenetic introduction. Her voice, her lyrics and her piano work were by turns full of longing and full of attitude, sometimes eerie, sometimes ebullient.

The band, with its odd combination of instruments, seemed to fit her perfectly, showing her off but shining in its own right. The bar's patrons swayed, sometimes dancing, and cheered mightily when the band finished its first set.

"Did you like it? I think she's awesome," Cali said, her cheeks rosy from drinking. I wondered if mine were, too. I was almost done with the extra-large second Old-Fashioned.

"She's great! They're great together," I said, feeling light and happy. And part of something. I liked this place, these people. I felt my phone buzz in my bag and pulled it out.

"Has Cinderella turned into a pumpkin?" said Alex's text.

Shit. What time was it? My phone told me it was 9:30. I could wait and hear the second set. I could go home. But if the latter, I wasn't sure I should drive. As soon as I started thinking about it, I felt a wave of fatigue. Maybe I should bag it, so I could survive the week.

Gary materialized at my elbow. "Aren't they awesome?" he said. "Ez is terrific." His eyes were glowing.

"A bit of a crush, eh?" I asked, feeling loose enough to tease him.

"Maybe," he said. "I'm vulnerable to pretty women." He wiggled his eyebrows at me.

I blushed. "I think I have to go home, or I'm not going to be able to drag myself into school tomorrow."

"Well, we don't have Montrose's class in the morning. Do you have something else?"

"Yeah, glazing techniques."

"Right," he said. "Do you want me to walk you to your car?"

"I don't think I can drive right now. So maybe I just need to hang out a while till I'm OK." I knew I sounded confused, but that's what a buzz will do for you.

"I can drive you. I've only had a couple of beers. For me, that's like water with fizz."

"Oh, I can't ask you to do that," I said, but I was relieved at the offer.

"No problem," he said, laid back as always. "Hey, guys, I'm going to drive Sloane home, and then I'll come back for the second set," he told my cousins.

"Right," Damien said with sarcasm.

"Thank you," Cali said to Gary, while glaring at Damien. "You OK?" she said to me.

"Absolutely fine," I said, "except for the not being able to drive part."

She laughed. "OK. I'll call you tomorrow."

I pulled out my phone and texted Alex. "Heading home." Noncommittal. I'd text him again when I got there.

Gary enthused about Ez and her band as we walked back to the art school parking lot, and then again during the ride in his van to my place.

"They should be on the national scene," he declared. "They should get discovered!"

"Maybe they will be," I said. "They're really good."

"You know, I play a little drums myself. And ukulele. But that's nothing. Everybody plays ukulele."

"I guess I'll have to learn then," I said, amazed and amused as we pulled into my driveway. "Thanks so much for the ride."

"No problem!" Gary said, happy, still high from the music. "I'll see you tomorrow."

He looked at me for a long moment, his warm smile transmitting some of his glow, and I felt it radiate to my skin. I smiled awkwardly and waved and got out of the van, a little flummoxed by the flutter of attraction between us, and headed for my door, not watching to see him leave.

As I put my key in the lock, I saw a shift in my shadow — headlights behind me. Gary again?

I turned to see Alex's Mustang pulling up as Gary's van headed down the street.

Ah. This could be interesting.

I turned the key the rest of the way and went inside, turning on a lamp, leaving the door open behind me. I dropped my satchel on my work table next to a pile of books I'd been sorting and turned to watch Alex slip into the room and close the door.

"Who was that in the van?" he asked, his face not quite as controlled as usual.

I leaned against the table. I was cool. I had nothing to hide. "My ride? Gary. I work with him at the school."

"Gary. Your pottery friend, right?"

"Right. He's a good guy. I'd had a little too much to drink, so he offered me a ride."

Alex took a few more steps into the room, looking around as if to convince himself we were alone. "I could have given you a ride."

"I didn't want to trouble you. It was getting late."

"It's never too late for you to call me." He walked up to me and wrapped an arm around my waist. "Besides, I'll give you the best ride in town." He leaned close and kissed my neck. My body responded, buzzed and pliant, but I realized part of me was annoyed with him, with his presumptuousness.

"I told you I'd let you know if I could see you," I said.

He pulled back. "Didn't you? You said you were going home."

"That wasn't an invitation."

"Oh, I think it was."

The power in his voice sent a thrill up my spine. He wrapped both arms around me, pushing up against me, against the table. I felt his erection through his jeans, his jeans to mine. I still had my pottery clothes on; no carefully chosen outfit, no feminine lures. Except for lipstick. Which fell victim to his own lips, now on mine, working me slowly, opening me, electrifying me from my mouth outward.

My annoyance melted into lust. My hands snaked around his neck, pulling him to me. I moaned under his kiss as his hands worked their way to my jeans, unbuttoning, unzipping, pulling them and my underwear down and off with my shoes and socks. I felt a chill breeze over my exposed skin and shivered with cold and need.

And then it was urgent. Alex pushed down his jeans and hoisted me up to the work table, shoving me back, scattering the pile of books. I grunted as he leaned against me, ramming hard inside me. I wasn't quite ready, and there was pain with the pleasure, but it only heightened my excitement. He wanted me so much, he would take me like this, with a fever, with a brutal hunger, and I loved knowing that I could do this to him. I loved being his object of desire.

My pussy grew wetter by the second, easing his passage, and he plunged more deeply into me. I lay back on the hard table, its surface a punishment upon my shoulders, my hips, as he fucked me. I spread my palms on the worn, polished wood, crying out with each powerful thrust. I could feel the buttons of his shirt pressing into my torso.

With one hand, he reached up under my T-shirt, my bra, pinching a nipple hard, and I came with a shuddering, rough climax. I felt him release inside me, and I responded with another convulsion of pleasure as he groaned, replete.

He lay his head against my chest, spent, his breath hot, and then he eased himself off me and took me by the hand, helping me down. He kicked away his jeans and picked me up, and I clung to him, beyond thought.

He took me behind the beautiful screen of wood and stained glass to my unmade bed and lay me there. He pulled my shirt off, my bra, finally stripping me completely, watching me watching him.

He vanished for a moment; the lamp went off, and he was back, lit only by the dim and distant street lights sliding through the Venetian blinds.

He crawled into bed next to me, holding me, caressing me, his now naked body still emanating heat as I clutched him tightly.

"Alex," I whispered.

"My Sloane."

I AWOKE WELL before I had to. Something was different.

It was Alex. Someone else in my space. I heard him in the kitchenette, opening cabinets and the fridge, rattling pans. I stretched and looked around for something to wear. I ended up reaching under my pillow for my sleep shirt and putting that on. I used the bathroom and came out into the open space. Alex wore jeans and the shirt from last night, unbuttoned, casual and sexy. He was frying a couple of eggs. The tiny two-cup coffee maker was gurgling, too, and two pieces of bread hopped up from the old chrome toaster.

"Good morning." He looked me over appreciatively. "If you didn't have eggs and bread, I think you'd starve," he said, leaving the pan so he could butter the toast.

"Someone keeps feeding me. I haven't had a chance to stock up," I said, crossing my arms as I sat at the small chrome and Formica table, another great thrift-store find.

"How do you feel this morning?" There was a hint of worry in his tone that I found endearing. He wasn't just a steamroller, then.

"I'm OK." I smiled at his look of relief.

He poured two coffees in mugs I'd made and put them on the table.

"Black OK?"

"Perfect," I said. "You should have come out to the bar last night. You'd have liked the band, especially since you're a musician."

He looked at me sharply. "Why do you say that?"

"What?"

"That I'm a musician. I'm not." He put the toast and eggs on two plates, vintage Fiestaware, and placed them on the table. "Silverware?"

"That drawer," I pointed, and he grabbed forks for both of us and sat down. I ate a bite of the eggs and made an appreciative sound before I continued. "You have that cello in your wine room."

"Oh," he said, taking a sip of the coffee. "That was a gift."

"So you do play?" I asked.

"No," he said. "No. That was a gift I gave someone else, who gave it back."

My ears pricked up at this news.

"Who?" I asked, trying to keep my cool.

"A woman I dated last year. Not for long. Not really dated."

"Oh, really?"

He took another sip of coffee and then a bite of toast, maybe to put off answering me. "She's in the symphony."

"Where'd you meet?"

"I saw her perform many times, but I met her at — one of my parties."

He looked uncomfortable. After all, I'd met him at one of his parties.

"In the wine room?" I asked, trying unsuccessfully to squelch my sarcasm.

"No," Alex said. "Just at a party. We only went out twice."

"How much did you stay in?" I asked, trying to make a joke out of it.

His eyes flashed, a hint of anger. "We didn't last more than a week. I thought at first it was more than it was. It was just an affair. She broke it off. I sent her the cello, and she sent it back."

"Well, two more days, then."

"What?" He looked at me keenly.

"Two more days, and we have a week," I said. "You and I."

He slammed a hand on the table, startling me. "This is not like that!"

"OK!" I said, a tumble of emotions — jealousy, trepidation, an impulse to shut him out, to flee my own feelings. "So you sent her a cello after a week."

His laugh was bitter. "Sooner. It was impulsive. Some guys send flowers. I sent a cello. I could afford it."

"Then why do you keep it?

"As a reminder." I looked at him expectantly. "Not of her! A reminder not to take these things lightly."

"These things," I said, picking at my eggs.

"It's not like that with you," he said, his voice now a hoarse whisper. "You're different. We're different."

I wasn't sure if I should be laughing or crying or putting all this down to past history. So I swallowed a bite of the eggs, looking at the plate. "Can you give me a ride to school?"

"Yes."

I couldn't look him in the eye, but I felt him watching me as I got up and walked toward my bed and the bathroom, past the beautiful screen he'd given me, his extravagant gift. And I pictured the womanly curves of the burnished cello aglow in his wine den, a strange and constant reminder. Perhaps a warning.

I took my shower and dressed in my casual pottery clothes — loose, black pants that tied at the ankle, with big pockets, and a close-fitting army-green T-shirt — and emerged from behind the screen.

I hadn't come to any conclusions under the hot water, only that I was a naive fool who didn't know how to handle my feelings.

Alex was leaning against the table where'd we made love last night. Love? Was it? Would it ever be? Is that what I wanted?

Right now, what I knew I felt was compulsion. And passion. A passion I'd never felt before, addictive and all-consuming.

As conflicted as I was, I felt it now, looking at him, his eyes cloudy with emotion.

"I'm ready," I said, moving next to him, grabbing my satchel from the table, where the books still lay scattered.

He followed me to the door, putting a hand lightly on my back. I felt the current between us, a low pulse, undeniable. I locked the door behind us and followed him to the car.

We headed down the drive and onto the river road, foggy this morning, the oaks and their necklaces of Spanish moss ghostly in the veil of gray.

"I didn't come to the club last night because I couldn't," he said in a low voice.

"Why not?"

"The same reason I couldn't go into the bar the night before. I just get overwhelmed in situations like that."

"I don't understand," I said. There was a lot I didn't understand. "You have parties."

"At my place. My boundaries. My rules."

"You said you do work in the community."

"Board meetings," he said. "Gallery openings and things like that; sometimes they're OK, a nice quiet event. But when I get into a crowd like that —"

"What, at bars? Or is it the art crowd? Your peers. They *are* your peers, Alex. You're one of them. You're creative and smart. You belong."

"It's fucking irrational, all right?" he said, turning off the river road and into the maze of streets that would take us into downtown Bohemia. "My therapist is trying to help me with it."

So he had a therapist. That was probably a good thing.

"Do you want to talk about it?" I asked softly.

He was quiet for a while, until we pulled up to the main entrance of the school. "Can we talk later? You will see me later, won't you, Sloane?" His voice was full of anxiety. He wasn't looking at me.

I took a deep breath and leaned over to him, grasped his chin and made him face me. "Yes, Alex," I whispered, and I felt him relax as I leaned toward him and kissed him.

As I pulled back, he reached up and pulled me to him again for a deeper kiss, that passion that seemed to heal him, if only for a little while.

"I can pick you up at 6," he said.

"No, I'll drive to you," I said. "I'll text you when I'm on my way."

He nodded with something like relief in his eyes, relief and longing, as I exited the car and watched him drive away.

PART 2

To say I was distracted at school was an understatement. I took notes during the glazing class as our teacher, a slender, blond MFA with geeky black-rimmed glasses and an impressive resume of exhibits and credits, talked about chemistry and techniques we might try. Of course, she told us, we'd need pieces to glaze first, which meant I spent my studio time trimming a pot that I hoped would be dry enough for the kiln by Friday.

I met up with Gary in Pottery Studio C at 4 p.m. for what turned into a complete reorganization of the tools and shelves, getting ready for a night class. He was cheerful, still enthused about Ez's band and, I thought, somewhat warmer toward me. He was so, I don't know, *normal*. Well-adjusted. All in comparison with Alex, of course. And maybe it's just because my body's strings were tuned so tightly, but I also found a certain resonance in Gary, an attraction more subtle than the one I had with Alex. It was disconcerting. Alluring. I finished the job with him as quickly as I could, turned down his offer to get a coffee, and hurried home to get ready for the evening.

I had no idea what to expect. It didn't feel like a date. Would we go out to dinner? Stay in and talk? Should I bring something?

My angst bordered on ridiculous. After what Alex and I had shared, why was I hung up on trivialities? Maybe because we hadn't really shared trivialities, the normal little things that people do. That couples do.

Exasperated, I donned loose cotton pants, made from a soft, opaque green gauze, and a satiny champagne-colored tank top. Over that, I pulled a brown cardigan sweater. It was just cold enough for that — that, and a gauzy scarf that pulled all the colors together. I pulled back part of my hair and fastened it with a bronze barrette and put on some bronze-colored leaf earrings. On my feet, I wore brown sandals. Fall in Florida, I thought wryly as I checked myself out in the mirror. I added lipstick almost as an afterthought.

Then I texted Alex. "Is it OK to come over? Should I bring dinner?"

"Already taken care of. Can't wait to see you."

So, he was being sweet. Maybe. I hated texts. There was no nuance, no tone.

I headed out and, using my phone's GPS to make sure I would get there, drove toward Alex's place.

When I got to the causeway and turned east, my eyes filled with moonlight. The disc was nearly full and almost daylight-bright in the clear, dark sky. I couldn't wait to see the beach in this light. But for the first time, I felt ambivalent about seeing Alex. I realized that I was afraid of what he might tell me. I'd been living a fantasy that was about to get real.

I found his condo with barely a glance at the GPS and parked in one of the few guest spaces. At the door, I punched in the code he'd sent me, entered the lobby and got into the elevator. "I'm here," I texted him.

"I'll push the button," he typed back. In a minute, the elevator started to rise. It was funny how a stranger in the elevator was completely at the mercy of the floors above. Whoever pressed their "down" button had a shot at getting a present: a keyless guest.

I was relieved when I arrived at the eighth floor. When the doors opened, Alex was waiting for me, in loose jeans, a black T-shirt and bare feet. He didn't like shoes much, I was starting to realize. At least at home. Maybe it was the beach calling. He grasped my hand and gave me a soft, succinct kiss.

"You look festive," he said.

"That's what I was going for," I said drily.

"It's a good thing," he said. "You give this place life."

I followed him into the kitchen, where the delicious aroma of garlic and tomato sauce suggested something Italian for dinner.

"Lasagna," Alex said. "Keeping it simple."

"You call lasagna simple?"

"You don't cook much, do you?" he teased. "It doesn't get much simpler. It's almost ready. Come out on the balcony. I've got a nice Montepulciano open for you."

I dropped my purse on the counter and followed him. There was a trace of tension between us. I wanted to address it, to feel in sync with him again. But I told myself to be patient, and as I walked onto the balcony, I was again distracted by the moon. I headed for the railing to drink it in, the cool white light that lit up the sand and gleamed in a wide swath of glimmering reflection on the waves of the ocean. There was that bracing scent of the sea, carried by the salty breeze, cool enough that I was glad I wore my sweater.

Alex joined me and handed me a glass of wine. He held his up to the moonlight. "It's more mysterious in this half-light," he said. "Just think, this grew up in the Tuscan sun. Under the Tuscan moon. It traveled halfway around the world to be with us, carrying Italy with it, all its beauty and flavor." He took a sip. "Not bad," he said, a funny coda to his poetic description.

I chuckled and took a sip. "It's very good," I agreed. "Lighter than some of the other wines you've given me, but I think I can taste *la luna*."

He held out one hand and caressed my cheek. His kiss, when it came, was languorous and deep, tasting of wine and longing. My lips answered his, but I stood almost still, like a flower opening to a hummingbird, the willing vessel for his deft touch. I drifted in the feeling until he released me, and I opened my eyes to see his still closed, as if he were savoring a perfect wine.

His eyelids fluttered open. "Let's go inside and talk for a few minutes before dinner," he said.

He took the bottle and his glass. I took mine. To my surprise, he led me not to the living area or the library, but through the kitchen to the wine room.

"I put up the temperature a few degrees so you wouldn't be too cold," he said as we entered. It was pretty much as I remembered it, with the countless bottles, the jewel-tone painting over the fireplace, the coffee table and the red couch. But the cello was gone.

Alex saw me looking. "It's in the storage closet. I'm going to donate it to one of the local schools that has an orchestra program. About time I got it out of here, anyway."

He sat on the couch, putting his bottle and glass on the coffee table, and I followed. He picked up a remote, a touch-screen panel, from the table and hit a button so the fireplace lit up and the rest of the lights in the room dimmed.

"You do have a way with mood lighting," I said.

He gave me a half-smile. "This is not that kind of mood. The darkness sometimes helps me think. Helps me work through things. Earlier, you asked me if I wanted to talk. I'm going to tell you something I've only told my therapist. And I hope you —"

He stopped, as if he couldn't say more. I put the wine glass down and took his hand in mine.

"I'm here to listen," I said.

When he spoke, he spoke hesitantly. "OK. It's been a long time since this happened, what I'm going to tell you, but sometimes, that anxiety I was telling you about comes rushing back. To be honest, anxiety isn't a strong enough word. It's panic. It didn't develop right away. It was some time after my parents died that it started."

"Was it your parents' death that triggered it?"

"I'm not sure entirely why, but it's not that. Or not just that. My therapist thinks it's because I don't feel safe."

I had the feeling I wasn't going to like hearing what came next.

"Why not?" I asked softly.

He sighed and withdrew his hand. He sat forward, his head down, leaning his elbows against his knees, his hands folded. *He can't look at me,* I thought. I sat still, hoping he would talk. I noticed how quiet it was in here, with no music, the merest suggestion of waves, and Alex's breathing.

"I had trouble in school, especially middle school," he finally said. "I was a skinny kid, a brain, a geek, pretty much every awkward teen stereotype you can imagine. And a handful of the other kids beat me up. Jocks, to call upon another teen stereotype. But that's what they were. And they added another stereotype to the mix: They called me a faggot. I wasn't, but you know, there were so many other names, what was one more?

"When I got into my first year of high school, I had hopes things would get better. Most kids seemed to be more mature, as a rule, and we freshmen were all the low men on the totem pole. Everything seemed to calm down. And so when one of the jocks announced he was having a homecoming party and included me on the invite list, I just thought, OK, the whole class is invited, this is no big deal, and maybe I'm one of the crowd now. Maybe it's OK. I was actually kind of excited about going."

I could hear the strain in his voice, the rising tension. I felt my eyes moisten in empathy. He was suffering. I wanted to reach out to him. But I sat very still and waited.

"I walked to the party, since it was only half a mile down the river road and up a block, and I figured if there's drinking, I don't want to drive. The house was in one of the newer neighborhoods. I get there and notice there are a few cars, but it didn't really seem like a party. I got to the doorstep and just had a feeling things weren't right. I was turning around when the door opened and the guy who was supposed to be the host grabbed me and pulled me inside. He and three of his friends were waiting. They were drunk, really drunk. That's probably what saved me. Later.

"They called me all of the names they'd called me in middle school. Especially faggot. They really liked that one. They beat me up, worse than they ever had before. And then they — they stripped me. They held me down and beat me with a belt, especially my backside. They beat me until I bled. And then they flipped me over." He paused. I looked at the fire — this was an electric fire, I realized, devoid of warmth, not like the one in the other room. I felt cold as he continued.

"They — touched me. They held me down and manipulated me until — until I got hard. It was just biology, I guess, but I was horrified. I was fighting them the whole time. I'm pretty sure the ringleader had his own issues. Repressed impulses, I don't know. He was the one who touched me. He seemed to enjoy it a lot. But once he'd got me in that state, the others started giving him a hard time, and they let go of me. While they were yelling at each other, I stumbled up. I got out. I ran out into the night. No clothes. I ran all the way home, hiding behind the trees when cars came down the road. I had a terrible feeling of being lost. When I got home, my feet were bloody, and I was bruised all over, bleeding from the lashes. I could barely move from the pain. I snuck into the house, patched myself up. I didn't tell my parents. Jesus, it would've broken their hearts to see me like that. But my mom knew the next day something had happened. She tried to get it out of me, but I never told her."

Alex's voice had become so quiet, so thready, I feared I would lose him somehow to the terrible memory. I was shaking, too, imagining the boy he once was, beaten, violated.

"You didn't report it?"

He shook his head and looked up to see the tears running down my cheeks. His face opened up as he came out of his trance.

"Oh, sweetie. I didn't mean to upset you," he said.

"Alex," I said, wrapping my arms around him, wanting to banish the memory, the darkness. "I wish I could have been there to protect you."

He made a sound in my ear that might have been amusement and held me tight. "You probably could have kicked their ass," he joked.

I gave a half-laugh, half-sob and held him even more tightly. Eventually, he relaxed his embrace, and I sat back, grabbing one of his hands, not wanting to let go. "Did you go back to school right away?"

"Yes, I did. Those bastards were not going to ruin my fucking life." He sounded angry. "I made it a point to get stronger. I worked out. I was ready to fight them if the need ever came up again. But it was funny. After that, they seemed to lose the taste for beating me up. Maybe they learned something about themselves, something they didn't want to know. The ringleader got kicked out about two months later for drugs. I never saw him again."

"You were strong then," I said. "You're still strong."

"But I still have this thing," he said. "This fear. Not of them. It was a long time ago. But it runs deep. A strange party, or a drunk crowd in a bar — Sloane, I want to be like everybody else. I want to go with you. Be with you."

"It's OK," I said with a sniffle. "It's no big deal. I just want you to feel safe."

"It *is* a big deal. It's been constricting me for so long." He took a deep breath. "I met with my therapist today. We decided to do a couple of things. One is a different kind of therapy. It involves looking at moving lights and focusing on the memory. I'm going back to her tomorrow to try it."

"What does that do?" It sounded strange to me.

"Apparently, quite a lot."

"What's the other thing?"

"She says I should test myself," he said. "With you, if you will go with me."

"How can I help?"

"This is a kind of agoraphobia," he said. "Sometimes it helps to have a friend along — someone you trust. I trust you."

"I'll do whatever it takes," I said.

"There's a Halloween party at your landlords' house the weekend after next. Did they mention it?"

"Mrs. Doctor mentioned it. She said I was invited, and that it would be hard to get out of the driveway."

The corner of his mouth turned up, almost a smile. "Dr. Doctor, don't you mean?" he teased. "It's a huge event. A mix of the society people and the art crowd. I hear it's a lot of fun. And I can go in disguise."

"Will that help?"

"No, but you will."

"So we'll go to the party? Together?"

"Yes," he said, a vulnerable note in his voice, as if he expected rejection. "I promise. If you're willing to go with me."

I shot him a coquettish smile. "Will you dress as a pirate?"

Alex laughed, then, a real laugh, and I was relieved to hear it. "You have a thing for pirates?"

"Something about the boots and the hat. And all that swashbuckling."

"It's a deal," he said, "but you'd better be a wench. And a hot one. I don't want you going as Margaret Thatcher or something."

It was my turn to laugh. "I'll be the most lustful wench you ever pillaged," I promised.

He let out a long breath and put a hand on my knee.

"Let's eat our dinner, wench," he said, and his mischievous tone made me feel better still. But he looked drawn and thoughtful as we picked up the wine and headed out to the kitchen.

ALEX and I ate at the island in the kitchen, sitting on barstools. Delicate piano, Chopin, played in the background thanks to more magic with another of Alex's remote controls. The lasagna was delicious, and the garlic bread was even better.

"Did you make this, too?" I asked, savoring a buttery bite. I figured the second piece was my dessert.

"I bought the bread, but I doctored it up."

"What's your secret?"

"I just broil it with butter, olive oil, fresh garlic and paprika," he said.

"The red sprinkle," I nodded. "When did you get to be such a good cook?"

"I hate going to restaurants alone," Alex said. "So I learned."

"You are amazing." I meant it.

He looked me over with something like appreciation. "How am I so lucky to have you here?"

"Well, obviously, it's the lasagna," I said. "Otherwise I'd be out of here by now."

He shook his head with a smile. "No, really. I wish I knew. But since you're here . . . "

"Yes?" I asked, feeling a flutter of anticipation as I sipped my wine to wash down the last bite.

"I want my muse report."

"Your muse report," I repeated, feeling my brow furrow.

"Tell me about the school. About your day. Your life."

"You don't need me to do that," I said. "Not really. Or you won't need me to, soon."

He ignored my response. "Tell me about your classes with that genius you were telling me about."

"I don't know if he's a genius," I said. "I'm starting to think he's a little creepy."

Concern flared in Alex's eyes. "Why do you say that?"

"Oh, it's nothing," I assured him. "He's mean, but I'm sure he's going to help me be a better potter. It was — just this vibe I got. And something Gary said."

"Gary," Alex said, a flicker in his eye. "Your pottery friend."

"Yes. He said Montrose seems to like some students more than others."

"It sounds as if a lot of people like you," Alex said. "Not that I blame them."

"That's silly." I sipped my wine, hoping he wouldn't ask me more.

"Do you like Gary?"

"I like him a lot," I said, then wondered if I shouldn't have. Alex was twirling his wine glass on the granite countertop, staring into its garnet depths. "I mean, he just seems like a good guy. Friendly. Nice. I have a part-time job there, now, and we work together, cleaning the studios and stuff." Whoa. Now I was babbling.

Alex looked me in the eye. "As my muse, you have a contractual obligation to tell me everything," he said. His teasing had an edge.

"We don't have a contract," I countered, trying to keep my tone light.

"Indulge me." He filled my glass again.

I drank more wine, feeling put on the spot, stewing. "So this is like truth or dare, in which I always say the truth?"

"I have tried to tell you the truth. And I reserve the right to ask for a dare later," he said with a wicked smile.

"Hmph," I said, my nose in my wine glass, drinking more than I should, trying to deflect him.

"Are you attracted to Gary?"

I looked into Alex's gray eyes. OK. Fine. If he wanted it, I was going to let him have it.

"Yes," I said, not elaborating.

Alex shifted on his stool as discomfort, jealousy and an icy calm shifted over his features in quick succession.

"Has he kissed you?"

"Why don't you ask me if I've kissed him?" I asked, angry suddenly.

He looked shocked. "Have you?"

"No, but this interrogation is uncalled for."

"This is research," Alex said, back in control, "for my writing. Anything you do as part of this research project would be fair game."

"You can't be serious," I said, even angrier. "What is this, then, between us, if you're just going to throw me to the wolves and write about it later?"

"Is Gary a wolf?"

"A lot less of one than you are."

I stomped out of the kitchen, not sure which way to go. I'd left my purse back there, so stomping out of the condo wasn't an immediate option. I ran through the dark living area, where moonlight edged the furniture, square ghosts, silent witnesses. I fled to the balcony, where the cool air still streamed in the doors, and gulped deep breaths, trying to figure out just what was happening in my head as the waves roared below.

"Sloane!" I heard Alex call behind me. He ran out onto the balcony and grabbed me by the arm. I looked down at his hand, and he let go. When I looked back into his face, his cool had crumbled.

"I'm sorry," he said. "The idea of you with someone else kills me. But at the same time, you might be happier with someone who is less — damaged than I am. And I am OK with you entertaining that possibility. I want you to be happy."

I shook my head. The wind blew my hair, my scarf, amplifying my wild emotions. "Do you think this makes me happy? This double talk about me being with someone else?"

"I mean it honestly," he said. "You would probably be a lot happier with someone else."

"I — you — isn't that for me to decide? Alex . . . " All my words, my fury crammed up in my throat. I clenched my fists and started to cry. Oh, great.

He gathered me in his arms, and damn him, I let him.

"Sloane," he whispered, stroking my hair. "Shhhh."

After a moment, I shrugged him off. "What does this mean to you, then?" I asked hoarsely. "Nothing at all?"

His eyes were glittering with moonlight, and I thought he was going to walk away, tell me to leave. But he reached out and held my face between his hands.

"Everything," he whispered. "You mean everything." He crushed his mouth to mine, with twice the passion he'd shown me before, and I believed it, wanted to believe him. Wanted to suspend disbelief and lose myself in his kiss, his embrace, and to hell with the consequences.

He ended the kiss, grasped my hand and pulled me back

into the condo, to the nearest seating area, to a soft white couch. He pushed me into it, teasing my lips with his, stretching his body against mine.

The ocean wind flowed around us, suspending us in the gossamer darkness. He pulled off my sandals, and then the soft pants. He pulled off the scarf and wrapped it around his own neck as he continued to undress me. My skin prickled, gooseflesh in the chill October wind, as he tossed aside my barrette. He was still fully dressed when he had me naked. I felt limp, emotionally drained, yet alert, my nerves singing as he touched me, as I gave myself up to him. He trailed kisses down my neck to my breasts, my nipples, which were hard from cold and arousal, and flicked them with his tongue. He pulled at one lightly with his teeth and I let out a small cry at this twinge of pain and pleasure. He kissed my belly, my thighs; he ran his tongue up my wet slit, and I moaned as he licked and teased my bud until I squirmed beneath him.

He stopped as I was just shy of release, and I groaned with something like frustration. He unwrapped the scarf from around his neck, my scarf, and held it over my body, trailing the end up my legs and over my highly sensitized sex. This light touch offered only a whisper of sensation, but I felt myself clench, my want intensifying. He let the scarf skim my breasts; he let it float over my lips, my nose, my hair. And then he leaned down and wrapped it around my eyes, blind-folding me.

I felt a double jolt of trepidation and intense desire. To be at Alex's mercy, however symbolically, was alarming, thrilling. Now my world was all touch and scent and sound; I didn't know where he was, but I felt the caress of the wind on my skin, smelled and heard the sea, and reached out with my senses to find him. Where had he gone?

I heard it first, a low buzz, and I had an idea of what he had brought me. But until he touched me with the vibrator, I had no idea how erotic this cold, impersonal object could be in his hands.

He played me like an instrument, played with me like a toy. He touched the hard plastic to my already swollen clit with the deftness of a painter, my body a canvas for his pleasure and mine. He pressed and released and circled my nub until my body hummed along. And then I felt the magic wand move, teasing my opening, and I braced for its alien penetration. My slick cleft accepted the vibrator's smooth length easily, and I groaned as he pushed it inside me, fucking me with it. I wanted him, not this toy, but I couldn't help myself; as he rubbed it against my G-spot, waves of pleasure swept through my core. I climaxed with a soft moan, lifting my hips, my legs open wide. Still he said nothing. It could have been anyone probing me in the dark, a stranger who watched my body writhe with pleasure, and the thought aroused me further. When he pulled it out and turned it off, I was left empty, wondering what was next, hearing rustling in the dark. And then his hands guided me, lifted me, turned me until I was on all fours on the couch.

I felt him against my back. I could feel his skin, now free of clothes. His body was hot against mine. He pushed my legs apart and found my wet slit first with his fingers, and then with his cock. He eased it deep inside me and I moaned again, blind, knowing I was fucked by Alex, imagining I was being fucked by a stranger. Alex was both: an intimate. A stranger. My lover. I pushed back against him, hovering on the edge of another climax as he thrust into me harder, harder, his hands roaming over my buttocks, his sac slapping against me.

Even as he screwed me, he reached around me and rubbed my clit, dipping a finger into my creamy cleft. Not being able to see what he was doing only added to my suspense, my excitement. He withdrew the finger and, in a moment, I felt it again — on my anus. I gasped and puckered at this unfamiliar touch, feeling a tremor of fear and forbidden arousal. He pushed his wet finger gently against my tight hole. My orgasm was almost instantaneous, a surge around him, and I released a groan of complete abandon. He came with his own growl of ecstasy, mingling with mine. He collapsed against me, pushing me face-down into the soft cushions, and I burned under his heat.

After a moment, he withdrew and pulled the scarf away from my eyes. I blinked, seeing red and then, turning on my side against him, I saw the room etched in bright moonlight. It no longer seemed so empty. The ocean still crashed outside, and the cool breeze enveloped us. Alex settled against my back and embraced me, warming me, and we relaxed into the couch.

"I just want you to be happy," he whispered in my ear.

Irrationally, instinctively, as I fell asleep in his arms, I was.

I AWOKE COLD, without the benefit of Alex's warmth, as the unfiltered morning light poured in the doors. I got up awkwardly, feeling the aftermath of the night before, and wandered to the powder room. On the way back into the living space, I saw the wall clock: 9:15 a.m. *Shit!* I was almost certainly going to be late.

I dashed to get my clothes, dressed, grabbed my purse from the kitchen. I thought of leaving without saying goodbye to Alex, but after his revelation last night — and after our subsequent quarrel and collision — I felt an impulse to connect with him. A quick look into his bedroom, the library and the wine room revealed no one; I didn't have time to explore the other rooms, and besides, the place was quiet. He was gone. I got into the elevator, descended to my car, and sped off toward my place.

A quick shower and a change into jeans, pink sneakers and a simple white T-shirt, and then I was on the way to school. I got into Pottery Studio B at 10:10 a.m.

Figures. It was the one day Montrose wasn't late.

"Kind of you to join us, Sloane," the teacher said as I gathered my bucket and projects in process and sat next to Gary.

"Sorry," I said.

"Do you want to tell us why you kept us waiting?" Montrose asked, moving to lean over me as I lifted a plastic bag from the tentacle I'd shaped two days before.

The other students were working around me to the music of the radio, and nobody else seemed to care that I was late. No one had even noticed. Gary had a look of barely contained amusement, and I wanted to smack him for making me want to laugh, too. I didn't think Montrose cared, either. He was just giving me a hard time.

I could have lied. Said I had car trouble. But I chose to be obscure.

"I'd rather not say," I told Montrose.

"That's your right," the teacher said. "It's not like this is high school. But *nice* students are never late."

I shot a glance at him over my shoulder and saw that he, too, looked amused — but in a much less pleasant way, as if he knew what I'd been doing. Unbidden, I thought of Alex fucking me from behind as I, blindfolded, relished his possession of me. I fought to keep my face impassive as I turned to my work, but I knew I didn't have that much control.

"I look forward to seeing what you make of that interesting, elongated piece there," Montrose nodded at the tentacle-in-progress as he walked away.

"Elongated," Gary enunciated mockingly under his breath.

"Oh, fuck me," I muttered in frustration, pulling a trimming tool from my box.

"What?" Gary exclaimed with a startled half-laugh as he looked up at me.

"Sorry. Just getting the idea that I have no idea how to communicate with men."

"Really," he said with interest, turning back toward the new vase he was throwing. "I think you're doing fine." I glanced at him and saw he was smiling.

"You have no idea," I said, focusing on my work. The piece, more than two feet tall, was already sinuous and twisting. I shaped and trimmed it, the imagined arm of a sinister squid, giving it suckers, texture and angles. At one point I looked up to see Montrose sitting at the front of the room staring at me as I worked — or, more accurately, staring at my hands as I manipulated the long piece. Was he observing my technique, or imagining something else?

My oversexed imagination was getting away from me. *Not everyone wants to screw you, Sloane,* I told myself. This week, it just seemed like it.

"Want to grab lunch?" Gary asked as we cleaned out our buckets at the sink after class.

I thought of Alex's jealous turn, and then him telling me

to be happy. I thought of his absence this morning. And, I thought, I'm thinking way too much.

"Sure," I said.

We ate at Picasso's, at the same table where I'd lunched with Cali. This time, I got the chicken salad sandwich, and Gary ordered a Philly cheese steak.

"You want to talk about it?" he asked after a few minutes of not saying much at all.

"What?" I asked innocently, sipping my iced tea, waiting for the food.

"Men."

I laughed. "Definitely not."

"You have a boyfriend?" he persisted.

Now that was an interesting question. Was Alex my boyfriend? My sexual obsession? Something in between? I decided that honesty was the best policy.

"It's hard to say."

He sipped his Coke. "So this would be an 'it's complicated' thing on Facebook?"

"This would *never* be on Facebook," I said. I could feel my face burning.

"You are an intriguing woman, Abbey," he said neutrally as the waitress arrived with plates of food, but I saw the interest in his eyes.

"And you're a nice guy, Gorski," I answered, taking a bite of the delicious chicken salad sandwich.

"Ugh. How could you say that?" he groaned before taking an enormous bite out of his huge sandwich, which seemed almost small in his big hands.

"What's wrong?"

"Nice?" Gary said between bites. "*Nice? I can't do any better than nice?*"

"That's a good thing, isn't it?"

"And here I thought I was a devastatingly handsome, edgy artist," he joked.

"Sure," I said, grinning. "You're that, too."

"Don't freaking tease me," he said, eating a potato chip.

"You're cute," I said, and he made a face. "Sorry. Handsome."

He regarded me over another mouthful of cheese steak. "Want to go out tonight?" he asked.

"You should be a lawyer. You led your witness right into that trap."

"It's a tender trap," he teased, referring to one of the old movies we'd talked about the other night.

"I would love to, but as I said — or didn't say, really — I am seeing someone."

"Ah," Gary said. "But he's not a boyfriend."

No, I thought, *but he's screwing my brains out and has told me his darkest secret.*

"Boyfriend may be an inadequate word," I said honestly. "Let's drop it, Gary. I have Rose's class this afternoon, and then I have some time. Have any work for me?"

"Always," he said.

As it turned out, we spent two hours in the late afternoon cleaning up the courtyard, where, in one corner, three gas kilns sat on a patio under a high metal roof. The kilns were mostly fire brick, rougher-looking than the clean, new equipment in use inside the building.

While Gary worked to repair the connections on the biggest kiln, I straightened up shelves full of old cooking pots. I dumped new material into the bins that held paper for the raku firings. And I piled up clutter by the courtyard gate, where it could be sorted before most of it was discarded.

It was almost dark by the time we were done. I felt a longing to leave and connect with Alex, but I hadn't heard from him all day. He hadn't responded to my texts. I wondered at his lack of communication. It worried me.

"We should test this big kiln," Gary said, interrupting my thoughts. "They have a Saturday workshop, and they'll be using these kilns at the end of the day. I want to make sure this one will get up to temperature."

It wasn't like I had plans. "What do we have to do?"

"Let's glaze a couple of pieces real quick and fire them. It'll be fun."

"Oh, that's right," I said as I followed him into the building. "You're into fire."

"Definitely," he said with relish. "Have you done raku before?"

"Only a couple of times."

Gary grabbed two bisque-fired vases, white, hard and slightly rough, and handed me one. "You glaze this one."

"Really?" I examined the handsomely shaped vase, about the size of my head, smooth with a flaring lip and a crisp foot.

"Sure. It's just a test object," he said. I marveled at how quickly Gary turned out elegant pieces of pottery.

I followed him into another studio, where he turned on the electric pan that held the wax we would use to coat the base of each piece. The wax would repel the glaze, so the vases wouldn't stick to the shelf during firing. He sifted through the buckets of glaze stacked along one wall until he found a selection formulated for raku.

"Try this," he said. "It's iridescent and shiny when it works well, with hints of green, blue and copper. I'm going to do a crackle I've been working on."

"Your own formula?" I asked as I stirred the glaze he'd given me, getting it smooth and ready for dipping.

"Yeah. It has lead. We try to keep the children away." He grinned as he stirred his soupy glaze.

In a few minutes, we dipped the foot of each piece in the thin layer of melted wax in the electric pan before dipping the vases into the glazes. They looked dull and uninteresting now, but high heat would cause chemical reactions in the coatings that would create unpredictable and, with luck, pretty colors and texture.

We both washed our hands of stray chemicals, grabbed our safety gear and headed out to the kiln. Darkness had settled in, but a couple of outdoor lights lessened the gloom. We placed the vases in the top shelf of the kiln, and Gary lit it and covered it; the gas flame made a gushing sound as it burned.

Gary checked the temperature with a digital pyrometer.

"Just a few minutes," he said. "Let's get the pots ready."

We each got one of the large metal cooking pots, lined them with a thick nest of shredded paper and set them on the ground next to the kiln.

"Get your gloves on," he said. "I think it's time."

The pyrometer confirmed peak temperature. Gary pulled a welder's mask over his head to protect his eyes from the light and heat of the kiln, and I stood back. Wearing elbow-length, protective gloves, he pulled the lid aside. The glowing-hot kiln lit him up, a towering devil, as he used a pair of long tongs to remove the first vase. It glowed red-hot.

He gently placed it in the first metal pot, and the intense heat of the vase caught the paper on fire. Also wearing gloves and safety glasses, I popped the lid onto the flaming pot, allowing the fire inside to consume the paper and oxygen, creating the reduction environment that would transform the glazes. We repeated the process with the second vase and pot, and Gary shut off the kiln.

He pulled off his mask, sweating, beaming.

"God, I love that," he said. "Let's give it about twenty minutes, and then we'll see what magic we've created."

I smiled at his enthusiasm, his happiness. Here was someone who knew what he loved, who was pursuing it with passion. That's what I wanted — not him, I told myself, but to be like him. Alive in the pure joy of creativity.

When the time came, wearing my gloves, I pulled the lids off the metal pots, revealing a dark, charred mass of paper and ashes and the vases themselves. Gary hosed them down, cooling them off, arresting the reduction process, and in a few minutes, I was able to pull the warm vases out of their pots. Gary fired water at them again, managing to spray quite a bit of it on me.

"Hey!" I said, laughing. "Careful, or I'll drop your masterpieces!"

"It would be worth it to get your shirt wet. Unfortunately, my aim isn't that good."

Crap. He was still flirting with me. Though I didn't mind all that much. I laughed nervously as he sprayed the inside and outside of the vases one more time while I held them.

"Done yet?" I asked.

"OK, fine," he said with dramatic reluctance. We set aside the vases, cleaned up the metal pots, and took the fired pieces inside to see what we had.

After a few minutes of scrubbing off the excess carbon with Comet and rinsing the vases, we saw we had very nice pots indeed. The one Gary had glazed had a wealth of fine dark crackles in the white finish, and the lip, which he had not glazed, was an attractive charcoal black.

The glaze I had used had generated a mottled blue-green on one side of the vase and a bright, shiny copper on the other, with threads of gold and blue and even burgundy mingling on the rest of the surface.

"This is really beautiful," I said, feeling the thrill of holding the warm vessel in my hand, seeing the light and color dance across its surface as I turned it.

"Yes, you are," Gary said. He leaned toward me and planted a warm kiss on my lips.

I was so surprised, my reaction was more instinct than thought: to kiss him back. And I did, if only for a minute, tasting his eagerness as my mouth opened under his, before I remembered myself and withdrew.

"You weren't supposed to do that," I whispered.

"Why?" he asked gently. "Because you have a non-boyfriend?"

"No," I said. I was confused.

"You're upset. I'm sorry. Are you mad at me?"

"No," I said, looking up at him. "It's OK. Honestly — I enjoyed it." He smiled more broadly, but I held up one hand. "I can't. I'm committed to this other thing, this other man — and I'm just kind of overwhelmed."

Gary lowered his eyes and nodded slowly, turning his vase over in his hands, looking at it distractedly.

"It's cool," he said. "You can't blame a guy for trying." He shot me a small smile. "And I'm here if you change your mind."

"Thank you," I said. "I should go. Do you want me to help clean up?"

"I've got it. We're pretty much done. I'll just turn off the lights."

"Here's your vase." I held out the glimmering piece.

"Keep it," he said. "Sloane?"

"Yes?"

"I didn't screw up this friendship-working-together thing, did I?"

"No," I said. "Really, this is one of the most normal things that's happened this week." I shot him a reassuring smile, took the vase, gathered my things and left the building.

Sitting in my car in the parking lot, I pulled out my phone. Still nothing from Alex. Maybe I should have left him a note this morning. Maybe he was upset. I'd seen him every day since I'd met him. Could I go a day without him?

I pretty much already had. I debated whether to text again or call or do nothing. Finally, I called.

His phone rang several times, and then I got his no-frills voicemail. "This is Alex. Please leave a message." I felt warm hearing his voice and a little distressed, thinking about what had just passed between Gary and me. I hesitated at the tone.

"Alex, are you OK?" I finally said. "I'm just getting out of school. Call me if you like. I'd like to see you."

I ended the call, feeling lost. I abruptly felt a huge hole in my existence where Alex should have been, the feel of him, his presence. His possession. Why had I responded so willingly to Gary's kiss? I knew I was undergoing a wrenching change. Alex had opened me up in ways I never expected. My body was twanging like a plucked guitar string; something deep in my soul was resonating, a temple bell struck and vibrating, reverberating at the core of my sex, my psyche.

I didn't want to go hunting for Alex as he had done for me two nights ago. But I needed him.

I drove home to a noticeably empty apartment. I changed

into a loose, white cotton nightgown, had popcorn for dinner — I really did need to buy groceries — read a few chapters of a Florida crime novel and, unnerved on more than one level, curled up under my grandma's quilt and slipped into uneasy sleep.

FRIDAY, I had no classes. It was a day for professional students like me to work independently, and I used it to deal with clay at various stages of doneness, trimming and adding texture to leather-hard pots, shaping and joining wetter pieces, even throwing a couple of new ones.

I submitted a couple of thoroughly dry greenware pieces for bisque firing as I helped Gary load the kilns late in the morning. He seemed quiet, even a little shy around me, and we worked together in companionable if slightly tense silence.

I left the school at noon, heading to my place, calling Alex as I went. Still no answer. It was so strange. He'd been at my elbow for every minute of the past week, it had seemed, and when he wasn't, he was deep in my thoughts.

When I pulled into the driveway of the doctors' Victorian house and my apartment, I saw Mrs. Doctor walking into her rose garden with a basket of tools. Damn it, I had to stop thinking of her as that; she was Daisy Pullman, I reminded myself. After I parked by the carriage house, I wandered out into the beautifully landscaped yard to see if she had any knowledge to share.

I skirted the head-high hedge that bordered the round rose garden and entered through the circle's one opening, an arched arbor. The garden was laid out around a crisscrossing path with two curved concrete benches at its center. Bright pink, red and yellow blooms fluttered at the tops of tall bushes with glossy green leaves.

"Gorgeous flowers," I called out to Dr. Pullman as I approached her.

She looked up and smiled. "Thanks, Sloane." She was pretty, youthful at somewhere twice my age, with Mediterranean-brown skin and glossy black hair pulled back in a ponytail. The wide-brimmed hat she was wearing probably helped preserve her appearance, keeping out the brutal Florida sun everyone had warned me about. It was a cool day, but she worked in a T-shirt and shorts, pruning a luscious red rose bush. She wore thick leather gloves on her hands.

"How are you settling in?" she asked. "Is the carriage house OK?"

"I love it," I said.

"Making friends?" She stood up, pausing in her pruning, arching her back in a graceful stretch. Her lively brown eyes looked me over. "I hear you've met Alex."

At least she'd brought up the subject, saving me the trouble. "Yes. He's a nice guy."

She nodded as if she were weighing the accuracy of this description. "He's very considerate," she said. "And generous."

"You work with him sometimes, don't you, Dr. Pullman?"

"Please call me Daisy. We're both on the art museum board and occasionally join forces on other projects, and I see him at a few events, though he doesn't get out as often as a lot of people in his position. We help each other out sometimes. It's good to have an ally among the movers and shakers."

I needed to get to the point, but I tried to keep my anxiety out of my voice. "You haven't by chance seen him in the past couple of days? I — needed to talk to him about something, and he hasn't called me back."

Concern softened her gaze, and I had the feeling she knew I was worried about more than a phone call. "He was at the board meeting this morning."

"Oh," I said, taken aback. That seemed so — normal. "Did he seem OK?"

"It's not always easy to tell with Alex, but he seemed fine. Are you all right, my dear?"

I wasn't. I wasn't feeling good at all. I groped for one of the two benches that faced each other at the heart of the crossed paths and sat down.

"I'm OK," I said weakly as I sat on the cold surface.

The doctor dropped her pruners and came quickly to my side.

"Do you feel faint?" she asked. I nodded. "Just lean over a little. Put your head down." She lay one gloved hand gently on my back, and for one second, I missed my mother, the way she'd bring me a cool washcloth and bathe my forehead when I was sick in bed as a child. Daisy dropped her gloves to the ground, picked up one of my hands and felt the pulse at my wrist. Then she rubbed my back again.

"Just breathe deeply," she said. "You're going to be fine."

I listened to the wind in the oak trees, smelled the sweet bouquet of the roses. It was a beautiful day. There was no reason for me to feel like this. I was always healthy. This was nothing. Except I had a sickening feeling. A sickening feeling that I had lost Alex.

After a few minutes, I looked up. I still felt strange, but my head no longer felt like a runaway helium balloon. I smiled awkwardly up at Daisy, who straightened and returned my smile. "Feel better?"

"Yes," I said. "Thank you. I'm sorry. That was embarrassing."

"It happens to everyone sometime," she said. "Still, let me know if it happens again. You might want to go lie down for a bit. Drink some water. And if there's anything in particular you're worried about, just try to put it aside and focus on being well."

Anything in particular. God, I was so transparent.

"Thank you," I said. "Lucky I'm staying here, I guess. If I was renting from a plumber, they'd have told me I needed to unclog my drains."

She laughed. "Glad to help. You sure you're OK?"

"Yes," I said with as much emphasis as I could muster as I got up and unsteadily began the short walk back to my place. "Thank you," I called out.

It was a relief to get inside the door, turn the lock and lie down on the couch. I closed my eyes and tried to process what I'd heard. Alex was out in the world, living his normal life, completely without me.

I went back over our strangely clashing conversations of two nights ago — the sweet moment by the ocean, his terrible story, the pleasant dinner and his unnerving talk of muses and letting me be happy. And then his possession of me. He said I was everything. He took me over. Filled me up. I shivered, thinking of how my body had thrilled to his touch in the dark.

He'd said something about more therapy. He'd said he had planned a session for yesterday. I wondered what that had been like. Did his therapist tell him to stay away from me or something?

Oh, shit, Sloane, it's not all about you, I told myself.

He had issues. He had to work through them. But I thought he'd understood that I would help him.

I made up my mind. I would try to see him. If he could tell me to go away, tell me to my face, then I would. I wouldn't beg.

But still. In a very short time, he had worked his way deep inside me, and not just physically. I felt like the tin man with a new heart, a heart that was already breaking.

Or maybe I was a junkie, addicted to Alex, in painful withdrawal.

I allowed myself a mordant smile, sitting up and hugging my knees on my plush, worn couch, as the light of late afternoon washed up at the windows like a golden wave. If I was going into battle, I would go armed.

Unfortunately, my wardrobe's armaments were wanting. I didn't have all that many outfits that hip girls would call cute, and most of the ones I hadn't worn on our dates tended to have a northern vibe.

I sighed, looking into the clothes that hung there, and wondered if I might stretch my budget a tiny bit and get a little something. I'd seen a big discount fashion store on my drives into downtown.

I checked my phone compulsively. Still no response, though Cali had invited me to the Junction Box to hear another band tonight. No matter how this all came out, I might as well do some targeted shopping.

In forty minutes of roaming the cluttered aisles of the discount store, I found a handful of strategically priced garments that would do for multiple outings, with a little creative mixing and matching. Because if Alex wasn't going to see me anymore, I wasn't going to sit at home crying. At least, that's what I told myself.

A thrift shop next door yielded a few more treasures for even less money, including a black velvet jacket that tapered at the waist and flared around my hips, stopping around mid-thigh. It would go perfectly with the translucent silver-gray tunic I'd found — I had a satiny black bra I'd wear underneath — and a fun black belt that looped around my waist twice. I'd don it all over clingy black pants, almost tights, that would work nicely with a pair of high-heeled black boots I'd found among the crazy collection of used shoes. They looked brand new.

I stopped at the drugstore for a new lipstick and found a few fun hair baubles while I was there. They went into my purse, and I went home and assembled the outfit, adding bangle bracelets and a long necklace with a tiny crystal bottle pendant, a piece with a whimsical secret that I'd found while in college. I added earrings made with black and silver beads mixed with clear crystals, along with carefully applied eyeliner, mascara and lipstick. I combed out my hair, leaving it loose, considering a hat but deciding against it. The bra peeked through the shirt with what I hoped was tasteful allure.

I wasn't displeased. This was a power outfit on a pauper budget. For a second I almost forgot I was dressing for a confrontation, not a date. Though I still had hope.

Packing my black purse, I headed out to my car, trying one more time to call Alex. I didn't leave a message. I didn't want him to know I was coming.

Last night, the moon had been full, and tonight, it still seemed to brim over its milky saucer. The light shimmered on the lagoon; the subtle river waves were calm, now that the wind had eased. This was a magical place, I thought, or it could be, if I would just let it in. I didn't need one man to make me happy.

So went the few brain cells that were predicting and rationalizing. The rest told me to drive faster, faster, toward Bohemia Beach.

~

I PARKED in a guest space and used the keypad to get into the lobby. I had the code, but there was the problem of getting up to Alex's floor. I didn't have a key that would work in the elevator, and I didn't want to use the intercom; it was too easy for him to ignore.

But I had some luck as I approached the elevator. Good luck and bad luck. A sign on it said "Out of Order." So how did these people get to their condos in the sky?

I looked around and saw a door propped open — a door to the stairway.

"Why couldn't he live on the second floor?" I muttered. First I peeked in the garage; I saw his car parked in his space. He was probably here. So I took a deep breath and began the climb in my high-heeled boots.

I was more out of shape than I'd thought. I should probably start running again. I had to stop at five for a quick breather, and then I was back on the real-life stair-stepper.

I discovered that while eight was the top floor, another flight of stairs headed to the roof, probably for maintenance. Interesting. And probably not accessible. Besides, was I planning to fly onto his balcony?

The other problem was, the door on eight, which I figured led to the foyer, was locked. And I had no idea if it was alarmed. I thought perhaps not, given the door downstairs was wide open for anyone who happened in. I wasn't much of a lock breaker. Would he even hear my knock? Should I call again? He'd been ignoring my calls and texts.

I considered my options as I caught my breath, and then I remembered the little packet of hair adornments in my purse. Perhaps one of those would do.

Feeling like a burglar or a stalker, I wasn't sure which, I popped open the plastic packaging, browsed through the sparkles and found a bobby pin adorned with a rhinestone flower. It was worth a try. I'd come all the way up here, after all.

I got on my knees in front of the lock, pushed in the two-pronged pin and tried to find something to catch and twist, to make it yield. I tried for a good ten minutes, taking breaks to peer hopelessly into the tiny dark slot of the lock.

I'd just told myself I'd give it one more minute when the door slowly opened.

It pulled away from me with the pin still in the lock, and I was left with my hands comically poised in midair, on my knees, looking up at the shadowy figure of Alex Alwend.

"I just couldn't stand watching anymore," he said, his tone wry. "Why don't you come in? Although you're certainly attractive on your knees."

He turned back toward the foyer and the double doors that led into his condo.

"You were watching me? How?" I asked, too flummoxed to start my planned demands and recriminations. I climbed to my feet, following him, and popped my trinket out of the lock before the door closed behind me.

"There's a security camera aimed at the door. I give you points for persistence."

He held open the double doors for me, and I got a good look at him. He seemed exhausted. He wore a soft, navy-blue sweater that set off his gray eyes and honey hair, over a pair of loose khakis. And he was barefoot.

Alex barely looked at me, at least not until we got out into the main room. Then he turned around and took me in, and I detected a slight widening of his eyes, a subtle rise to attention. He shook his head slowly.

"You look incredible," he said. "But why are you here?"

"Why didn't you respond to me?" I asked, unsuccessfully trying to keep the anguish out of my voice. I was tired, too, and angry and sad. He wasn't trapped under a piece of furniture or dying of the flu. He'd just been ignoring me.

He let out a long breath of air.

"Come into the library," he said. "Just to talk. We need to talk."

I had the horrible feeling this conversation was already off the rails, but I followed him into the room and put my purse on a table by the door. He lit the space much the way he had on our first incredible night, turning on the gas fire in the fireplace and the stained-glass sconces flanking the mantel. But the mood was decidedly different, and no wine was in sight.

I realized I hadn't eaten since some toast at breakfast. No wonder I'd almost fainted this afternoon. But now I was anything but hungry.

As I sat on the couch, I felt a sudden comfort in the books that surrounded me, the stories of struggle and triumph, the eons of research and knowledge, all so much bigger than my little problem. My little, gigantic feelings for Alex.

He sat next to me, not touching me.

"It's not you," was the first thing he said.

"Oh, great." I knew I sounded miserable. " 'It's not you, it's me.' "

"What? No," he declared, and he reached out and touched my hand briefly before withdrawing. "I didn't want you to see me like this, Sloane. And — I was afraid to draw you into this."

"Into this what?"

"This black hole. It's been a very difficult couple of days, and I feel like — I'm like one big eggshell. One wrong word, and I'll shatter into a million pieces."

"I'm here to help you," I said. "And why do you feel that way?"

He stared into the fire, his strong features half in shadow. "I had an incredible therapy session yesterday," he said. "Incredible and incredibly difficult. It was EMDR therapy. Do you know what that is?"

"No."

"It sounds like hocus-pocus, but it actually works. The therapist guides the session, but mostly it was me. I focused on a traumatic memory." He paused. "In this case, I chose the one we talked about."

Because, I realized, he had a choice of trauma. His parents dying horribly and suddenly when he was nineteen wasn't so pleasant, either.

"And then I focused on the lights, small lights moving back and forth on this narrow bar," he continued. "You move your eyes back and forth, focusing on the memory. And then it's like you're there again, reliving it, in hyperfocus. Watching it from afar, but living it, working it out. It was like popping the cork off a bottle. My contents just spilled out, all the horror and the fear, all the degradation, everything. I can't even quantify it. I ended up weeping on the therapist's floor."

I felt as if I'd intruded into a very, very private space.

"I'm sorry," I whispered. "I was just so worried about you. And then I heard you were at your meeting today . . . "

He looked over at me. "You did?" The corner of his mouth turned up. "You asked about me?"

"I wanted to help you."

"I should have let you." He reached out and took my hand, and I felt some of my chill leave me, though he turned back to the fire. "I got myself together for the meeting. I wrote — more writing than I've done in a long time, though it was disjointed and frantic. I doubt any of it made much sense. And I went back to the therapist to talk everything over this afternoon, to work through the emotional experience. It's strange. For the first time, I felt like I could deal with it. Like the fear and the horror of it wasn't so bad anymore. I have more sessions ahead of me, but it's like a dam has broken."

"That's good, isn't it?" I didn't want to ask him about me, but I needed to. "Why did you not want to see me?"

"I desperately wanted to see you. But that was part of the dilemma. This was emotionally intense, but more than that: The therapist warned me — she said that once I got through the process, I'd probably want to get rid of a lot of people in my old life. In a way, I've done that already, but I'd just met you, and I couldn't imagine tossing you overboard with the flotsam. I didn't want to be in any situation in which I have to tell you goodbye. My mind's in a muddle, but I think you're the best thing that's happened to me for a long time. I mean, if I hadn't met you, I never would have tried this therapy."

"It sounds like you need therapy for the therapy," I joked, because joking seemed better than breaking down at the idea I might never see him again.

He offered a grim smile. "It's a process, and I have to work through it. But what she said concerned me. She said people who go through this therapy tend to destroy everything they've built up to protect themselves, all their illusions, their defenses. And I had another reason." He looked at me with a mix of torment and yearning. "I didn't want to feel like I was using you for some kind of twisted therapy of my own. I — I really care for you, and I needed to work through some stuff before I saw you again. Before I was sure I should see you again."

"I don't fully understand what you're going through, Alex. But any way I can help you through this, you know I will."

He brought my hand to his lips, kissing it gently. Not seductively, but with care. "My needs get a little dark. I think you've seen that with me. I just wanted to be sure I was in control — or understood my lack of control — before I saw you again. Because I cannot resist you." Now his eyes burned into mine, and the sweetness melted into something more searing.

I felt the slightest tremor through my body.

"Are you OK now?" I asked in a hushed voice, embracing my own truth. "I mean, are you OK to see me? Because whatever you call it — even if it's darkness — whatever you have, I need it the way a tree needs sunlight."

Alex's face underwent a transformation. Its sculpted lines seemed to shift, his strong jaw now sensuous, his eyes bright and ardent, his mouth vulnerable and divine. He moved closer to me and began touching me, lightly, as if he were drawing my outline: my cheekbones, my chin, my lips; my ears and neck, my shoulders, my waist and hips and legs. I began trembling in earnest, and he pulled me close to him, wrapping his arms around me in a warm, tight embrace.

"Are you sure?" he whispered, the way he had that first night.

"Yes, Alex," I said, burying my face in his neck, hugging him close.

We stayed that way for a long time. And then he released me.

"What do you want to do tonight?" he asked.

"Whatever you want," I murmured, and I was sure my tone told him what I wanted. I wanted him.

He straightened up on the couch and lifted my hands, beckoning me to stand. "Let me look at you," he said. "You look incredible. You look way too chic for Bohemia Beach."

I smiled as I stood and turned slowly for him in front of the fire, happy he admired my carefully chosen ensemble. He watched me, his impudent gaze roving over every inch of my body. I realized he wasn't just complimenting my clothes. And a switch had flipped. He was no longer focused on his pain. He was focused on me.

"Those boots look dangerous," he said impassively. "Take them off."

I swallowed, noting the glint in his eye. I bent down and slowly worked them off, setting them to the side of the hearth.

"I love that soft jacket," he said. "Throw it over here, won't you?"

Under his cool expression, I thought, he was having dastardly fun. I shrugged the jacket off my shoulders and tossed it to him.

"You must be warm in those tight pants," he said. "Maybe you'd better take them off, since you're so close to the fire."

I raised my eyebrows and began to work off the pants,

slowly, prolonging the moment, until his face betrayed more than a hint of hunger.

"Shouldn't we be playing poker or something?" I asked innocently.

"I lost my cards," he said. "That shirt is so pretty over that bra, but it hides so much of you. I think I'll need that next."

"What do I get in return?"

"The satisfaction of doing what I say," he said with a lazy smile. Yes, he was feeling better.

"Maybe that's not enough."

"Oh, I think it is," he said. "Because you know what you're doing to me." He rested a hand lightly on his crotch, where his hardness was evident through the thin fabric of the khakis.

I felt an ache, a wetness between my legs. I unbuckled the double belt and dropped it to the floor, matching his stare. I pulled the thin shirt over my head, taking care to tuck the bottle pendant under it before I did so. I tossed him the shirt.

Alex took it in both hands and held it up to his nose, inhaling deeply.

"You smell like flowers," he said, his voice more husky. "But you look wicked in that black underwear. And now I can see how little was under those pants. You look very, very nice, Sloane."

I glanced down at myself. My breasts were pointed and high in the bra, cleavage mounding over the fabric, and the firelight cast a deep shadow between them. The pendant dangled there, almost to my belly button.

I hitched a thumb in the stretchy waistband of the thong, pulling it slightly away from my body as I turned around again, and I thought I saw him swallow. The thong was the only one I had, but he was right. It was wicked. His hand was resting again on his crotch, and it looked as if it took all his effort not to do more.

"What's that necklace?" he asked.

Silently, I grasped the small crystal bottle and unscrewed the top. I dipped the attached wand into the bottle, held it to my lips and blew. A stream of bubbles drifted toward him, sparkling in the firelight.

He smirked, but he was just as intent on his agenda.

"You'd better put that aside, because I think that bra has to come off," he said.

He began moving his hand lightly over the surface of his bulge as I put the necklace aside. It was heady, seeing my effect on him.

I unclasped the bra in the back and eased the straps slowly off each shoulder. I dropped it next to me and cupped my breasts, running my fingers over my nipples, pinching them lightly, pulling them as he watched.

"Touch yourself," he whispered, unfastening his pants and pulling them off with his briefs. He began caressing himself lightly. His shaft looked big, magnified by my lust, and my wetness increased as I slipped a finger under the tiny triangle of fabric and touched my own rosebud, the tiny pleasure point that, under his gaze, quivered with need.

"Penetration," he said, demanding, increasing his own pace. "Push your fingers inside."

I pushed two fingers inside my slick cleft and tried to find joy there, but I was too distracted by Alex, who had removed his sweater and now sat naked on the couch, gorgeous, lustful, watching me intently, slowly moving his hand up and down his erection.

"Please," I whispered as I touched myself.

"Take it off," he ordered.

The wisp of fabric came off. Now all I wore was jewelry. I sank to my knees in front of the fire. "Please, Alex."

"Are you ready for me?" he asked, getting up, his hard cock leading the way as he walked toward me.

In response, I reached up to him and lifted it toward me, licking the tip of it, tasting the wetness there. And then I touched him with my lips, just the wide crown at first, making much use of my tongue, before taking him in more deeply, melting into the heat and hardness of him.

After a few hypnotic moments, he clutched my hair and pulled me away, and I looked up at him, my lips still slick. He pushed me back in front of the fire, onto the soft rug there, and loomed over me, primitive man, a warrior taking his prize, and lowered himself to me. I felt his tip probing my entrance, and then he thrust his cock inside me.

I closed my eyes and spread out my arms and moaned, a long, licentious moan, every cell of my body alive for him. He worked me slowly, as he had while undressing me, and I opened my eyes to see his gray gaze drilling into mine, no longer impassive. His glowing eyes spoke of molten passion, and I met them with equal feeling, lifting my hips to take his thrusts, as he grunted and moved faster and faster, at last pushing deeply into me with an explosive orgasm. My body responded in kind. As he pulled out of me, a last shot of his seed iced my belly. He ran two fingers through it, brushing it away, and put those fingers in my mouth. I sucked dreamily as I looked into his eyes, delirious with him, feeling as if I'd gone through the fire, ecstatic to be burned.

He withdrew his fingers, bent down and kissed me deeply. And then he got up, pulling me up with him, and took me to the couch, where he cradled me, kissing me endlessly, until I couldn't distinguish my mouth from his. Limp and sated, I let him lead me to his bedroom, where I curled up under the covers with him, listening to the ocean as I drifted into dreams.

I AWOKE in the middle of the night, starving. The bedside clock said it was 2:53 a.m. Alex was sleeping quietly beside me, and the ocean's muted roar flowed around us. I could see the water through the sheer curtains, a surreal sight at night, thanks to the unusually bright moon.

I slipped out of bed, feeling chilly without clothes. I wanted to go to the kitchen, maybe steal a snack, but it would be nicer with something on my back. I remembered my velvet jacket and went back to the library to retrieve it, putting it on over my naked skin and pulling it close around me. Then I went out to the kitchen and opened the gigantic refrigerator.

It was hardly full, but what was there looked good — fresh fruits and vegetables, juices, beer, cheeses, condiments, and snacks with potential, like hummus. There were a couple of bottles of champagne that I resisted; instead, I poured myself a small glass of the orange juice Alex had raved about. I cut a few pieces of cheese — Jarlsberg — and grabbed a cluster of white grapes. I found some nice sesame crackers after nosing into several cabinets and fixed up a little plate of food. I was just debating where to eat it when I heard cries from the bedroom.

I didn't think. I ran. I found Alex sitting up in bed, sweating, distressed. I climbed into bed with him and wrapped my arms around him.

"Are you OK?" I asked, kissing his hair, his cheek.

"Yeah, I'm OK," he said hoarsely. He shook his head. "Nightmare. Everything crumbling in a massive storm. The condo swept into the sea, into the giant waves. I couldn't find you."

"I'm right here," I said, moved that he would dream of me.

"Yes, you are." He pulled back, trying to smile. "Hey, what are you wearing?"

"You don't recognize it?" I plucked at the lapels of the velvet jacket. "I guess I got it off so fast earlier, you didn't have much time to think about it."

"You getting ready to leave me?"

"Yes, Alex," I said drily. "I'm going out in public in just this jacket."

"Excellent," he said, his salacious sense of humor restored in an instant.

"Actually, I was stealing a snack from the kitchen. I haven't eaten all day."

"That's not stealing," he said. "*Mi casa es su casa.* Mind if I join you?"

"Since it's your larder, I can hardly object," I said, hopping back out of bed. He climbed out, too, and followed me out of the bedroom and across the living area toward the kitchen. He let out a low whistle behind me.

"You're looking very cheeky in that jacket," he said, and I felt myself blush. Amazing, after all we'd done, that I still blushed. I sensed him get closer, and he cupped a buttock with his hand. "I don't know if I'm hungry for food, now."

"You're incorrigible," I said, breaking into a run for the kitchen, laughing.

Still naked, he dashed after me, catching me at the island, turning me toward him, slipping his hands under the jacket and onto my waist as he kissed me.

I came up for air. "I have to eat, or I'm going to pass out," I said, an image of the rose garden flitting through my brain.

"OK," he said reluctantly. "Then I'm opening champagne." He released me and headed for the fridge.

"Is this odd behavior for 3 a.m.?" I asked as I popped a cracker with cheese into my mouth. "Mmm. Good cheese," I said around my mouthful, which I followed with the divine orange juice.

He removed the muselet on the bottle he'd chosen and used a towel to work out the cork. A Greek statue casually opening champagne.

"These are normal hours around here. Sometimes I can't sleep. I'm up any old time, writing if inspiration strikes, or reading or watching an old movie. Sometimes I sleep half the day."

"And drink champagne in the middle of the night."

"No," he said with a smile, filling two glasses. "I never pour myself champagne in the middle of the night. Maybe cognac, but never champagne. I open champagne for you."

Alex handed me a glass, and I took a sip.

"Mmm, you have the most amazing taste," I said.

"You're living proof of that." He sipped his glass with satisfaction. I ate more cheese and crackers and grapes and tried unsuccessfully not to stare at his body. He noticed, a small smile playing around his lips.

"Where do you think your dream came from?" I asked to change the subject.

"Hmm," he said, his eyes unfocusing as he thought. "It probably came from therapy, at least partly. The therapist said her patients often have dreams that signify the destruction of old ways of thinking. But they are often paired with images of rebirth. This wasn't. It was terrifying."

"And me being lost at sea?"

"I'm sure I have anxiety about what would happen to me if I pushed you away and what you might do. I've pictured you pairing off with another guy. Maybe your friend Gary. I don't know, but the idea makes me crazy, and my subconscious could be picking up on that."

I merely nodded, trying to control my features. But I didn't count on Alex's perceptive skills.

"Have you seen Gary again?" he asked.

"Of course. In class. And I work with him. I did grab lunch with him the other day." I stuffed the last piece of cheese and a cracker in my mouth and chewed, unwilling to say more.

"There's something else." Alex's eyes were cool again, holding mine.

I finished my bite. "Even if there were, it's not like I knew where I stood with you. You wouldn't even answer my calls. I want to be with you, Alex. You know that."

"I think I do, but something happened, didn't it? It's OK. You can tell me."

"This is ridiculous."

"Tell me. I won't mind." He had a curious look on his face, almost of delight, like a researcher who'd found a particularly good subject, and it made me feel contrary.

"It's nothing worth reporting," I said.

"Then he kissed you. Because sex would be worth reporting."

"I wouldn't sleep with him!"

"But kissing . . ." Alex put down his glass and moved close to me, pressing up against me, against the counter. His nose was an inch from mine; I could feel his warm breath, smell the champagne. He pushed the jacket down around my shoulders so it effectively bound me in place. My breasts were exposed, and my heartbeat ticked up as he leaned in and kissed me with sexy confidence, deeper by the second. He paused, murmured, "I'll make you forget that boy." And he dove in again.

I moaned an objection, but to what, I wasn't sure.

He paused again, looked into my eyes. "Admit it."

"Admit what?"

"Confess. It will make this more fun."

"What will be more fun?" I breathed.

"Revenge sex."

"He kissed me," I said without hesitation. "He was nice about it."

Alex smiled wickedly. "A nice kisser?"

"That, too," I whispered, feeling Alex getting hard against me.

"You little slut," he murmured, but I could hear the teasing in his tone.

I almost laughed out loud, but he shut my mouth with a fierce kiss. This was not the reaction I would have expected, not that I'd ever planned to tell him what happened. Alex's perverse sense of humor detached me from the moment, but it also made me feel more safe.

"Time for your punishment," he said, his voice low and commanding. He pulled the jacket down in back and twisted it, and me, so he could hold my wrists in place. He marched me in front of him into the dim living space. He pushed me down on my knees on a hassock and tied the sleeves of the jacket around my wrists, wrapping the rest of the fabric around the knot so I couldn't move my hands. I probably could have escaped if I'd wanted to. I didn't. I felt my excitement grow as he manhandled me.

"Bend over," he whispered, grasping my hips so I wouldn't fall. As soon as I did, he pushed my legs apart with one knee and, holding me firmly, plunged into my pussy.

I gasped at the rough pleasure of it, secretly glad he hadn't taken me another way. I wasn't sure I'd ever be ready for him there, given his size. He was already more than adequate for my sex.

He pulled me to him with each stab of his cock. Being held this way was a new thrill, and it pushed me to a new edge. Somewhere between his humor and his sober passion and his manifest need for control, between my fear and my acceptance and my capitulation, I found a new realm of pleasure. I moaned.

"Shhh," he warned. "I'll tell you when you can talk."

I bit my lip and held back my cries with effort, because this was an intense, physical fucking. He met his release quickly, with a half-groan, half-sigh, still pushing into me.

"Now," he whispered.

Already clenching around him, I let out a long, low exhalation of satisfaction, arching my back into him.

"Yes," he whispered in my ear. "I like you like this. My prisoner of love."

In the aftermath, I didn't say anything; he had used the word *love,* in an unlikely context, and I tried not to take it for more than it was. But I wondered what it would take to extract that sentiment from Alex. Especially when I had begun to feel — even to worry — I was falling in love with him.

He gently unbound my arms, lifted me up and turned me toward him, kissing my neck as he rested his hands on my hips.

"Is it your goal to do that on every piece of furniture you have?" I murmured.

He chuckled into my ear.

"I hope so," Alex said. "I have a lot of furniture."

WE MOVED the champagne to his bedroom, drank and chatted a while, and drifted off to sleep to the ocean's lullaby.

When I awoke, the sun shone brightly outside, already high in the sky. To my delight, Alex was still in bed with me, not vanished on some errand. And it was Saturday. I was free. We were free.

I turned on my side to watch him sleep, but his sixth sense must have been awake. He opened those crystal gray eyes to mine, and a slow smile widened across his face.

"You're here," he said from his pillow.

"And it's Saturday."

"Can it be that just a week ago I was picking you up at your apartment and dragging you to brunch?"

"That was nice."

"Bah," Alex said. "All part of my evil plan."

"And now you've turned me into a strumpet."

"Exactly." He touched my toes with his, and I wriggled happily under the covers. He answered my movements until we were skin to skin, and he kissed me. "I feel like I should keep you entertained. What do you want to do today?"

"Oh, you keep me entertained," I giggled. "But I would really like to do something outside. It's so beautiful."

He looked thoughtful, and then he smiled. "I have just the thing."

An hour and a half later, with my tummy full of Alex's

French toast, he picked me up at my place — where I'd had to drive to get appropriate clothes — and we were back on the river road. The car's top was down, and the dappled sunlight piercing the trees dazzled my eyes.

We pulled into the driveway of Alex's childhood home and walked around the back to the dock to get the kayaks. One by one, we carried them to the front.

"What's wrong with paddling here?" I asked as we set the second one down in the driveway.

"It's pretty, but we can do better," Alex said, entering a code into the garage keypad. The door opened to reveal a shiny black sport-utility vehicle with a kayak rack on the top. He must really like black cars.

"Ah," I said. "I wondered how we were going to carry them in the Mustang."

We strapped the yellow and blue boats onto the roof — well, mostly Alex did, because he was taller than I was — and made our leisurely way north to Cocoa Beach.

The Thousand Islands access point was not amid the carnival revelry I associated with this town. Instead, Alex explained, it was on the less commercial, west side of the barrier island, allowing kayakers to paddle through a network of small waterways that would bring us in touch with nature.

"Are there alligators?" I asked, nervous, as Alex lifted the kayaks off the roof with a little help from me. I'd been told every puddle of water in Florida had alligators.

"This is brackish water, which they don't love, but every once in a while you'll see one," he said. "Have you done this before?"

"I've done some canoeing, especially when I was in Girl Scouts." He smiled at this; I guess I wouldn't get a merit badge for our activities of the past week. "I've only kayaked once, on a lake."

"This is similar, which is why we're using open kayaks," he said as we carried the boats and paddles to the ramp. "The Indian River Lagoon is pretty calm, though it's a little windy today. We can expect some chop. Most of the lagoon is only four or five feet deep, though there are some deeper holes. And the Intracoastal channel for the bigger boats, of course. The life vest is in the bow, but if you feel more comfortable with it on, go ahead."

"I'll be fine." I was really looking forward to getting on the water, especially because it was a chance to have a regular day with Alex.

He helped push off my kayak at the ramp, and he waded into the water to board his.

In a few minutes, we were paddling free and clear in a wide canal that curved off toward wild, narrower passages. They twisted and looped, bringing us through small islands covered in thickets of dark green vegetation.

We passed through one shady mangrove tunnel whose primeval greenery almost made me forget civilization was so near. Even smaller passages wandered off its enclosed channel. I drifted close to one so narrow it seemed to vanish into leafy green shadows. As I pondered whether to go in, Alex waved me off.

"Some of those runs are like caves," he said. "Sometimes you have to battle your way through the thicket, all while looking out for snakes and spiders falling on your head."

"Sounds divine."

"We can try one later," he said, not hearing my dry tone. "For now, let's just get out of this shade and enjoy the sun."

"Oh, believe me, I am."

We glided out of the tunnel and back into sunlight, and I immediately felt warmer.

I watched the light gleam in rivulets of water running off my paddle every time I lifted it out of the water. And I watched Alex smoothly working his — right, left, right, left — his muscles rippling in the short sleeves of his tight gray T-shirt. I didn't have nearly that machinelike power and efficiency, but making pottery had made me strong. I had no trouble keeping up.

We moved swiftly, in near silence, listening to the cries of an osprey and the beating wings of a flock of ibis, flashing white over the lagoon as they took off in front of us. Once, a snuffle and a spritz heralded a giant potato of a creature breaking the surface of the water — a manatee that could have easily displaced one of our boats, if it had borne a hint of aggression.

I caught a glimpse of a shiny dark thing swimming down one waterway — a narrow and twisty passage, bending quickly out of sight, but not quite as bad as the mangrove channels. I turned to pursue it.

"Hey, wait up!" Alex called.

"I think it's an otter! I want to see it!" I pulled harder, enjoying the burn in my muscles as I accelerated. In a moment, I caught a blur of movement out of the corner of my eye and saw Alex whoosh past me in his kayak, a grin on his face.

"Oh, no, you don't!" I called out, doubling my efforts on the sinuous turns of the channel. The otter flipped and sank under the water in front of me, but he was free to go. This race had become about more than chasing down an adorable otter.

I was catching up to Alex when I heard new sounds, not

of birds, but of people — whooping, shouting and arguing. Alex had already slowed. As I shot past him toward the wide turn in the channel where the unknown party waited, hidden by palms and mangroves, I saw an expression of alarm on his face.

"Asshole!" came a drunken male voice from around the corner. "You drank my last beer!"

"Fuck you and the ski you rode in on," came an equal response, to a round of laughter.

"I'm outta here, man," came the first voice. I started back-paddling, not wanting to get in the middle of the confrontation, just wanting to get back to Alex and make sure he was all right. And then the Jet Ski appeared from behind the thicket, plowing through the water, throwing up a wave as it made a sharp turn and banged off my boat.

I was underwater before I knew what had happened. *It must have flipped my kayak,* was my first fleeting thought. The other was: *Find the riverbed. If the water is as shallow as they say it is, I can stand up.*

Here, though, it wasn't. Or I was so turned around that I couldn't find it.

Stunned and running out of air, I started to panic. I opened my eyes in the murky water, looking for the light, and saw little more than plants, silt and an eye. And a grin. Of an alligator.

I inadvertently took in a gulp of water as I kicked away from it. Disgusting water. Terrifying dinosaur. The gator shifted slightly, eyeing me, but I must not have been worth his trouble. I broke the surface sputtering, and then I threw up.

I looked around, trying to figure out where my boat was, where Alex was. I could hear him calling my name. I swam toward the sound, and after a moment, I could see a shoal underneath me. I lowered my feet, and I was standing in the lagoon, head well above water.

So that's how people drown in just a few feet of water.

The drunken boaters were long gone. I coughed and took deep breaths, trying to get some air in my lungs, and I heard Alex's frantic call again. "Sloane!"

He sounded far away, but I shouted back anyway, my voice still creaky. "Here! Alex!"

Alex's blue kayak glided into view, from behind a thicket of green mangroves, and he paddled toward me with rapid strokes.

"Sloane!" His voice sounded as if it would break. "Are you all right?"

"Fine," I said as he pulled up, though I was still struggling to get a clean breath. "A little shaken up, is all. Are you OK?"

Alex looked much worse off than I was — pale and sick. He just nodded.

"Have you seen my kayak?" I asked, more worried about him than myself.

"It's around those bushes, tangled up in a mangrove," he said. "It should be OK. We might have to bail a little. Let me get it."

Before I could object, he was powering back around the point. I waded gingerly in that direction, coughing again, trying to get that salty algae taste out of my mouth.

In a few minutes, he reappeared, my yellow boat hitched to his by a tether.

"I'm sorry," I said when he came back. "I guess I just didn't see it coming."

"I could hear them coming. I should have gotten us both

out of there," Alex said grimly, as if he were describing combat.

"It was just an accident," I said. He steadied my kayak against his, but I almost spilled the boat again as I climbed awkwardly back in. "Nothing you could have done."

"I could have tried to help you," he said with a distant look, handing me my rescued paddle. "Called you off. They were drunk. They were dangerous. I just froze."

I knew he was back in his scary place, and I felt terrible for him. "I was OK, Alex," I said softly. "It was no big deal. Just an accident. Don't worry."

"I'm always going to worry," he said, his voice still rough. "Let's get back to the ramp."

I paddled behind him quietly, thinking of his entrenched fears. All the while, I shivered. The wan fall sun no longer seemed enough to keep me warm, soaked to the skin as I was. My T-shirt and especially my canvas shorts clung to me uncomfortably, and my wet sneakers felt as if they were full of sand.

"I can't wait to take off these shorts," I said as we disembarked at the boat ramp. There was a beat, a moment when I would have expected one of Alex's deliciously inappropriate jokes, but he had nothing.

"I'll get you home right away so you can get out of those clothes." He sounded frightfully mature.

"Can't wait," I said, drawing him on, but still he said nothing.

The silence made the drive home even longer. By the time we got back to my place, I was really worried.

"Please don't be upset," I said.

He turned to me and turned off the car.

"Sloane, don't ever, ever think that I was angry with you.

I'm furious with myself. I let you get ahead of me, and those rednecks almost killed you. They were screaming and laughing the whole time, even when they saw your boat face-down in the water. I could have strangled them. But I was paralyzed. It's that same damn thing again."

"But nothing really happened," I said. "We're OK. It's OK."

"It is not OK!"

"OK," I repeated lamely. "I'm just worried about you."

"Worried about me?" He shook his head. "You never cease to surprise me."

Alex got out of the car and came around to open the door and let me out. He escorted me to the door of the carriage house, his arm in mine, and then he let go.

I fumbled with my key — which, fortunately, I'd left in his SUV with my purse, instead of at the bottom of the river — and finally got the door open.

He spoke very quietly as I entered the room. "I have to work this out before I endanger you again, Sloane."

I spun on my heel. He was still in the doorway, head bowed, looking wretched.

"Don't you dare." I was surprised at the cold rage in my voice. "Don't you dare blame yourself. And what do you think you are? Superman? My protector? Your strength is attractive, Alex, but I can handle myself. And I can help you, too, if you'll let me."

"I'll see you next Saturday for the Halloween party," he said mechanically. "That will give me a few days to work on this. To work on myself. Not sure if it will be enough, but I have to try. I promised to take you, and I will."

I stood there, chilled by more than my damp clothes, my mouth gaping.

"You can't shut me out again," I said. "You can't. I won't stand for it."

He looked up at me. "You have to. For your sake and mine."

"Ridiculous," I said, feeling the creep of dread. I was losing him again.

He nodded. "Yes, it is."

"Alex, no."

"Listen," he said. "It's only a week. And — I'll answer my phone. Will that work?"

"Not really." I walked over to him and gently picked up his hand, lifting it to my lips as he had mine when we first met. The look in his eyes was a mix of despair and — at least I hoped — longing.

"You don't have to do this," I told him. "But if you think you do — you'd better call me."

"Of course," he said. I wasn't sure if I believed him. "But I just need you to respect my space now."

And to my disbelief, he left, shutting the door behind him.

"The hell I will," I muttered to my empty little house.

Hot shower. Dry clothes. Cereal for dinner. And the silence of my apartment. I didn't want to play music. I didn't have a TV. And I still felt cold. So cold.

I went to bed early and woke up in the morning in a cold sweat. Was I getting sick? I didn't feel feverish, but I didn't feel well, either. I had a dull headache that no amount of sleep could quell, and I had a lot of sleep. I slept most of the day, interrupted only by nightmares. No calls.

No Alex. And should I call him? After he'd all but said goodbye, with a promise to take me to a party in a week, a promise he'd made only out of some twisted sense of obligation?

I wasn't going to let him go that easily, when letting him go meant letting him go alone into that scary place inside himself.

I called him about 5 p.m. There was no answer, and I left a message.

"Hey, Alex. I want to know how you're doing. Please call me back. You said you would talk to me."

I waited for forty minutes, and then I put the phone into my pocket. It was foolish to sit around waiting for a miracle. I needed a walk to clear the cotton from my head.

The late-day light had a subtle golden quality as it filtered through the oaks and palms along the river road. The fine weather and the beautiful setting had drawn a legion of runners, dog walkers and cyclists. And me.

My head started to feel more clear in the delicate warmth of early evening, in the fresh air. I started to have a little hope.

A group of cyclists swished by me, and I heard a familiar voice I couldn't quite place. "Sloane!"

One of the cyclists broke off from the peloton and curved back to where I was walking. The lanky fellow dismounted and removed his helmet, revealing a mop of dark curls. Gary.

He walked his bike alongside me so he could keep my pace. "What a surprise to see you out here," he said.

"It's because I'm so lazy." I shot him a wry look. "I haven't walked or run since I moved here. I need to get back to it."

"At least you live near the river. It's a great location, especially if you have a bike."

"I don't."

"Then you'll have to get one," he grinned. "You can bike to school, too."

"Not with all my tools and the crazy traffic!"

"That's just the influx of snowbirds. They double the traffic this time of year. Florida has such a bad rep for drivers, but we natives all know it's the northerners' fault."

I smirked. "I resemble that remark."

"You may be from up north, but I'm sure you can drive," Gary said with confidence. He popped a water bottle out of a rack on his bike and took a long gulp. "Need any?" he offered.

"I'm fine." It was true. I felt better.

"So how's your non-boyfriend?" Gary asked.

"Not a great day to ask."

"Uh-oh. You didn't tell him about me, did you?"

It was a joke, but my response dashed the smile from Gary's lips.

"Actually, I did. But he seemed to take it rather well," I said, remembering Alex's satisfying way of taking me to task.

Calm slowly returned to Gary's face.

"If he didn't mind, maybe . . . " His smile was flirtatious again.

"No," I said, shaking my head, but I couldn't help but smile at him, too. "I have to try to work this out."

"I get the sense you're making life hard, when it could be so easy," Gary said.

I nodded, looking up at him, this cute, considerate, talented guy. "I'm not going to deny that you have a point. But I'm starting to think there is something in my nature that makes it impossible to turn away. It's attraction at a fundamental level. And so I choose the difficult path because that's the only one I can choose."

"We do these things not because they are easy, but

because they are hard," Gary said in a passable John F. Kennedy accent before returning to his normal voice. "You know. Launching to the moon. Chasing a non-boyfriend."

I laughed. It felt good to laugh.

"It might be easier going to the moon," I acknowledged.

"See you in class tomorrow?" he asked.

"Sure," I said. "See you then."

He swung onto his bike, secured his helmet and pedaled off into the sunset.

I turned back toward my place and felt a buzz in my pocket. I pulled out my phone to see a text message from Alex. "I will talk to you but it must be tomorrow. I have an appointment tomorrow morning. Patience. I'm sorry."

"Don't be sorry," I texted back, relieved to hear from him. "Are you OK?"

"Not yet but I regret being a jerk yesterday evening. I went into robot mode. I shut you out. I will talk to you tomorrow. I promise. Are you OK with that?"

He'd apologized. He knew he'd been hurtful. That was a start. A small weight lifted from my heart.

"Yes," I typed.

Always yes for Alex. But part of me wondered if I should say no.

MONDAY WENT QUICKLY. Montrose said little about my work in progress, except to remark on a texture he liked or a different way I might shape a piece.

"I see you thinking," he said with approval. "You're thinking through your clay."

He was right. I had a vision now for a larger piece, a self-contained fountain that would feature a monster emerging from the deep, the image clashing with the peaceful sea motifs that were so common in beach art. Beach art was a big thing here, and I now saw there was a big difference between decorative art and *art*.

Despite my teacher's constructive criticism, it was still unnerving to watch him watch me work. I tried to ignore his stares from the front of the room. Instead, I chatted with Gary, who was keeping a friendly distance but was still a comforting presence as I split my time between my art and my work for the school.

In the back of my mind, I thought about Alex. Those thoughts also worked their way into the clay, informing my monster, the thing from the murk of the subconscious.

As soon as I got out to my car that evening, I called him. And he didn't answer. Again. I was frustrated. Even angry. I was driving home, reminding myself that his isolation wasn't necessarily about me, when he called me back.

I popped my Bluetooth earpiece on and answered. "Alex?"

"The one and only," he said, and I could hear a hint of humor in his tone. I felt relieved and also sheepish for my selfishness.

"How did it go today?"

"It was hard. But it was better. I felt better after my session." He sounded tense.

"I detect another 'but' in there," I said as I pulled into the parking lot of the grocery store closest to my house. It was time to buy groceries as if I actually lived here, instead of foraging between dates.

"But — I still worry about where this is taking me," he

replied. "I feel different. It's scary. And I worry I'll feel differently about you when I'm done."

I wanted to ask him how he felt about me. My feelings for him had entrenched themselves; they were sleeping in my bed, dreaming in my head. I didn't know how to describe them, yet, but I didn't expect they would leave anytime soon.

"Do you feel differently?" was all I asked.

"No," he said. "I still want to see you. Today, I missed you."

I felt a pulse of excitement. He missed me. "Want me to come over?"

"No."

Pop. There went my balloon.

"I'm just not there yet, Sloane, in my own mind," he said. "What I mean is, I won't be acting out of my best interests or yours if I see you now. But I want to see you. I'm looking forward to the party Saturday. I couldn't say that two days ago."

I watched people stepping out of their cars, lugging children by the hand, walking out of the store with carts full of groceries, living normal lives. But all I could think about was breathing the same air as Alex, feeling him touch me again.

"I never thought five days could seem so long," I told him in a quiet voice.

"Do you miss me?" he asked, and my heart ached for the loneliness in his voice.

"So much." And so much for playing my cards close to the vest.

"Sweet Sloane," Alex said. "I feel better talking to you. I'll call you tomorrow, OK?"

And so it went through the week, with tentative but encouraging conversations. We talked longer each time, and about more topics; I was getting to know him in a way I hadn't before. He was a thinker under that powerful libido. He was informed about the world. I learned more about how he spent his days — writing, community work, exercise, the business of life and tending to his finances — all in all, I thought, a forlorn existence.

I got into a routine with work and school. I added walking to the mix, taking long evening strolls and occasional runs along the river road, studying its bends and trees and shadows, meeting the regulars who exercised on the same route, learning their dogs' names, memorizing the beautiful architectural details of the late-19th-century houses there.

My landlords were obviously getting ready for the party; I came home on Tuesday to several ghosts hanging in the trees around the driveway and a newly planted faux graveyard not far from my carriage house. Tiki torches appeared the next day, marking arbitrary paths through the large, heavily landscaped yard, where more creepy props appeared daily. This was going to be a big deal.

Friday, I came home to a sign on my door with a biohazard symbol that said: "QUARANTINE — ZOMBIE PLAGUE — DO NOT ENTER." On it was a sticky note: "This should keep the guests from knocking on your door. Daisy."

I laughed, the first real laugh I'd had in days. My refined doctor landlords had a sick sense of humor. I crumpled the sticky note as I went inside, settled into the couch and called Alex.

He answered the phone this time.

"You know what this has been like?" he asked after we said our hellos. "It's been like getting on a toboggan and hurtling down a ski run with no idea what's waiting around the bend — rocks, trees, hot chocolate. Just a crazy plunge into the unknown. But exhilarating. Like I'm shedding my clothes as I go, my old clothes, anyway."

"I wouldn't mind witnessing that." I'd refrained from flirting with him in the past couple of days, but it was hard to turn down that kind of opening.

"I'd like you to be there," he said. "I want to tell you something: I feel pretty good now. And I am pretty sure you're going to be in the ski lodge at the bottom of the hill. I can't wait to see you."

"Tomorrow, right?" I asked, hoping he would say "tonight."

"I think that's best," he said. "Just because I have certain expectations for myself. For how I feel. Broken wide open but getting better. This all started with me wanting to be able to be with you. And going to this party is going to be huge for me. It will be the first real test."

"If it gets too bad, my place is right here," I said. "We have a place to go."

"So how's your lusty wench costume coming along?"

That was a good sign. I smiled. "Still working on it."

"Arrr, and ye'll be walkin' the plank if I'm not happy with ye," he said, putting on a pirate accent.

"I look forward to seeing your plank," I said, feeling warm at hearing that flirtatious tone I'd missed.

"Oh, ho, missy," he said, still putting on the accent. "Just hearing you talk that way makes my plank stand at attention."

"Really?"

"Really," Alex said, suddenly losing the accent.

"If you put out your plank, I'll have to board you," I teased.

"Damn." His voice was low, intense. "If you could see what a few words from your lips do to me."

"I'd like to see what my lips do to you," I pressed him further, loosening the button and zipper on my jeans, reaching my free hand down to touch myself. After the previous week, I was like a can of gasoline, waiting for a match. If he only knew.

"If you were here, you'd see exactly what you do to me," he said.

"We could switch to video, and then I really could see you," I purred.

There was silence for several seconds. I started to wonder if I'd gone too far. And then the call ended, startling me. *Damn it.*

Almost immediately, my phone chirped. He was requesting a video call. I accepted it and found myself looking into his eyes, or as much of his eyes as the less-than-perfect video call could show me.

He'd taken off his shirt. That much I could see. I touched myself lightly, but I didn't show him. Not yet. I'd never done this before, this kind of seduction. And I sensed a role reversal, perhaps because I was shielded by the technology.

"Let me see you," I said, running my tongue over my lips.

"OK, beautiful." The video image changed as he held his phone farther back, revealing his muscular torso and his jeans, open like mine, his bulge straining against his black briefs.

"Set yourself free," I whispered. He wordlessly complied, easing his jeans down with his free hand, and then his briefs. His hard cock sprang forward, and I let out a little gasp. To see him this way was revealing not just visually, but emotionally. I was seriously turned on, perhaps because I was driving, perhaps because *he* was so turned on.

I pulled my free hand out of my jeans and, giving my best smoldering glance to the little lens in the phone, put my thumb in my mouth and began to suck it.

"God, Sloane," he croaked, setting his hand on his cock. He ran his hand down his hard length, and I almost lost it.

He propped the phone on something — something on the coffee table in the wine room, I thought, because he sank back into the red couch, and I could see all of him, his sculpted, naked body, as he stroked himself to the beat of my sucking.

I got up, looking for a place where I could set up my phone, too, and propped it against a pile of books on my work table. I took my thumb out of my mouth and pulled my T-shirt up over my head and dropped it on the floor. I slowly released the clasp on my bra, just a simple white one today, and dropped my brassiere, too. Watching him, I cupped my breasts, squeezing them, and traced my fingers over the areolas until he groaned.

He did not stop watching me as he touched himself. His eyes were fixed on the phone, as if he were in a trance. So I stepped back and pulled off my jeans and underpants, kicking away my sneakers in the process. And I reached between my legs and penetrated myself with my fingers.

"Yes," I heard him say. His pace accelerated. "Fuck yourself. Yes. That's my cock inside you, Sloane. You are mine. I don't care how far away you are. *You are mine.*"

It was these words that made me lose whatever self-control had gotten me to this point, and I pushed deeper inside myself, into the slickness there. I closed my eyes as I felt him inside me, imagined his hands on my body. I was breathless. Aching. Aching for him. I came with a low moan. Panting, I opened my eyes as I prolonged the orgasm, and he was fast joining me.

"*Yes,*" he groaned, and he came under his fast-moving hand, his seed spurting from his big cock in virile pulses.

Even as I felt my own pleasure, I felt a curious detachment. It was strange to see him do this without me there, like some lonely video troll on the Internet — but this was Alex. Talking to *me*. I couldn't imagine opening up this way for anyone but him.

I withdrew my fingers and put them in my mouth, sucking, tasting myself, my own arousal, lost in the thought of him watching me, still electrified.

At last, he was at rest. His head fell back against the couch. I could hear his breathing.

When he lifted his eyes, I was close to the phone, smiling at him, still wanting him, my hands clasped in front of me.

"Are you sure we have to wait until tomorrow?" I asked.

"God, yes, Sloane, or you'll kill me. I'll forget about anything but fucking you. Party first."

"Get the work out of the way, huh?" Because for him, the party probably would be work.

"The party might be fun," Alex admitted. "But being with you will be better. You are so sexy. How did it take me so long to find you?"

"Whatever I am, you make me that and more," I said. "I wasn't the 'me' you know until I met you."

He sighed, picked up the phone and held it close so I could see his face, now relaxed, even happy. "Until tomorrow, wench. I'll be there at eight."

"Bring your Jolly Roger," I said slyly, and hung up.

I AWOKE Saturday with one agenda: become the sexiest pirate wench possible.

Since modern Halloween costumes seemed to be primarily about exploiting women's sluttiest instincts, my goal didn't seem too hard — except I was thrifting most of it. I'd already bought a flouncy black skirt from Goodwill. I'd ripped and re-stitched it strategically so it had a jagged hem that, at least at points, was definitely daring.

I'd wear my high-heeled boots, but I needed a little something extra. With my appetite whetted by last night's virtual encounter with Alex, I wanted to wear an outfit he'd never forget.

I laid out the bits and pieces of my costume on my bed and called Cali.

"So you're going to the party tonight, too? Excellent," she said. "So is Damien and a bunch of our friends."

"Yeah, and I'm still working on my costume. Can I ask you an embarrassing question?"

"Shoot."

"Where you do buy sexy lingerie around here?"

Cali laughed. "*Really* sexy?"

"I can't lie to you. Yes. As sexy as it gets."

"So Alex is making an appearance," my cousin surmised.

"Yes. He has trouble sometimes in social situations. So I can't guarantee how long we'll stay. But I figure I might be an excellent distraction."

"I'm sure," Cali said drily. "OK — I think the best bet for you might be The Velvet Glove." She gave me directions. "Want me to go with you?"

"No," I said, already contemplating my embarrassment. "I would die. Do I need an escort?'

Cali laughed again. "No. It's a clean place. Nice people. I've shopped there for bridal showers before. They don't seem to realize they're selling dildos and porn along with the pretty clothes. It's like shopping at a Hallmark store, but the greeting cards all have naked people on them."

"Oh, boy," I said, getting nervous.

"You'll be fine. Eyes on the prize," Cali teased.

The store was on a less-traveled street in downtown Bohemia. I parked in the small lot and, working up my courage, headed inside. A few women were chatting as they browsed through the clothes; one man was looking at magazines. Pop music played on the speakers. I could see a doorway into more rooms in the back of the store that no doubt held all sorts of paraphernalia that would make my mother faint.

"Good afternoon, darlin'," the older lady behind the counter said when I entered. "What can I help you find?" She had a Southern accent, red hair coiffed like Lucille Ball's, drawn-on eyebrows, a conservative blouse with a floral print and synthetic pink stretch pants. Not exactly a diva of sin. I felt a bit less intimidated.

"I need some — accessories for a Halloween costume," I said.

"Well, you came to the right place," she said in her friendly drawl. "We have tons of costumes, and it's all twenty percent off this weekend. What do you need? Naughty nurse? Sexy zombie? Those are very big this year."

I suppressed a giggle. Prurient potter, perhaps?

"Pirate," I said, leaving out the bit about being a wench. That was a given.

"Oh, then the first thing you need is a corset or bustier. Shirt optional." She led me to a round rack bursting with colorful costumes trimmed with satin, lace, bows, strings, leather and buckles.

"I have a skirt and shoes," I said as she fished through the hangers. "The skirt is black. Maybe something that will coordinate with it in green or red?"

She paused to look me over, taking in my dimensions, and pulled out a shiny emerald-green brocade corset trimmed in black.

"This will look so pretty with your eyes," the woman said. "Now, this is strapless for easy access." She winked. "You have a nice C-cup there, don't you? These will make you look like a D. And the cups have a little extra feature . . . "

By the time she was done with me, I felt thoroughly tarted up. With my little pink bag of unmentionables and a few shreds of my innocence intact, I hit the road and returned home to take a nap before my elaborate preparations for the party.

When I awoke, I ate an apple, took a shower, did some personal grooming, wrapped a towel around myself, cranked up a rock and roll playlist on my iPod dock, and contemplated how I would put it all together.

"Dressing" was a funny word for such scant clothing, I thought, as I emptied the contents of the pink bag onto the bed.

Just as I was about to begin, my phone rang. With horror, I saw it was my mother, but I made myself answer — it was better than getting a call later, when Alex was here. I peppered our short, awkward conversation with vague, reassuring updates as I stared at the evidence of my depravity. Though it was nice hearing her voice, I had too recently escaped her repressive ways, and in the end, it was a relief to hang up.

Once I'd reset my brain, I started with the panties, the naughtiest things I'd ever owned, black and lacy, with a gap where the crotch should be. At least they had a little back coverage, if high-cut mesh lace could be called coverage. Next, I pulled on the fishnet stockings and the garter belt. As I clipped the stockings in place, I had to admit the combination was scorching hot.

The corset was next. I zipped up the snug front and arranged my breasts in the cups. The lady in the store was right: My cleavage mounded high above the green and black bodice. No straps interrupted the creamy curve of my skin from my shoulders all the way to my breasts. And the shiny green-and-black fabric was gorgeous, trimmed generously in black seams and lace.

The skirt was comfortable, with an elastic waistband, and it hid the most wayward aspects of my undergarments. At least, if I didn't bend over too far.

I'd purchased one more accessory to help me feel a little less exposed: elbow-length black satin gloves, fingerless, with just a black cord that looped around my middle finger to hold them in place. They added a touch of elegance to my brazen outfit.

I opened the wardrobe so I could check myself out in the long mirror and had a rush of confidence. This ensemble, I was sure, would make Alex happy. And, I thought with a small smile, to look this sexy, to be this unfamiliar siren, made me happy, too. It felt good to escape myself — or to reveal a part of myself that had long been hidden. If Alex was on a journey, so was I.

I dried my hair and added ringlets with the curling iron,

and I found a long, sheer black scarf to pull the locks away from my face. Eye makeup was next, and my favorite dark red lipstick. Last, I donned a pair of dangling faux-pearl earrings accented with tiny rhinestones that put me in an eighteenth-century mood.

Twilight had faded to near night. I glanced at the clock. 7:30 already! Alex would be here soon. And I was hearing more activity outside.

I peeked through the blinds and looked up toward the house. In the light of the tiki torches and a few atmospheric, blood-red spotlights, I saw a handful of vehicles parked along the long driveway, including a catering van. There was also a crew putting final touches on the outdoor decor, its surprises hidden by the near-darkness. I wondered where the doctors found people who installed ghouls on demand. Probably the same people who installed Christmas lights for the well-off.

I checked my phone just to be sure I hadn't missed anything. Suppose Alex didn't come? What if the prospect of the party was just too much for him? Would he visit me anyway?

I fretted while I pulled on the high-heeled boots I'd worn when I'd scaled his mountain of a stairway. Maybe tonight was not a sure thing, not the happy reunion I'd hoped for. Even if he went to the party, we had yet to see how he would handle being in a crowd in an unfamiliar environment. I had almost worked myself up into real distress when a knock came at the door.

I clip-clopped to the door and opened it, and there was a dashing, sexy, sinister buccaneer beyond my wildest dreams: Broad hat with gray, white and black plumes. White shirt with laces that revealed just enough of his muscled chest. Eggplant overcoat with black leather trim and big brass buttons. A black leather vest. A purple sash with a sword at his waist. Noticeably tight black pants. And black leather boots that folded down at the knee, trimmed with straps and buckles. He'd even allowed himself a day's growth of stubble, adding to his ruffian charm.

"Alex," I breathed as I stepped aside to let him in. "Or should I call you Captain?"

Alex, in turn staring at me as he entered, took a moment to find his voice.

"Wench," he said in a pirate accent with English over-tones, his eyes boring into mine, "I'm sure you will call me Captain before the night is over. But I want you to mean it."

"So," I said, "you're going to make me?"

"Damn right." He grabbed me around the waist and dipped me, covering my mouth with his in a fierce kiss that turned my blood into boiling lava. When he released me, I could barely stand, and his hat was askew.

"You want to make me now?" I asked breathlessly.

The accent was gone when he answered. "Business before pleasure," he said in a low voice as he straightened his hat. I could tell he was tempted, but he wanted to brave the party first. "I have something for you, wench."

He reached into a pocket of his coat and pulled out a black velvet bag, dangling it in front of me.

"For me?" I took the bag, feeling the slippery movement of something inside — jewelry, I thought.

I shot him a smile and opened the drawstring. I turned the bag over, and a gorgeous double string of coin pearls slipped into my hand. I let out a little gasp.

"Straight from the treasure chest," my pirate said, a hint of a smile on his lips.

"These are incredible." I turned the rough, flat pearls

over so their subtle, iridescent colors caught the light — hints of pink, gold and green. "I don't have anything for you."

"You have you," he said simply, reaching forward to take the pearls from me, holding them up. I turned my back toward him, and he lay them against my skin, clasping the choker around my neck, clicking the magnetic clasp together. He kissed my shoulder, his lips lingering. He kissed my neck, my earlobe, and fingered the faux pearls in my ear. "It even matches."

"But the earrings aren't real," I said.

"I'll remedy that someday," Alex murmured as he turned me back to him and kissed my mouth, a kiss I returned with more emotion than I thought I could contain.

He straightened, and a wicked smile slowly took over his face. I swear, he really did look like a pirate. A goddamn sexy pirate.

He looked me over. "I want you now, wench. But since I have to wait, I think I'll do a little reconnaissance before I start plundering. Sometimes I enjoy deprivation combined with anticipation." He circled me slowly. "Your breasts! That corset is delicious. And those stockings. My God. What else is under there?"

"You'll have to plunder me to find out."

"Don't tempt me, wench," he said, his voice a throaty growl. "I'm inspecting you now for boarding later."

"Where are your gloves? I thought pirates wore gloves," I teased him, wiggling my fingers at him so he could take note of mine.

"The better to touch you with, my dear," he said, moving closer. With achingly deliberate slowness, he lifted my skirt. I heard his sharp intake of breath as he saw the garters, the panties. I swiveled my hips so he would have no doubt what kind of wench he was dealing with.

"You are no mere wench," he purred in my ear. "You are a temptress. Leaving your pussy exposed for any rake who comes along with a hot cock."

His naughty words intensified my longing. I reached out one hand and grazed his crotch. He was hard as a rock.

"Are you sure you don't want me to do something about that?" I asked.

He dropped the edge of the skirt and moved away, then turned back to me, his eyes molten silver. He spoke slowly, enunciating every syllable. "The deprivation is going to make ravishing you all that much more delicious later."

I felt an ache, a rush of heat between my legs. How were we ever going to navigate the party in this aroused state? He saw the yearning in my face, and he gave me that wicked smile again. He held out one arm.

"Shall we go, dear hot wench?"

"Yes, Alex," I managed to utter. At least I'd distracted him from anxiety about the party. And confounded myself in the bargain.

I locked the door behind us and handed him my spare key, on a keychain with a ceramic, star-shaped fob I'd made myself. "No pockets," I explained.

"I should say not." He slipped the key into his coat pocket, and we strolled off toward the torches and the spooky mysteries beyond.

THERE WERE many more cars in the driveway; Alex's was next

to mine, along with a few others I didn't know. Dr. Daisy was right. I wasn't going anywhere tonight.

Not that I wanted to. Not with Alex back on my arm. With other arriving revelers, we walked up the driveway to the main sidewalk, well-lit by tiki torches as it wound through the trees and bushes. As we approached the porch, I saw a sign pointing in the opposite direction that said "Haunted Trail."

"Things like that scare me," I confessed.

"*That* I can handle," Alex said drily. As we climbed the steps, he gripped my arm more securely. It almost felt as if he were protecting me, but I knew he was steadying himself.

I gave his arm a squeeze back. "You ready?"

"Actually," he said, smiling down at me, "I feel pretty good."

We walked through the doors and entered a world of noise and color, shadow and light — LED candles where there weren't real ones, colored spotlights, strings of fairy lights. Music formed a thumping but not overwhelming backdrop and seemed to come from everywhere. A kaleido-scope of costumed partiers washed around us.

And the decor! There was the occasional witch or mummy or hanging bat, but mostly, there were skeletons. Skeletons everywhere. Big ones, small ones, even smaller ones, all having a skeleton party, in party hats, holding goblets, entwined in the staircase railing, hanging off a chandelier.

I laughed at the macabre energy of it. I looked up at Alex, and he was grinning, too.

We stopped by a punch bowl and filled a couple of clear cups. I took a sip and sighed. Something with gin and cham-pagne and citrus. Very nice.

"I hope that's not from the crate of champagne I sent over," Alex said after taking a sip. "It shouldn't be mixed with anything."

"Are you being a snob again?"

"Absolutely," he said as we reached one of the food tables and filled small, clear plates with exquisite hors d'oeuvres that tasted as good as they looked: crab pastries; shrimp skewers; bruschetta; roasted fig halves with goat cheese; sushi tuna, wasabi and cucumber bites; dollops of egg, crème fraiche and caviar in decorative spoons; English, French and Spanish cheeses, and almond cookies that looked like fingers, a nod to Halloween. There was also a brain that I assumed was made from gelatin, but these *were* doctors. One never knew.

We found Daisy and her husband, dressed as Morticia and Gomez Addams, holding court in the large, crowded back screened porch. A hired bartender mixed mai tais behind a thatched tiki bar.

I spotted Ez, the singer I'd met at the Junction Box, knocking back shots with a couple of her band mates, and we exchanged a wave.

"Alex!" Daisy said with genuine pleasure and not a little surprise as she realized who accompanied him. "Sloane! Glad you could make it."

"How could we miss it?" I replied.

"Thanks for inviting us," Alex said, almost shyly. He was tentative but holding his own, I thought.

"Of course, my dear. Evan, look who's here!"

Evan, or Mr. Doctor, as we might call him in private, took his cigar out of his mouth and offered my date a hearty handshake.

"Alex! And can this be our tenant?" His eyes just about

popped out of his head as his gaze swept over my body, and I got the impression he'd had more than a few mai tais.

"Hi, Dr. Pullman," I said, suddenly feeling a bit shy myself.

"You need a mai tai!" he bellowed, waving his cigar at the bartender, a young woman in black who looked more than a little harried as people shouted out drink orders. After a moment, she handed two drinks over the bar in ceramic, moai-shaped tiki mugs topped with bunches of mint. We traded our empty glasses for them, and I took a sip.

"Oh, wow," I said.

Alex nodded after sipping his. "Strong and delicious. This is the way they're supposed to be made."

"Sloane!" came a familiar voice — my nicer cousin's. I whipped around to see Cali and Damien coming toward me from the other end of the porch.

Calista was dressed as what I could only call a white fairy, all sparkles and tulle and goodness, with diaphanous wings and her blond hair piled high on her head, spiked with glittering adornments. In contrast, she had a serious black camera hanging from her shoulder.

Damien sported his usual shock of black hair, but out of it poked red horns, and he wore a shiny red jacket, red shirt, black tie and black pants. He had a pitchfork in one hand and a mai tai in the other. It was the most dressed up I'd ever seen him, and the most devilish.

"Coz," he said to me. "Alwend," he said to Alex.

"Damien. Nice to see you," Alex said neutrally.

"And this is Cali — Calista," I said. "The other cousin I told you about."

"The photographer," said Alex, and I was pleased he

remembered. "I think we went to school together, but a few years apart, right? So our paths didn't really cross."

"That's right," she said. "You look very — "

I failed to suppress a smile as she searched for a word that meant *incredibly sexy* without actually saying it.

"Hot," Damien interjected indifferently. Cali jabbed him with an elbow. "What? He does. Don't worry, I'm not out to jump his bones. That's my cousin's department."

"Damien!" I exclaimed.

Alex just laughed, and what a pleasant sound it was.

"Have a good time," Alex said. "We're going to walk around some more."

"OK," said Cali, who then whispered to me, "I see you found The Velvet Glove."

She raised an eyebrow at me and I smiled more widely. I waved goodbye as I followed Alex out of the seething crowd and back into the house.

At the bottom of the back staircase, there was a relative dearth of bodies, and we took advantage of the break to sit side by side on the stairs and sip our mai tais.

"You OK?" I asked him.

"It was a little tight back there, but I'm OK," he said. "I really feel like I've been let out of a cage. It's wild. I find myself forgetting I'm in a crowd. I'm enjoying a drink or a snippet of conversation, or looking at you."

He put a hand on my knee and drew it up slightly, lifting my skirt just above where the stocking ended and my skin began.

"Careful," I whispered.

"How can I be careful when what you're wearing is so reckless?" he whispered back, nibbling my neck. My pirate fantasies were nothing compared with Alex, his hand on my leg, his lips on my skin.

I heard an "ahem" and looked up.

"Gary!" I said.

My friend was dressed as a court jester, a costume that seemed especially appropriate given the dumbfounded look on his face.

"Sloane! *This* is your non —?" He clammed up before he could say "non-boyfriend."

Alex stood up to shake Gary's hand. "Gary — nice to see you again."

"Uh, yeah," Gary said. "How you doing, Alex?"

"Great. I understand you know Sloane. I'm her boyfriend."

Now it was my turn to be dumbfounded. I looked at Alex with my mouth open. Did he just say he was my boyfriend? I started to grin. But wait . . .

"You know Gary?" I asked.

"Everybody knows Gary," said Alex, who seemed to be enjoying both of our reactions. "He's a mainstay of the art school. And his mom just about single-handedly drove the campaign that raised the money for its endowment. It wouldn't be the Bohemia School of Art and Design without Gary's family."

Gary swallowed, looking silly but kind of cute in his jester hat. The bells on the tips jingled as he nodded. His curly hair stuck out from beneath its confines.

"She just raised the money. We weren't major contributors or anything," Gary explained.

"Raising it is the hardest job of all," Alex said.

"Nice," I managed to remark.

Alex nodded at Gary and began to move down the stairs. "Take it easy."

"You, too, Alex," Gary said.

I gave my pottery partner a half-smile as I walked down the steps and edged past him. I could see him trying and failing not to take in every inch of my wenchiness, astonishment in his eyes.

As Alex and I got back into the flow of the crowd, we set down our empty mugs, and I bumped my hip hard against him.

"You knew who Gary was all along?"

"I wasn't sure," Alex said, "but I couldn't think of another Gary who'd be working with you in the pottery studio."

"You're devious," I said. "I'd better keep an eye on you."

"I'm a pirate. What do you expect, wench?"

"I don't know, *boyfriend.*" I looked up to see his mischievous smile. And amid the push and pull of people, he bent down and touched his lips to mine. With my slight buzz from the booze and my more intense buzz from the whole boyfriend thing, I almost forgot we weren't alone as his tongue plumbed my mouth, as he pressed my body close to his.

When he lifted his head, removing the shield created by his grand hat, I saw a much more unpleasant face leering at me.

"Miss Abbey," said Montrose King. He had a glass of red wine in his hand and swayed on his feet. He was dressed in something medieval, a costume with a lot of black velvet and silver trim. It set off his goatee and made him look more sinister than usual.

"Mr. King," I said, echoing his formal address, feeling self-conscious in my outfit for the first time.

"You look ravishing. And who is this lucky pirate?"

"Alex Alwend," I said faintly. "This is Montrose King, the potter-in-residence at the school."

"I've heard much about your work," Alex said, but his response was cold. He didn't like Montrose's tone either.

Montrose ignored Alex and spoke to me.

"I should have recruited you to be Maid Marian to my Sheriff of Nottingham." He took a deep drink of his wine. "Though you aren't looking very maidenly tonight."

Alex took half a step toward him, and I put a hand on his arm.

"Now, now," said Montrose, drinking again, "if you were Robin Hood, we'd have a quarrel, but you're just one of the rich he set out to rob, aren't you?"

"Just," Alex said, seething.

"Let's go see the haunted trail," I said, tugging at Alex's sleeve. With difficulty, I got him to move, and we pushed past Montrose.

"We'll meet again," Montrose muttered in my ear as I slid past him, and I thought I felt his hand brush my leg. I shivered.

Alex was quaking. I could feel it. I got him to the front door and out on the porch.

"Are you all right?" I asked.

"Me? I'm fine!" he said, looking down at me, cupping my chin. "Are you OK? Is he always like that with you?"

"He's drunk," I said dismissively, hoping Alex would cool down.

He searched my eyes, then let go of my chin.

"Come on," I coaxed. "Forget about him. Let's take our walk. Are you really OK?"

"Of course," he said, but he still sounded out of sorts, if not quite so furious.

"Then you did it."

"What?"

"You survived a party. You know. You did it!"

He looked confused for a second, as if he'd forgotten what I was talking about, and then a look of wonder overtook his features.

"You know, you're right." He gave me a quick kiss. "But all in all, I'd still rather be alone with you."

"Haunted trail first," I said as I stepped onto the walkway, pulling him behind me. "Remember how exciting deprivation is?"

"I just remember how tantalizing your pussy looked under that skirt," he said in a low voice, and I giggled, skipping ahead to the shadows beyond the next tiki torch.

He caught up with me, grabbed me in a hungry kiss and ran a hand up under my skirt, touching me there. I felt the heat build between my legs, mixed with trepidation.

"Someone will see," I whispered. "And there are scary things on this trail, I think."

"Then we'd better hurry," he murmured, kissing me deeply, reaching farther beneath my skirt, probing me with one finger as his tongue entwined with mine. A wave of pleasure engulfed me as I ground against him, as I sucked on his tongue. God, I wanted him. But this wasn't the place.

With a little bleat, I broke the kiss reluctantly, pulled away and walked down the path delineated by the torches, with Alex close behind me. We wound through clusters of palm trees, shrubbery and flowering plants that created sinister, dancing shadows in the variable light.

"Something smells wonderful," I said softly, afraid to awaken the ghosts.

"Night-blooming jasmine," Alex said.

"You know everything."

"Almost."

I laughed. Just then, a figure in a hockey mask jumped out of the bushes, revving a chainsaw. I screamed and clutched at Alex.

He laughed, waving away the actor. "There's not even a blade on it, Sloane. Oldest trick in the book."

"Let's just get through this," I said, steeling myself for the next hurdle.

A few more people jumped out at us from dark clusters of plants and various bloody tableaus, scaring me a little less each time, but I was glad when we saw the sign that said "You survived!"

The trail ended by the rose garden, not all that far from my place.

"Thank God," I said, a little exhausted from the tension.

"What's this?" he asked, noting the tall hedge.

"The rose garden. You've never seen it? Oh, it's so pretty. I'm not sure what it will be like in the dark, but it already smells good."

I took him by the hand and walked him around to the entrance.

The garden felt more intimate at night, enclosed on all sides, the scent of the flowers more intense than anything we could see. Only ambient light reached in here, and barely that — stars and the distant flicker of the torches. Still holding hands, we walked around the circle and through the crossed paths until coming to the center. This place seemed magical; connected, somehow, to the energy of the earth.

Alex took both my hands and pulled me backward toward one of the benches. Pushing his sword out of the way, he sat and pulled me on top of his lap.

Straddling him, I could feel how hard he was through the tight pants. He took off his hat, lay it carefully beside us, and pulled me closer for a deep, bone-melting kiss. I wrapped my legs around him, wrapped my arms around his neck, got lost in my mouth being ravaged by his.

He ended the kiss and looked into my eyes.

"I want to fuck you now," he whispered.

I wanted him so much, but something troubled me. Maybe I was still spooked by the ghouls.

"We should go to my place," I said.

"I'm through with deprivation." He touched my clit, rubbing it lightly, and I couldn't hold back a low moan as his pace increased.

"It's only a few steps away," I said breathlessly. "Let's go."

"OK," he said, withdrawing his hand. "But we need champagne. I'm going to get one of the bottles I sent up to the house. And then we'll go to your place. I promise. Wait for me here?"

"OK," I said. "Hurry."

"I'll take a shortcut." Alex grimaced as I eased myself off him. "No chainsaws." He kissed me again, donned his hat and dashed for the opening.

I laughed in delight. My cavalier. My pirate. I closed my eyes, breathing in the scent of the roses, feeling the delicate breeze in my hair.

"Alone at last."

My eyes flew open, and I whirled to see Montrose King standing at the edge of the rose garden. In front of the only exit.

PART 3

"*T*houghtless of your pirate to abandon his harlot to any villain who happens by," Montrose said, walking unsteadily toward me.

"He'll be right back." I quickly stepped backward.

"You're a beautiful woman, Ms. Abbey." From him, the compliment sounded menacing.

I just shook my head — no to what he was saying, no to his approach. No. *No.*

"A beautiful face," he slurred. "Beautiful breasts. That beautiful ass you so willingly showed off just now, sitting like a slut on your pirate's lap."

"Montrose!" I was shocked he would go this far, even in words. I was his student, for Christ's sake. "Get out of here!" I said with more emphasis, but he walked closer still. I began to move around the circle, putting the benches between me and him, hoping to get a shot at the exit.

"Makes me wonder what there is to see under that skirt. Are you offended?" He shook his head at my horrified expression. "How could you be? My dear, you said you weren't a nice girl. And artists should stick together. We can work together, you know. We could make amazing art. This could be very, very pleasant."

Montrose lunged as I tried to make a dash for it and grabbed my arm with a grip of steel, pushing me back toward the bench where Alex had just held me.

"Get away from her." Alex's low voice filled me with relief. I looked toward the entrance to the rose garden and saw him there, dimly outlined by the lights beyond. I tried to move toward him, but Montrose still had a fierce grip on my arm.

"Let go!" I growled through gritted teeth, struggling to pull away.

In an alarming and absurd movement, Alex put down the bottle of champagne he was carrying and drew his sword.

"You can't be serious," Montrose said, but he released me. I ran and hid behind Alex, shaking in anger and relief. At the same time, I wanted to laugh hysterically. This was like some kind of sick movie.

Alex touched my shoulder, silently asking me to stay where I was, and strode up to Montrose with the blade in his hand. Like the rest of Alex's costume — the leather, the plumes — the sword looked real. And, knowing Alex and his penchant for buying the very best, I felt sure it was.

"Don't, Alex!" I called out. "It's not worth it."

"It's all right, Maid Marian," Montrose said, sounding even more drunk. He backed up, his hands in the air, and sat hard on the bench. "I surrender the booty."

"You will stay away from her," Alex said coldly, waving the point of the sword under Montrose's nose. "You will treat her with respect. And no matter what you think of me, I have the power to have you thrown out of the school tomorrow. However, in deference to discretion, I will not, unless you cross that line. *And you will not cross that line.* Do I make myself clear?"

In response, Montrose waved his hands dismissively, as if he could make Alex disappear. After a moment of swaying, my teacher passed out, rolling off the bench and onto the stone path with a *thunk*.

Alex lowered his sword. "Well, that was anticlimactic."

I walked up beside him as we both regarded the snoring, drunken lump that was Montrose King.

"Do you think he heard you?" I asked, surprised by the tremor in my voice.

"He heard me," Alex said. "And if he didn't, I'll skewer him."

I reached my arms around Alex's waist and buried my face in his buccaneer's coat. He held me until my breathing slowed, and then he walked me back to the entrance of the rose garden. He sheathed his sword, grabbed the bottle of champagne, and escorted me outside and toward my place.

THE CHAMPAGNE WAS FANTASTIC, even if we drank it out of mismatched wine glasses, and it did much to calm my nerves. We enjoyed it on the couch, curled up together, still in our costumes, sans boots, though Alex also had removed his hat and sword. His wavy hair was charmingly rumpled.

"That's a real sword, isn't it?" I asked.

"A rapier. Of course. As a sometime science-fiction-fantasy geek, I relish any chance to get authentic with a costume."

I chuckled. "Do you know how to use it?"

"Actually, yes. I studied fencing."

"It was pretty hot," I said, sipping the champagne, "being rescued by a guy with an actual sword. Talk about taking my pirate fantasy up a notch."

"I wish it hadn't been necessary," he said seriously. "I hope he doesn't make an issue out of this."

"He can't. What he was suggesting — what he might have done — "

"I will *never* let anything happen to you," Alex said fiercely, pulling me closer to him.

I took a deep breath. "I admit, he scared me for a minute. But you can't always be there for everything. You have to trust that I can take care of myself, too."

Alex looked thoughtful. "I respect that. Though my protective instincts are going to kick in sometimes."

"I'm really glad that you were there tonight, but I'm generally not a damsel in distress. I'm kind of embarrassed that I was. Don't get used to it."

"Acknowledged. And don't be embarrassed. He grabbed you."

"I know." I suppressed a shiver, turned my face up to his and kissed him. "Thank you."

Heat flickered in his eyes, and the corner of his mouth turned up. "It's interesting, isn't it, how we come together? Do you know what I mean? I like that even though you can be tough, sometimes you yield to me. I know you choose to do it, and that makes it all the more arousing when you do."

"I love it when you talk about sex. I'm serious," I said to his quizzical expression. "I feel like I can talk about anything with you. And yes," my voice grew softer, "I like yielding to you. I like it when you — take charge. But I also liked seducing you over the phone."

His eyes darkened with that smoky look I was starting to know so well.

"Are you ready?" Alex asked. "I didn't want to push you after what happened."

I nodded. "Give me a minute. Pour us some more champagne."

I got up from the couch, feeling him watching me as I padded back toward my "bedroom" in my stockinged feet. On the short dresser was a cluster of candles I'd bought at The Velvet Glove, and I lit them with a wooden match. My heart turned over at their beautiful, amber light, the inviting circle of warmth that would bring me together with Alex.

I picked up a lipstick, refreshed my color, and called out to him.

"Turn off the lamp and come back here."

"As you wish, wench," Alex replied, and I smiled.

The room got darker as the lamp went out, emphasizing the warm glow around me.

Alex poked his head around the wall created by the screen he'd given me. He had a serious look in his eyes, the look of desire. He walked into the space, set the two glasses on the dresser next to the candles, shrugged off the handsome buccaneer coat and dropped it to the floor.

I sighed to look at him, his muscular chest accentuated by the loose pirate shirt and vest, the rest of his physique dangerously delineated by those pants.

"What do you want, wench?" he asked softly.

An interesting beginning, I thought. I moved to pick up a glass and, as he watched, drained it of champagne. I wanted to be drunk. To let all my inhibitions melt away in the golden bubbles.

"I'm going to prepare myself for you," I said.

"What do you want me to do?"

"Sit. Watch."

A faraway look entered his eyes. He climbed on the bed and made himself comfortable, leaned against the pile of pillows and the headboard, crossed his legs, entwined his fingers over his stomach.

I pulled off the gloves first, slowly, not quite strip-tease style, and set them on the dresser. I pulled the scarf out of my hair and dropped it on top of the gloves, shaking out my locks, letting them fall forward. Alex nodded in approval, saying nothing. But I watched his eyes get larger as I ran my fingers up my belly, over the corset, ready to reveal the secret of this lovely piece of lingerie. I reached to the black seams that ran across the cups of each breast and slowly unsnapped the hidden fasteners, three snaps on each side. As they were loosened, the fabric parted over each nipple. For effect, I widened the gap with my fingers, pushing my breasts out through the holes.

"Goddamn it, Sloane," Alex whispered hoarsely. His hands were clasped so tightly together, I thought he'd break a finger.

I smiled to see him so vexed. "Almost ready," I said, and with the tantalizing speed of a rivulet of honey, I worked my skirt painstakingly down over my hips, knees and legs and tossed it on top of his buccaneer coat.

My nipples got harder just watching him sit up to look at me — my peekaboo breasts, the garters, the fishnet stockings, the lacy panties with the slit that so clearly invited him to fuck me.

"You're so good at undressing yourself," he said, his voice throaty. "Get over here and undress me, wench."

"Yes, Alex," I said, excited by his words. He did like words.

I'd never met a man who talked so much in an intimate situation. I wondered if he knew how much his words turned me on.

He sat on the edge of the bed, and I untied his sash first and dropped it to the floor. Next, I unbuttoned and removed the vest. Then I worked at undoing his trousers, leaning in close to him so my breasts brushed his chest through the thin shirt. His face had a look of barely contained control as I did so. I unfastened the pants; he stood to make it easier to peel the snug fabric away from him.

Thin black briefs barely contained his erection. I cupped it gently, and he gasped. God, he was hard. I pulled the briefs down, lowering to my knees as I did so, and he stepped out of them. His thick cock stood at attention, and I resisted the urge to touch it, to lick it. Let *him* end the deprivation game.

I stood and reached to his waist, leaning my breasts up against him again. I could feel his warm breath on my neck. I grasped his shirt by the bottom and pulled it up over his head. And just like that, he was naked. I felt the sweet buzz of the champagne as I stepped back and looked him over.

"You're not so tough without your sword, are you?" I asked slyly.

"What do you call this?" He grasped his cock. He walked over to me, so close we were chest to chest, my nipples brushing against his skin. "Wench, I enjoyed your little demonstration. But you are my prisoner, and I intend to have my way with you."

"But, sir, would you steal my virtue?"

"I would fuck your virtue into next week," Alex said, and I giggled. "The prisoner may not laugh," he said, looking around. He spied my scarf on the dresser and picked it up.

"Such a convenient scarf. Such a convenient four-poster bed. I believe I shall have to teach the prisoner a lesson."

He pulled me toward him and kissed me hard. I moaned under the sudden pressure of his lips, under the sensation of his erection brushing against my sex through the gap in the panties. He grasped my wrists in front of me and tied one end of the scarf around them. And then he pushed me toward the end of the bed and tied the scarf to the bedpost while I was still standing up. With me facing the bed. I felt a flutter. He was going to take me from behind.

"Lower yourself," he said, pushing my bound arms down on the post. I bent forward. "What a nice view of your pussy. I wonder if it's wet." I felt him reach between my legs and dip a finger into my slit. "Why, yes. I think someone's virtue is in terrible need of a good screw. Fortunately, as a pirate, plundering is my specialty."

I felt my breath release in stuttering anticipation at his naughty words. He lay his hands on my buttocks, pushing his fingers up under the mesh lace of the crotchless panties, and he probed me lightly with his cock. I breathed in sharply as he eased inside my folds. I had never felt so full, so needy, as he began to thrust, to pump slowly against me. I remained bent over, standing with my legs apart, my arms in front of me, tethered by my wrists to the post. My breasts pointed toward the floor, pendulous through the holes in the lingerie, and he reached around and pinched them, hard. I cried out as the pain transmuted into pleasure.

"You want this, don't you, wench?" Alex grunted.

"Yes," I breathed.

"Tell me what you want me to do to you."

"I want you to fuck me." Which, of course, he was doing very well.

"Where do you want me to fuck you?" He trailed a finger suggestively between my butt cheeks. I hesitated. I wanted to do what he wanted. But there were things I didn't think I could do.

"Your finger excites me," I confessed, my voice tremulous. "But you are too big for me there, Captain."

He slowed his rhythm, reached down and kissed my shoulder. "Fear not, my prisoner. I am here for your pleasure as much as mine." He touched me there again. "And this is not important to me."

I exhaled in relief, taken out of the moment, but glad he respected my boundaries. I wanted to give him something in return.

I remembered our first night in Bohemia Beach.

"My mouth," I whispered. "Fuck my mouth."

His thrusting slowed, and he eased out of me. He untied my hands and spun me to face him, looping the scarf around the back of my neck, pulling me to him. With fevered eyes, and with a tenderness no pirate could possess, he kissed me deeply. Then he pointed to the bed.

I climbed onto the mattress, and he arranged me so my head was propped up on the pillows. I wondered what he was up to when he took my right wrist and tied the scarf around it, securing it to one bedpost. He looked around and grabbed his sash off the floor, using it to secure my other wrist, his face a handsome mask, his eyes ablaze as he raked me with his gaze. My heart beat faster at giving up so much control to him. In this position, I could surrender everything — all my pre-programmed guilt, all my childish reservations. I wanted him to take me. Hard.

Still, he leaned forward and whispered in my ear: "Tell me if you want me to stop. Do you?"

"Don't stop," I whispered.

The flame of excitement burned brighter in his eyes.

"You're beautiful like this, Sloane, all tied up and spread out for me." His gaze swept over me again, this time more slowly, possessing me. God, I was wet with wanting him. He was pushing buttons I never knew I had.

As he climbed onto the bed and straddled me, I felt a swoon of desire come over me. I moaned as he knelt over my chest, touching his wet cock to my lips.

I trembled as I took him in my mouth, tasting myself on his skin. He moved slowly back and forth, letting me set the pace. I felt the thrill of watching him in his abandonment — and in his complete control of me — as I sucked lovingly on his rigid shaft, a delicious feeling as I indulged him, as he moaned, as he released a guttural sigh, as he plunged deeper, teasing my throat. I loved seeing him relinquish his self-control, lose himself in me.

"Suck it, wench," he growled, laying a hand on top of my head as I moved. "Your mouth is made for my pleasure."

I hummed in acquiescence, hot for his words, taking him as deeply as I could, feeling him filling my mouth with his hard flesh. I tasted his need, the first few salty drops, but he pulled out before he was done.

He breathed heavily as he loomed over me. He ran a finger over my wet lips, and I sucked it for him. He watched me suck it, watched me watching him, fascinated, his eyes aflame with lust. At last he removed his finger, running it down my neck, the pearl necklace, the creamy mounds of my breasts, the hard nipples peeking through the fabric, the brocade-and-lace-covered belly, and then my bud, so aroused, so easily accessible through the opening in the lingerie. He began touching it lightly, then circling, flicking, squeezing, rubbing, until I whimpered and writhed with an almost overwhelming orgasm. While I was still coming, he pushed his cock inside me, and I almost sobbed with the ecstasy of it as he ravaged me. I strained at my bonds, wanting to touch him; I wrapped my stockinged legs around him. I felt so dirty in this lingerie. I wasn't a nice girl. I liked to suck cock and be tied up and fucked. By Alex. My *boyfriend* Alex.

He paused in his motion, still inside me, and reached up and freed my hands. I embraced him, pulling myself up to meet him, collide with him as he slammed into me anew, fucking me hard.

"Sloane," he hissed as he came explosively inside me, and a new wave of bliss drenched me in dark delight.

"Alex," I moaned, wanting to say his name, to convey how much I loved him as my body rocked with ecstasy.

Oh, hell.

I loved him.

This was a thrill ride for which I'd never had a ticket. Not just sex. Love. Sex *and* love.

He collapsed against me, kissing me tenderly, planting trails of kisses up and down my neck, my breasts, and I hoped he was on the same ride.

Gently, he stripped off my trappings, the corset, the garters and stockings, the panties, restoring me to myself, my comfortable skin, until I was nestled against the pillows, naked in his arms.

I'd been so bold this evening — bold in my costume, even in my submission. But I was afraid to articulate this new and perilous emotion. I was suddenly wide awake, despite the champagne and the lateness of the hour and the sweet drowsiness that followed our coupling.

Alex fell asleep next to me, one arm lying lazily across my

stomach, and I whispered the truth of my heart to his shadowy subconscious.

"I love you, Alex."

I AWOKE in the morning with the tiniest headache, feeling wee nails driving into my delicate skull. Nothing that a large glass of water and a nap wouldn't cure. I hoped. I rolled over to see Alex lying next to me, awake, watching me.

"Did you know you talk in your sleep?" he asked.

I felt my eyes widen. What could I have said?

Oh, shit. I wasn't ready to tell him what I'd figured out last night, especially when I didn't really know how he felt. I hoped my dreams hadn't done it for me.

I forced myself to reply. "What did I say?"

"You said, 'The cake is very good, but I prefer the bananas foster.' "

I giggled. "That's what I said? I couldn't have been hungry after all that good food at the party."

"I don't think it was about food."

"Hmm," I said. "Fiery bananas. I'll have to think about that."

He smiled. "Dreams are so rarely about what they seem. Or at least that's my experience. I've been working out a lot of my thought processes in some new writing, some fiction. It feels like the words are really starting to flow. And I've been keeping a journal as part of my therapy."

"Has it helped?" I reached out, skimming the sheet that lay over his body, letting my hand rest on his hip.

Alex inched a little closer, making it easier to touch him.

"The dreams have been pretty interesting. Last night I was

walking through a flaming landscape, trees on fire, palmettos, everything coal black. Except for a red rose growing there. " His voice became more distant as he relived the vision. "I didn't know what it was at first; I just saw the green shoot, the first leaves. But it grew rapidly in front of my eyes, and I lost sight of the fire around me as I focused on the rose, watching it bloom. I reached out and plucked the flower, but it pricked my hand. There was a bright drop of blood, and the bright red rose, and everything else was black and smoldering."

"I'm almost afraid to guess what that's about." I trailed my fingers over his shape, over the cool fabric of the sheet.

"Rebirth, for one thing. I was told to expect that. But the blood — that could mean many things. The pain I have to go through to get there. Or a fear of heartbreak."

" 'But he who dares not grasp the thorn should never crave the rose,' " I quoted.

"Anne Bronte?"

"That sounds right. Relic of an English class," I said.

"I suppose I crave the rose," Alex said, looking at me and then shifting his troubled eyes elsewhere, to the middle air beyond me.

I didn't like the way this was going. If the rose was love, and he wasn't looking at me, maybe he craved something else altogether.

"It's probably the rebirth dream you were talking about," I said, perhaps too quickly.

His eyes returned to mine, and my headache was forgotten as I wondered what he was thinking.

"Probably," was all Alex said. He rolled over onto his back, and I studied his profile. He could be so hard to read. And I was such a wimp for not speaking my heart.

But I wanted to protect his, even if he didn't know it. If he would give it to me to protect. I curled up next to him, kissing his shoulder, laying an arm over his stomach. Fatigue won the battle over anxiety, and I drifted back to sleep.

When we awoke, we decided an afternoon at the beach would be nice, especially when noisy workers came to clear away the party decorations and debris. First, I made pancakes for us, as Alex teased me about finally proving I could cook something.

He'd packed an overnight bag, so he put on jeans and a T-shirt rather than his pirate attire. I wore black capris and a light green V-neck knit shirt with three-quarter sleeves, just enough weight for the almost-cool air. I was learning that the Florida sun didn't allow the cold to linger for long.

"Maybe I should follow in my car," I said as we got ready to leave, "so you don't have to bring me back. I have class in the morning."

"Maybe I *should* bring you back — or drop you off at school in the morning," Alex said, "given last night's business."

"I think an escort to the classroom would be the worst possible strategy." I was packing a few things in a bag, just in case I stayed over. "I need to show up as if nothing bothers me. And I won't let it bother me, either."

He chuckled.

"Are you laughing at me?" I asked, only half-kidding. "I'm almost looking forward to confronting that asshole."

Alex shook his head. "Not laughing. Well, a little. I just like seeing you all fired up."

"That's what we potters do. Get fired up."

He groaned at the pun. "I'll drive you back. I like driving you, even if it's just to your house."

"OK." I smiled. He liked driving me. He liked being with me, of that I was sure. But did he love me? In the bald light of day, I wondered if I'd given my own feelings too much weight last night, amid the champagne and the heady sex. But I couldn't dismiss them. I felt them deeply. I hadn't known him long, but it seemed like a lifetime. My emotions weren't rational, but when were emotions ever rational? I felt my heart growing, and I couldn't believe that was a bad thing. Except that I'd let him inside, and if he decided to start breaking the china, there wasn't much I could do to stop the damage.

"Penny for your thoughts?" Alex was looking at me curiously.

"Just thinking about bananas foster," I joked, and he grinned.

It was a gorgeous beach day, and there were a lot of out-of-state license plates on the road in Bohemia Beach.

"That's how you can tell the tourists," Alex said as we walked into his condo. "They'll be swimming on a day like this. Floridians just look at the water and soak up the sun."

"I was considering it," I said.

"You're not a Floridian yet. You haven't acclimated. Wait till you do. You'll never want to go back north."

"I already feel that way," I said, then mentally kicked myself for all my words implied.

"Good," Alex said softly. "Do you want to put your bag in my room? Or — do you want another room?"

"Yours is good, if you don't mind," I said. I realized this was the first time I'd actually packed for an overnight stay.

"Good," he said again, this time with a smile. "Want to take a beach walk?"

"Sure. But I'm changing into my swimsuit first."

He gave me an exaggerated shiver. "Be my guest," he said.

Alex got a beverage in the kitchen while I went into his room to change. I loved the green and brown and white colors in here. It felt so organic and comfortable. The bed was rumpled, not quite made, as if he hadn't expected company. Or maybe I wasn't company; "company" implied a certain distance. Maybe I'd made the leap. I hoped so.

I emerged in my white bikini, with a thin, white-cotton cover-up that extended almost to my knees.

Alex was sitting in the living area with a glass of water, reading his computer tablet. He looked up when he heard me, then put down the tablet and stood up slowly, looking me over.

"It's amazing," he said.

"What?"

"How beautiful you are, no matter what you wear."

"Oh, stop," I said, but I couldn't suppress a smile.

"You may be wearing a bikini, but you look positively virginal compared with what you wore last night."

Now I was just a little embarrassed. "Was it too much?" I asked, and I cursed how tenuous I sounded.

"Of course not. There's no such thing." He smiled and walked up to me, kissing me sweetly. "I hope you'll honor me with your wench costume again sometime. In the meantime, I'll take the angel before me."

Damn. Flattery would get him everywhere.

"Do you have a beach towel?"

"Check the linen closet in the powder room," he said. "Tons in there. I'll put on my flip-flops."

In a few minutes, we headed down the elevator and took the back door through the garage and out to the beach. We left our towels, blanket and sandals at the foot of the wooden walkover. Alex rolled up the hems of his jeans, and then he took my hand. Was there anything so reassuring as a lover holding your hand? I didn't think so as we walked along the waterline, basking in the early afternoon sun, letting the foam tickle our toes, watching petite shore birds run on twinkling feet up and down the shifting wet borders left by the incoming waves.

It was almost low tide, and a smattering of tiny shells pricked the soles of my feet. I paused to scoop up a handful, and together we marveled at the variety of colors and textures and shapes in that world in my palm. A few minutes later, I saw a round form rolling in front of me and reached down to catch it in the foamy water: a beautiful shell, its spirals echoing the mathematical perfection of great art.

"Lightning whelk," Alex said. "A nice one. Take it home so you can hear the ocean."

We turned around after a while and headed back toward Alex's building, nodding pleasantly at other beach walkers, watching a couple of surfers trying to make the most of the subtle waves. I retrieved the towels and lay the blanket on the sand. I put down my shell and pulled off my cover-up as Alex watched.

"Didn't you bring a book?" I asked, warmly aware of his gaze on my body. This bikini had pretty good coverage, for a bikini, but I knew it accented my curves, especially my cleavage.

"Why do I need a book when I have you?" he asked impishly.

I just smiled and ran off toward the water, enjoying my beach bunny moment. I almost never got to wear this swimsuit up north.

I splashed in up to my chest and let the waves bump into me, crest over my shoulders. It was a pleasant, calming sensation. I watched a pelican plunge into the water nearby, coming up with a fish. The sky was deep blue, with just a few stray clouds, and the sparkling water echoed its color. But after a few minutes, the fall air got the better of my wet skin. *I must be acclimating,* I thought. I had goose bumps.

I waded out of the water and walked up to Alex, who was watching me with a thoughtful smile.

"Now I really like that bathing suit," he said, and I looked down to see my nipples showing hard and dark through the white fabric.

"I guess I'm damned to be a tramp wherever I go," I said drily.

"I like that," he grinned, handing me a towel. I dried off as best I could, wrapped it around me and dropped beside him on the blanket. He put an arm around me, and we watched the shadows lengthen until I warmed up, nestled against him.

"Ready?" he asked as I broke contact and pulled on my cover-up.

"I guess. I hate to leave it. It's so beautiful."

"The ocean will always be here," he whispered, leaning toward me, putting a finger under my chin, kissing me with a longing that made me ache. Did he mean the ocean would always be around? Or would it be here, at Alex's place in Bohemia Beach, waiting for me?

When we got into his apartment, I felt sleepy and relaxed, high on the tonic of the sea. I left the towels and blanket in the laundry room that Alex pointed out to me — yet another room, tucked between the powder room and the wine room — and followed him into the living area. I put my shell on a coffee table and admired it for a moment as I kicked off my sandals and doffed my cover-up.

"I'm going to rinse off," I said. "And then I might take a nap."

"Wait," Alex said. I turned to see a familiar spark in his eyes. "Let me help you."

God, he was insatiable. But I felt my instant response as he moved closer to me, took the cover-up from my hands and threw it over his shoulder.

He slowly lifted one bikini strap and slipped it off my shoulder. He did the same with the other, then reached behind my back and undid the clasp. He threw the wet garment to the wooden floor without a care and bent down to take one teat between his lips.

I released a long sigh as his tongue worked my nipple, as he pulled on it gently with his teeth, as he sucked harder, longer, until my every nerve was humming. Or so I thought, until he went to work on the other breast, and my pleasure doubled. I could hear the ocean; I could feel his mouth; I could feel the response in my core. I moaned with a rush of intense arousal as he pulled down my bikini bottoms, all the while still sucking and nibbling at my nipple. He began to travel down my belly, kissing and licking my skin as he went.

"Salty," he murmured as he continued his journey, grasping my buttocks, kneeling in front of me. His mouth found my clit, and his tongue offered a symphony of sensation, ever-changing, teasing me in a crescendo until I could barely stand the aching, throbbing orgasm that built and continued to mount as he relentlessly pleasured me.

"Stop," I whispered. "Too much." But he did not. With one finger, he caressed my anus, and I was surprised at the thrill I felt. He must have remembered me telling him his finger excited me; his finger I could accept.

"Yes," I breathed. First he dipped his finger into my wet cleft, and before I could beg for more, his hand moved back, between my cheeks. He pushed his finger gently inside my small hole, moving ever so slowly as his mouth possessed my sex. My orgasm intensified, strange and deep, with a sense of erotic violation as he took control of my body again. I cried out with my shuddering release, and in slow motion, he withdrew his finger and his tongue.

I dropped to my knees in front of him, exhausted, and covered his mouth with mine. His hungry lips were still slick with the taste of me, with the salt of the sea. When the connection finally broke, I wilted against him, wrapping my arms around his neck, holding him tightly.

"I hope this means you'll come to the beach more often," he said into my ear, humor in his tone.

"Anytime you want," I responded, still under the influence of the orgasm.

"Anytime *you* want." He pulled back, pushing my hair out of my face.

"Can I — can I do something for you?" I asked.

"Not this time," he said. "I wanted this to be about you."

"But pleasing you pleases me, too." And I still ached for him.

His eyes glittered. He pulled off his shirt, lay back on the floor and discarded his pants and briefs as I watched. There was no doubt he was as ready as I was.

"Come here, then," he said, and I moved to him, straddled him, lowered myself onto his jutting cock. I sighed as he filled me, excruciatingly deep, and I sat up and rocked him, riding him until I felt a different kind of orgasm building deep

inside me. I didn't explode until he touched my already stim-
ulated clit; I cried out, and he gasped as he came, crashing
through me like a hurricane. I clenched around him, milking
him, and he groaned.

As peace gradually overtook us, I eased off him and lay
down on the hard floor next to him, panting, feeling his
sticky come against my thighs.

"Who needs running when I've got you?" I joked.

"This is an exercise program I can endorse," he agreed.

"OK," I finally said, sitting up. "I'm going to take that
shower now."

"Want help?"

"If I keep taking help from you, I'll never get clean."

"That's the idea," he teased, but he let me go alone.

WE NAPPED AFTER MY SHOWER — or perhaps I should say our
shower, because Alex couldn't resist nipping in and soaping
my back and nether regions, and rinsing me thoroughly with
the hand shower. Otherwise, he let me retreat unmolested,
and he soon followed me to his bed.

When I awoke, the sky was nearly purple. The few streaks
of cloud were lit up orange over the gold-tipped waves. It was
sunset, I determined, for the sun was in the west; at least I
hadn't been unconscious all night. I let him sleep, pulled on
my V-neck shirt and panties, and padded out into the condo.

He'd offered me my own room. I wondered where the
guest room was. Or rooms? This place seemed to have a lot of
rooms.

Curiosity got the better of me, and I opened the next door
down the hallway from the master bath. It was, indeed, a

guest room, furnished with simple, modern furniture, with light blue walls that evoked the sky. I stepped inside. It showed no signs of habitation. There was a nice, normal bathroom, no stadium-size showers in sight.

Next down the hall was the library, cool and dark. And there was another room off the hall that I opened gingerly to find what might have been a bedroom, except, it seemed, it wasn't. There was a comfortable-looking couch facing a widescreen TV. There was a long, broad window seat that offered an oblique view of the ocean. There were more book-shelves, many accented with figurines from science-fiction TV and movies. A small table held a laser printer. And there was a fine, wide, old oak desk, mildly messy, with stacks of paper, books, a laptop computer and a lamp. I had finally stumbled upon Alex's writing lair.

I looked around, wondering if perhaps I shouldn't be here. Because this didn't seem like the public face of Alex. It was more intimate, less controlled, chaotic, even, and colorful with creativity.

I had never read any of Alex's writing. I had a sudden craving to do so. I was curious about how well he wrote, and, I had to admit, I was curious about *what* he wrote.

Now I was straying into dangerous territory. I could ask to see something he'd written. But peeking at just one story wouldn't hurt, I told myself. Just something to give me the flavor of it.

There was a composition notebook on top of a pile of magazines on the desk, the type common in school. I lifted the cover gingerly, as if it might explode. "Journal" was scrawled across the top of the first page in looping script. I slammed the notebook shut. That, I would not read. It didn't seem right. I was burning to know what he thought, but that wasn't the way to go about it.

Still — a story would be all right, wouldn't it? There might be something on his laptop, though I didn't relish feeling like a computer hacker. Instead I turned to a pile of what looked like typewritten sheets on one side of the desk — computer printouts, each chunk of paper stacked perpendicular to the next.

I picked up one titled "Deception in the Deep."

Intriguing words. And it looked like fiction. I sat down to read.

It was a pirate story, interestingly enough, yet it was set in outer space, which the space sailors called "the Deep." It was kind of steampunk, with Victorian-accented technology woven through it, but more to the point, it was about a devious spaceship captain who'd kidnapped a young woman of great fortune, planning to force her into marriage with his nobleman brother, then kill both of them and inherit the lot. The pirate was a bastard, it seemed, and in this society, he'd received no inheritance, so he'd turned to a life of crime.

Alex's descriptions were vivid, and the action was lively. The characters were interesting, partly because they seemed to be hoarding secrets along with their treasures. But what especially interested me was his descriptions of the young woman. As seen through the pirate's eyes, she was a pathetic innocent.

Sonia was beautiful and unmistakably intelligent, but when it came to Captain Artemis, she seemed woefully naive, read one paragraph. *She exuded goodness to the point where she expected it in other people, including him, no matter that he'd kidnapped her to effect her marriage to his rich and knavish brother. No matter that they had no cargo other than their ill-gotten gains. She seemed determined to win his heart, to make him honorable by sheer will. But he was determined to plunge her and his brother into the Deep as soon as they could be wed, before she discovered his true nature...*

I heard Alex call my name and, startled, dropped the papers on the carpeted floor. I gathered them quickly, trying to straighten the edges before I stacked them back in place. *Crap.* There was no use in pretending I hadn't been in here. Maybe being discovered might be a way to open up another avenue of conversation with him. Though I wasn't sure when I'd be brave enough to ask if he saw me as the foolish, sweet girl in his story.

Still feeling confused and unnerved, I ran to the window seat, curled up on the cushions and looked out at the view.

"In here!" I called.

A few seconds later, Alex, now clothed, opened the door with a look of concern on his face.

"I hadn't shown you this room," he said neutrally.

"I hope you don't mind," I said brightly. "I just wanted to see that guest room you mentioned, and I stumbled across this one and this wonderful window seat. Is this where you write?"

His expression eased slightly.

"Yes," he said. "There's a reason I didn't show it to you. This room is never really ready for guests. It kind of reflects my state of mind. Which is to say, not very orderly."

"It feels comfortable," I said. "Anyway — I hope I'm not just another guest."

Alex smiled ruefully, coming toward me, sitting next to me. "No, my dear *girlfriend*. And I don't want you to feel that way. It's OK. I just get a little worried about what kind of impression I'll make on people who see how I actually think."

"A good impression," I assured him. "And I want to know how you think. Always. So what are you writing?"

He looked at me closely. "It's all pretty rough fiction, but believe it or not, I'm trying science fiction again. I decided not to stifle that part of my imagination. And it's really working. I mean, I'm not sure the stories are working, but they're helping me work out the kinks in my brain, I guess. The words are starting to flow again."

"Because of therapy?"

"And you," he said, running a hand up my unclad leg.

I didn't like his answer. I hoped he didn't mean that I was his muse, or his model for the innocent girl who was being used, who was about to be thrown away and murdered for her fortune. Alex didn't think of me that way, did he? But in his story, there were turns of phrase, of dialogue, that suggested I was somewhere in that character.

I wasn't a writer. My inspiration didn't express itself in words, in pieces of other people's lives. It came out in shapes and textures, in color and image. Maybe the sea monster I was building in my ceramic art reflected something coiled in Alex's brain — or even the sinister forces in everyday life, represented by my loathsome teacher — but I didn't feel as if I was stealing anyone's soul, the way some Native Americans had looked on photographers. And I was starting to think a writer had that power.

"Are you OK?" he asked.

"Fine," I said. But I wasn't sure.

He gathered me to him, pulling me into his lap, cradling me. I let him, let his body talk, trying to forget his words. I liked what his body told me. Alex cared for me. Maybe this feeling was just an addiction, a pill I should stop taking for my own good. But it seemed so real as Alex stroked my hair, as I nestled against him and listened to the restless ocean.

ALEX DROVE me home early the next morning. The doctors' grounds were now ghoul-free, I was relieved to note, and even the zombie plague sign was gone from my door. But there was something else on the doorstep — a small box, about ten inches square, wrapped in brown craft paper and tied in twine.

Alex noted it, too, carrying my bag as he walked me to the door. "What is it?"

"No idea," I said, picking it up.

"Is it ticking?"

I laughed. "No. Let's go in and open it. And then I have to get ready for class."

I took the package to the work table, cut the twine with scissors and ripped off the paper. I gingerly opened the plain brown box. Inside, nestled in tissue paper, was a ceramic pot and an envelope addressed to "Miss Abbey."

"Oh, shit," I said.

"What?"

"That's what Montrose King calls me."

Alex's brow creased as I opened the envelope. An embossed white card was inside, and on it was scrawled, "My apologies. M."

I pulled out the pot. It was exquisite. It was a vase, but it looked like a seed pod, its textures eminently touchable, its colors a joyous mix of green and gold. It was one of the strangely beautiful organic pieces he was known for, and quite alien compared with the charming vase of Gary's I still had, sitting on one of my windowsills.

I let out my breath in a low whistle and looked up at Alex, who was glowering at the pot and shooting me worried glances.

"Well?" he finally said.

"He may be an asshole, but this is an incredible piece."

"Valuable?"

"Yes," I said. "He's very well known. This is worth hundreds or, more likely, well over a thousand."

"You like it?" Alex sounded concerned, as if he had something to fear from my creepy teacher.

"I admire it," I said. "But I don't want it. But one doesn't just throw away something this beautiful."

Alex looked relieved, then thoughtful. "The museum is having an auction in association with the regional show."

"Great idea!" I said. "And won't that just burn his buns."

Alex laughed. "I hope so," he said. "Or I could stuff him in a kiln and make sure of it."

"Death by kiln is even worse than the sword," I said. "Look, you'd better go. I have to get to school. I'm trying to make something that I hope will be accepted for that very show, and I have a lot to get done in the next few weeks."

"Really?" He looked interested. "Can't wait to see it."

"I hope you will and it doesn't end up exploding in the kiln. Now take this thing with you. I guess I have to face the monster himself this morning."

"Want me to go with you?" asked Alex, putting the vase back in its box.

"Of course not. Just don't leave that anywhere I have to see it."

"I'm taking it right to the museum," Alex said, leaning in for a kiss.

His mouth was warm and sweet this morning, and he released me far sooner than I would have liked. But it was time to get to school and get elbow-deep in clay. And I was really looking forward to it, no matter who might be looking over my shoulder.

I WAS SPARED the sight of Montrose King, at least for the day. Gary, who came in a few minutes late, said our teacher had called in sick, and we were to ask Gary for help if we needed it.

"But you know what I heard," Gary said confidentially as he cut a fine, lacy pattern in a tall, graceful vase, its clay not quite dry, the perfect consistency for embellishment.

"What did you hear?" I asked, hoping Alex and I didn't come into it, as I worked on shaping a sea creature for my piece.

"A couple of the guests found Montrose unconscious in the rose garden."

"Who found him?" I asked, trying to keep my voice even.

"A couple of society wives who, rumor has it, are having a lesbian affair."

"Now you're just making stuff up."

"No, really!" Gary said. "They ran up to the house and tried to get the Pullmans to check him out. They're doctors, you know."

"Yeah, I know. I live there, remember?"

"Oh, yeah, that's right. Anyway, Evan was already shit-faced, but Daisy came out to the garden in her Morticia

Addams outfit, trailed by a handful of curious drunks, and shook Montrose until he woke up. And he screamed."

I couldn't help but laugh, picturing the black-clad Daisy looming over our drunken teacher while a cluster of strangely costumed figures looked on. I had to pause in my work so I wouldn't damage the clay while I got myself under control.

"Yeah, I know, right?" Gary grinned at me. "They ended up getting him a cab. He was in a foul mood. I saw him sitting in the house waiting for the car, drinking more wine, of course."

"Of course," I said. "I'm just glad he's not here today. He's the last person I want to see right now."

"What do you mean?"

"Uh, nothing, really."

Gary looked skeptical. "What did he do? More drunken escapades?"

"You could say that. It's OK. We all escaped with our lives." I tried to make it into a joke, but Gary regarded me with a raised eyebrow.

"OK. Don't tell me if you don't want to." He turned back to his work, then added quietly: "So you looked pretty amazing on Saturday."

"Thanks," I said, a little sheepishly. "Halloween is that one day a year when all women are officially encouraged to dress like a vamp."

"Too bad it's only one day," Gary murmured.

I chuckled. "It was kind of fun," I admitted, turning my focus back to my own creation and thinking about the ravishing pirate who rescued me. And then, more darkly, wondering if he was planning to throw me overboard.

TIME RAN hard as it sped through the few weeks before the exhibition deadline, with me trying to keep up. Montrose returned to school but essentially ignored me in class, while I avoided him everywhere else. Either way, I'd managed to put off any further confrontation, though I knew he still eyed me with interest.

I met Alex less and less during the weekdays as I worked long hours on my sculpture or my job at the school. I tried to squeeze in as much studio time as possible as I shaped and finished the pieces. I kept late nights that had even the dedicated Gary shaking his head. I would let my pieces dry just enough so I could trim and enhance them, assembling several of the parts before firing. I had to let them dry thoroughly before they were fired, which meant a further crunch on my timeline, but I learned my lesson when a manta ray I'd created in a bed of seaweed exploded in the kiln because it still had moisture trapped in the clay. I recovered, re-created, and moved on. Each piece had to dry and go through its bisque firing; they had to cool and be glazed with just the right textures and colors; and in the end, I had to fit them all together, like a puzzle that just happened to have a working fountain inside it.

During one of these long stretches without Alex, my period arrived. It was normally a pest, but given my recent activities, I welcomed it with relief and quietly applauded modern birth control.

Alex and I tried to maintain our connection with phone calls and an occasional, brief mid-week meal, but my exhausting schedule made anything else too difficult for me to handle. I could hear his impatience as I put him off until the weekend. Somewhere in the back of my mind, I had an idea that a little distance between us might be healthy. But my resolve and our separations never lasted for long.

When Alex and I did meet — I kept weekends clear for him — we eased into each other's lives slowly at first, rehashing our week, before crashing into each other with a heat and a hunger that betrayed how hard it was for us to be apart. Or, at least, that's how I felt. My appetite was only whetted for more Alex. And it wasn't just his body. I missed his humor, his protective impulses, the cheerful way he took care of me, feeding me, loving me. It felt like love, even if he never said it. Still, I wondered what he really thought of me, deep in his heart. Or in the Deep of his fiction, if that was me in there, riding on a spaceship with an amoral pirate, awaiting my doom.

Alex asked me questions about the piece I was working on, and eventually, I told him the idea behind it, how he had partially inspired it — about the hidden darkness in all of us, hiding under every serene scene.

"So I'm your muse now?" he noted wryly over a steak dinner that he'd grilled on his balcony, where we enjoyed it in the last glimmer of a breezy twilight.

"I guess I needed one after all," I said. "But like any inspiration, most of it comes from within. You'll probably think I'm silly, but this is really important to me — getting into this exhibition. It would validate my decision to throw all my energy into pottery, to move here to Bohemia. It's a way to prove to myself that I'm good enough. That it was all worth it."

"It's been worth it for me," Alex said, and I felt a flutter.

"I'm definitely glad I'm here." *Because I love you, stupid.* "But I'm talking about my work. Do you know what I mean?"

"I know what you mean."

I took a sip of another fantastic cabernet he'd opened for us and smiled. He looked so handsome, so relaxed, in a button-up blue shirt open at the collar and rolled up at the sleeves, tucked into deliciously form-fitting jeans. And no shoes or socks, of course. The evenings were getting cooler — I was wearing a long black sweater over gray leggings, with my non-heeled black boots — but I guessed his manly toes could take the chill.

"So," I said, "my aunt and uncle have invited me to Thanksgiving dinner on Thursday, and you, too, if you'd like to be my date. It might be stressful, but at least I'll have turned in my pottery piece by then."

"I'm invited?" Alex asked. "So that would be with your cousins as well?"

"Yeah, I think so," I said. "You like them, don't you?"

"Calista seems nice. And Damien is Damien. I have nothing against him. And I'm starting to find him more amusing."

"Well, my aunt and uncle aren't amusing," I said. "My uncle's cool, but my aunt is my mom's sister, and it's like they have one mind — suspicious and ruthless. It's like the Spanish Inquisition."

"Nobody expects the Spanish Inquisition."

I chuckled at the Monty Python reference. "I said it was *like* the Spanish Inquisition. This is the Midwestern Inquisition, which is infinitely worse, and I fully expect my mother has authorized my Aunt Kay to employ full interrogation tactics."

Alex grinned as he poured himself more wine. "How bad can it be?"

I shook my head. "They're relentless, but they don't

realize how terrifying they are. They're '*nice,*' as in that Midwestern kind of nice that often results in passive-aggressive comments about living in sin and other such quaint notions."

"But I love living in sin. I'll bring up the topic, if you like," he teased.

"No way," I said, feeling my face go pink. "I don't think they know that much about you."

"They should," Alex said, "seeing as how I'm a pillar of the community and all that."

"A pillar, at least."

He laughed, and I grinned in return.

"My dear Sloane," he said. "You do have a dirty mind."

"So you'll go with me?"

"Of course," he said. "I can't let you face the inquisition alone."

I toyed with my long necklace, the one with the vial of bubbles that I'd teased him with before. I got up and went to the edge of the balcony, extracting the stopper with its wand and dipping it into the liquid. I blew a stream of bubbles into the strong breeze, and they flew crazily around the balcony and out into the air before diving toward the sea, caught in some invisible current. That's what being with Alex was like. I was caught in a current, flying high. When I was with Alex, I didn't care if I crashed to the ground.

He joined me at the railing, putting an arm around me.

"I remember those," he said as I blew another stream of bubbles into the evening.

"I would hope so," I said, remembering our night by the library fire. "I used to blow bubbles at college when I needed to relax. It sounds childish, I know, but I wasn't much of a partier, especially when I was always working or studying. I'd sit on the front steps of the dorm with a couple of friends, and we'd gossip and laugh, and I'd blow bubbles while they smoked."

Alex smiled. "I can't believe you adopted such a filthy habit. Do you know what your lungs look like after five years of blowing bubbles?"

"*Horribly* clean."

"While the rest of you got dirty?"

"Only my mind, as you pointed out. And that, only recently." I put the stopper back on the vial and reached up to touch his face.

He took me into his arms, kissing me with a pure wantonness — yes, pure, yet full of desire, raw sex and sweet emotion mingled, a powerful brew, lighter than air, iridescent and delicate and light like the bubbles.

And then his kiss darkened, deepened. He pressed his body against mine, and I clutched him more closely, feeling his bulge hard against me. I lost myself in the feel of him. I loved that he always wanted me. And, damn it, I loved *him*, despite any attempt to cool my heart. I would say it with my kiss, with my body. I still couldn't say it out loud.

He reached under my long sweater, pulling it up so his hands caressed the skin of my waist; he reached up farther under the soft black knit and cupped my breasts through the lacy bra that covered them. My nipples pebbled under his skilled touch, and he pinched them through the fabric until I moaned against his mouth, my yearning as sharp as ever.

It was dark now, and I don't know if the wild rhythms of the ocean drove me to my knees or my own desire to please him, but I fell at his feet and tugged open his jeans, pulling them and his briefs down far enough to reveal his magnificent erection. I took him in my mouth. He inhaled sharply at my first hard suck. And then he began to push back.

I knew this was one of his greatest pleasures, and I felt the ache of arousal as I took him deeper, pulling back to tease his tip with my tongue, then opening wide for another gentle thrust. Alex's rhythm increased, and he ran his hands through my hair as I devoured him. For the first time, groaning, he came in my mouth; the intensity of it surprised me, and I fought to control my gag reflex as I took his copious release. And then I was swallowing, and he pulled out, dropping to his knees with me, embracing me, kissing me hungrily, taking some of it back, until our lips became one again.

He tugged me up, pulling me toward the door, pulling me inside to the nearest couch. He pushed me back on the cushions, yanked off my boots, peeled off my leggings and underpants in one motion. He didn't bother to take off the sweater. He stepped out of his already undone jeans and briefs, knelt over me and probed my wet slit with his fingers. I stared into his eyes. He seemed transfixed by my increasing abandonment as my breathing grew more rapid, as my lips parted, as the waves of pleasure built into a familiar spasm of ecstasy. A spell shimmered between us in the dim light. And then, incredibly, he was ready for me again, probing at the gates, thrusting hard inside me. I let out a shuddering sigh as he drove into me, quickly building a pounding rhythm, not like his gentle treatment of my mouth. His fierce fucking almost hurt, but it was a pain edged with pleasure. And then I convulsed as a new quake spread outward from my core. I cried out as it overtook me.

"*Sloane.*" His voice quavered as he shared the zenith of our mutual orgasm. He eased his rhythm but still pushed into me, letting me bask in the waves still echoing in my body, slowing, receding, the tsunami returning to the sea. At last, he withdrew, and he lay on the couch next to me, pulling me to him for a languorous kiss that went on and on.

I could kiss him forever, I thought. I hoped I would.

My sculpture was due Wednesday at 5 p.m.

It was Wednesday at 3 p.m., and I was about to pull the last component out of the kiln.

I was also the last student around before the school closed for the holiday, or the last procrastinator, as Gary had suggested. But I hadn't procrastinated. I'd worked my ass off to make the deadline. If I didn't meet it, the jury would never see it, and my chance would be gone.

Gary had already left with the piece he was submitting to the show — one of his trademark vases, much simpler than mine, but deceptively so. It was tall but uniquely shaped; he'd cut facets into it and twisted the piece, and he'd impressed fine patterns into the clay and cut delicate, narrow slits through its walls. An iridescent raku glaze glimmered and glittered in shifting colors across its planes. When he turned the piece to show me all its angles, light glinted through the cuts in the surface, passing through the vase itself. The effect was magical.

Yes, mine was very different. I lifted the lid on the kiln that held the last piece of my sculpture, praying to the great gods of pottery that the glaze had worked out. I felt a familiar wave of heat wash over me as I looked inside. The kiln had cooled just enough to make the ceramics safe from cracking.

I reached in with gloved hands and lifted out the final

piece, happy to see my vision realized. The cluster of sea life was strange and stunning, foreboding and fanciful. The rubbings I'd done before the final glazing brought out detailed textures in my coral and creatures, which had bulging, creepy eyes and fat, thoughtful lips. I set the piece gently on the work table, where the other parts were ready for assembly.

My creatures, amid the undulating ceramic reef, would swim in a terraced loop around the sinister squid limbs emerging from the bottom of my imaginary sea. Water would drop from one terrace to another before recycling up from the wide, shallow bowl I'd created as a base.

As I prepared to fit the pieces together, just to make sure the fountain worked, I sensed movement behind me. I turned to see Montrose entering the room, and the space seemed to shrink.

"Miss Abbey," he said. "Still working?"

My throat felt dry. "Just pulling my last piece for my submission to the regional show."

"Nothing like pushing a deadline." He smiled. "I've always done the same thing."

Wearing a black sweater and black jeans, oddly reminiscent of his all-black Halloween costume, he circled me like a shark. I stood still, feeling strangely calm.

"Did you get my note?" Montrose asked, stopping next to me, next to all of my work of the past several weeks. I had visions of him sweeping everything to the floor, the way he'd destroyed my pot on the first day of class.

"Yes. Thank you."

"I hoped you did. I thought it — the piece — might make amends for my behavior at the party. I regret that night." He smoothed his goatee and leaned against the table, making me even more nervous, more for my sculpture than myself.

"It was more than was required," I said, trying to sound calm and assured. "I appreciate your apology. But I think we've already put it behind us."

"Have we?" He inched closer. "I said it crassly then, but I think we might have a connection, even if you can't see it. This work — it's very interesting. A good beginning. You might benefit from my mentorship. From a closer working relationship."

"I've appreciated being in your class. You've helped me learn a lot, and that's all I can ask for," I said, sounding like a robot, trying to stay cool, to deflect him. I just wanted him to leave. I needed to test my piece, get to the museum.

I glanced protectively at my work and was startled when he suddenly pressed toward me and grasped me around the waist, trying to kiss me. I turned my head, wanting to escape him, and his lips mashed against my ear.

Fueled by a rush of anger, I forcefully pushed him away. He stumbled backward, banging into the table, and my pieces rocked there, awaiting disaster.

"You will *not* cross that line," I spat, realizing a fraction of a second later that I had repeated Alex's words. If I'd had a sword, I would have gutted Montrose on the spot. Instead, I grasped one of my pieces and held it tightly, ready to throw it at his head, praying I wouldn't have to.

He looked stunned.

"You really are a proud little chit," Montrose said, his face assuming his usual contemptuous composure.

"Get out of here, Montrose," I replied, my fear of him evaporating. "We both know I'm too old for you."

"Ha," he said, not sounding the least bit amused. *"Good*

luck. You'll need it." He strode out of the room, leaving me flushed with fury.

Luck. With my luck, he was on the jury for the museum show. I didn't know who was on the jury. None of the artists did. Still, I was going forward with my submission, and I had just over an hour to make it happen.

Damn Montrose. I tried to ignore the writhing eels in my stomach and worked quickly to test the fit of the fragile, three-foot-high sculpture. The pieces had to support one another to create the flow required for the fountain. I added water, plugged in the pump and, after a moment, heard a satisfactory gurgle. The water danced around my creatures, enhancing the shine of the glazes, adding a welcome auditory component.

I smiled to see the dominant tentacle and the top of a squid head, with its one large and evil eye, emerge from the center, from the deep. It invaded the peaceful reef and its dopey inhabitants; the effect was sinister with just a touch of humor.

A few minutes later, the box of pieces packed safely in my car, I grabbed my bag and waved to the custodian on my way out. It was almost 5, and he was ready to lock up.

A three-block drive and a helpful docent later, and I was leaving the assembled sculpture at the museum. I paused in the doorway of a room crowded with entries and looked at it: weeks of work, lost in a pile of stuff like Citizen Kane's sled, left to the judgment of the experts.

"Don't worry, honey," the docent said. "We'll take good care of it."

I nodded, trying to match her smile. I felt a weariness overtake me as I left the art behind and walked out of the museum. The work was done. I'd fended off Montrose King.

And I had agreed to attend a Thanksgiving interrogation tomorrow with my new boyfriend.

I sat in my car and checked my phone. There was a text message from Alex: "Dinner?"

I called him, and just hearing his "Hello" brought up a gusher of emotion.

"Oh, Alex," I said.

"What is it?" he asked sharply.

I wasn't sure whether to tell him about Montrose. And then I decided I couldn't very well not tell him. So I did.

Alex was silent for several seconds. When he spoke, I could tell he was angry. "I'll make sure he doesn't work in that school again."

"Don't do that," I said, surprising myself. "My class with him is almost over, and I won't have him as an instructor again. He's not even teaching in the winter session — he's in residence, which means he can do whatever he wants. He's just giving a couple of lectures and a workshop."

"You're defending that guy?" Alex was incredulous.

"Not at all. I'm defending myself. I think it will be better if you don't go riding in like a white knight, using your power as a donor and board member to remove him. You'd have to explain why, at least to someone. And it wouldn't look good for you or for me."

He was silent again. Then: "Are you sure?"

"Yes," I said. "Look, he's done with me after today. He might try to make life kind of sucky for me, but the word is out on this guy. Almost everyone already thinks he's a jerk, even if they don't know my situation. Gary suspects, too. He even cautioned me about him early on."

"Gary," Alex said flatly.

"He's my friend."

"I know. I know." His tone was partially helpless, partially teasing. "They're drawn to you like bees to honey, Sloane. What can I say?"

"You're the only bee I want in my honeypot."

I thought I heard him emit a low growl. "Get over here right now."

I laughed. "I think maybe you should come to me. I'd like to wash the clay off me and change before we go out to dinner."

"Mmmm," he said. "All right. But you'd better wash fast, or I'll have to help you. And we both know that will take a lot longer."

"Yes, Alex," I said, feeling my stress start to melt away, knowing I'd see him soon. As the golden sun dipped toward the horizon, I put the car in drive, turned on the radio and headed home.

I CAME out of the shower and was startled to find Alex waiting for me on my bed, smiling, in jeans, a form-fitting blue T-shirt and a brown blazer. I about jumped out of my skin, which was all I was wearing.

"You scared me half to death," I said, pulling the towel off my hair and wrapping it around me. "How did you get in here?"

"You gave me a key at Halloween, remember?"

"Oh, right." I frowned. "I gave you a key because I didn't have any pockets. I just didn't — you're unexpected, is all. But I'm happy to see you," I added as a little wrinkle formed in his brow. I walked over to him and gave him a chaste kiss on the cheek.

"Hey," he said, grabbing my waist before I could escape. "Are you really glad to see me?"

"Always," I said.

"It's just that it almost seemed like you were avoiding me these past few weeks." I let him pull away my towel. There was something especially wanton about being caressed by my fully clothed boyfriend when I wasn't wearing a stitch. He pulled me to him for a sensuous kiss and lay back, taking me with him, so I was on top.

"We had the weekends," I said between kisses. "And now my project's done. You'll be sick of me pretty soon."

"I hope so." He rolled me over, caging me with his arms, kissing me more deeply. He kissed my neck; he licked and nibbled my breasts. He moved his mouth down my belly, a slow and stimulating journey, and licked my nub just about long enough for me to start melting — and then he stopped.

Alex sat up next to me. "Better get dressed."

"But don't you want to . . . ?" I tried to keep the pleading note out of my voice, but he'd kindled me to fiery want, only to throw cold water on me. I leaned on one elbow, nude and vulnerable on the bed, feeling cross.

He grinned. "I want you to think about how you'd like the evening to continue. I want you to think about it during dinner. And then, maybe, after dinner, we'll do something about it."

I sat up. "Maybe, huh? You might turn me down? Just drive me home?"

"Anticipation, Sloane," he said, his smile softer, warmer. "We dove in together so fast. And it's been wonderful. But I want an evening that lets us think about what it's going to be like to be together, unencumbered by parties and other distractions. I just want to go out to dinner with you and think hard about what I'm going to do to you later. Let's have another first date."

I sat up and wrapped the towel around my torso again. "So you *might* take me out to a lovely dinner only to find that I'm not interested. I might just give you the cold shoulder, and that will be it."

He bent down and kissed my shoulder, which was anything but cold under his lips. "I hope not. And I have to admit," he said, "when it comes to you, my restraint sucks." I laughed. "Still, I want to court you tonight. And watch. And wait."

Sometimes Alex could be such a weird duck. "Maybe you should wait in the living room," I said. "Guys don't usually watch their dates get dressed on the first date."

"Only if they're very, very lucky."

"Out!" I was joking, but I was also still a little annoyed at his power over me, the way he could make me vibrate with desire and then walk away. As he stood, so did I, letting the towel drop.

His gaze roved over me. "You are so delightfully evil when it comes to teasing me."

"You started it." I pointed, and he followed my direction, vanishing behind the wooden screen with one longing backward glance.

I got back to dressing. So what would I wear on a first date with Alex? When I really considered it a date? I'd go for the lacy black bra, with underpants to match, if only to make myself feel good. On a first date, I wasn't a sure thing. Or I hadn't been. Alex had changed all that.

Sheer black hose would be nice, I decided, with my low heels. A long-sleeved, black, discount-store dress that stopped above the knee, the skirt printed with delicate sprays of pink roses. The scoop neckline would let me wear the coin pearl necklace he'd given me, with its glimmers of pink.

I brushed out my hair, pinning up one side with a clip fixed with a small silk pink rose, and regarded myself in the mirror on the inside of the wardrobe door. Something was missing. I applied a little eye makeup and dabbed my mouth with deep pink lipstick.

When I emerged from my boudoir, a sweater over my arm, Alex was leaning against my work table, looking through one of my ceramics books. He closed it and walked over to me, kissing me sweetly.

"So pretty," he said. "I'd never know such a vixen lived under all those flowers."

"You may never know. After all, this is a first date." I gave him a cheeky smile, grabbed my black leather purse and walked to the door.

He drove me to dinner at a good Italian place in Bohemia — a nice counterpoint to the turkey we expected the next day for Thanksgiving — and we had a very good meal with an equally good chianti. We talked about art and movies and music. The conversation was pleasant, but every once in a while, I'd catch Alex looking at me intently, as if he had something else on his mind. Something that lit a fire inside me, that made me forget what I was saying.

When the waitress asked if we wanted dessert, he emphatically told her "no" and paid the check, despite my weak protestations.

"You'll have to accept that I want to spoil you," he said. "I have the means. Why does it bother you?"

"I'm used to paying my own way," I replied, donning my sweater against the evening's chill as we walked to the car.

"But you're not just an 'I.' We are a 'we,' aren't we?" he asked.

I didn't say anything right away. I let him open the car door for me, and I got in. He closed the door and came around, got in the driver's side, and started the engine. A lonely Chris Isaak tune started playing on the stereo.

"Well?" Alex asked.

My heart was full, but I still felt vulnerable. What was this about? Was his relationship with me for real? Or was it just about passion? Possession? I wondered sometimes, but I loved it when he whispered, *"You're mine."*

"I think we're a 'we,' " I told him. "But we are still individual people. I want to be fair. I don't want you to have to pay for everything."

"Sloane, you can't pay for everything anyway."

The truth, delivered in such a cavalier way, irked me. "Then maybe I shouldn't accept what I can't pay for."

"Why are you doing this?" He sounded frustrated. He put on his seat belt and pulled out of the parking space, then headed down the road. Toward what, I wasn't sure.

"I'm not doing anything."

"You're — I don't know. Blocking me. I pay not just because I can, but because it makes me happy. You don't owe me anything." The street lights shifted across his features as he drove, and for a moment I imagined us underwater, in a submarine, the ripples of light falling over us like waves, waiting for our oxygen to run out.

"I don't mean to be obstinate," I said. "I just feel like sometimes we're off-balance. I don't like being the epitome of the weaker sex. And the poor one in the relationship."

Alex shook his head. "You are anything but the weaker sex," he said. "And anything you yield to me is about your pleasure and mine. I want you to do what feels good to you. And it so happens that what feels good to you feels good to me, too. Doesn't it?" He shot me a quick smile. "Don't try to complicate things. Enjoy it."

The opposite of complicating things was keeping them simple. Complication meant things like love and a serious relationship. He wanted to keep it simple? So maybe he didn't want love and a relationship. He wanted casual dates and sex, maybe until it didn't seem simple anymore, and then he'd end it.

I thought all this without saying anything, wondering how my feelings had led me to this paranoid insecurity. Maybe I *was* being irrational, but traitorous tears welled up in my eyes. One slipped down my cheek. I looked out my window, trying to hide my face, not saying anything.

"Sloane?" Alex's voice was uncertain. "Are you OK?"

"Fine," I said, my voice husky. "Where are we going?"

"You'll see," he said, and he reached over and squeezed my hand.

Somehow this gesture widened the crack in my heart. His hand was warm and strong, communicating something more than a casual affair. Was I imagining the connection just because I wanted to?

I was definitely not the cool artist I imagined being when I first spent the night with Alex. I was an emotional girl who just might be playing out of her depth.

I noticed we were on the river road, but not headed toward my house. I recognized the road's turns, its climb. Alex pulled into the driveway of his childhood home. One small light shone by the front door.

"Why are we here?" I asked, curiosity momentarily quelling my qualms.

He didn't say anything as he parked and turned off the car. He got out and came around to my side, where I was already stepping out of the Mustang. He looped his right arm in my left and led me toward the house.

"You're taking me to see your family tomorrow. At least some of them," he said. "I thought I should do the same for you. Let you meet the ghosts."

I suppressed a shiver. "But I've been here before."

"Not as my girlfriend. Forget the first date thing for a minute. I'm not superstitious, but I feel sometimes like my parents are looking out for me when I'm here." He opened the front door, flipped a switch that turned on the arching floor lamp with the white globe on the end, and led me inside. "Sloane, I don't have any family left. So I want them to meet you. Get used to you. I know, it's all in my head," he said as my face gave away my concern. "But it's symbolic, too. This is all I have left of my family. And I want you to feel at home here."

He walked over to the orange flying-saucer fireplace, pulled a box of wooden matches out of it and lit one. He touched the flame to the newspapers and sticks already laid there, and the fire built and crackled and lapped around the log on top. He gestured toward the low, vintage couch, and I sat down. He flipped off the floor lamp so that only the fire lit the room, and he sat next to me and held my hand.

"They would have loved you," he said.

His parents. I wished I could have met them. How hard it must be to go through life without any kind of family. Even if a family was kind of hard and strict and old-school the way mine was, at least I had that connection, that link to the past. This house was all Alex had left of that, and I began to think his allusion to ghosts wasn't altogether wrong. All that remained of those lives was an echo in this empty home.

He said they would have loved me. "What about you?" I whispered.

"What about me?" He seemed genuinely puzzled. He didn't know what I was asking.

I shook my head, let the moment pass. "They would be so proud of you, Alex."

"Especially because I found you." He put an arm around me, kissed my neck, letting his lips linger there.

I let out a low breath, letting our physical link wash away my doubts, the way a junkie shoots up and forgets everything. Alex was my drug. But he was more, too — I couldn't think. His lips were on the move. He nipped my earlobe and used one hand to turn my head toward his. I let my head fall back, and he bent over me, pressing his mouth to mine, opening his, opening mine. I felt wide open in his arms. He lay his other hand on my knee, gently caressing my thigh, and through the fog of my desire, my emotion, I let go of my worry. He lifted his head and opened his eyes, staring into mine, his handsome face inscrutable.

He reached into my hair and pulled out the clip with the rose, tossing it onto the coffee table. He grasped my head with both his hands, digging his fingers into my hair, and kissed me with a scorching intensity that made my toes clench and pussy wet.

If it wasn't love, it was a lust of rare intensity, so pure in its heat that it burned away everything else.

I wrapped my arms around his waist and returned the kiss, repositioning my lips on his, tasting his mouth with my tongue, which danced with his as we drank of each other, trying to merge, to melt together into one shining quicksilver pool.

I pulled off his jacket. He pulled the dress up over my head, and then his shirt was off. His muscled chest, the wispy hairs at its center, were golden in the firelight. He let me unbutton his jeans, and he had them off in a flash, followed by his blue briefs. I marveled at the hard length of him as he touched me.

Alex ran his hands lightly over the lacy black bra and lifted my soft breasts so they were released from its confines, but still restricted, pushed up by it; my nipples prickled and hardened at his touch. He kissed and suckled each peak in turn, and then, gripping the waist of my hose, he ripped the garment so violently, the shreds fluttered as he yanked off the remains. I gasped at his rough haste as he pulled off the panties with equal speed. He pushed a finger inside my slit as he devoured me again with his mouth. I groaned with the urgent invasion, the sudden, harsh pleasure of it. He finger-fucked me first, waiting until I moaned again before pushing me back on the couch, positioning himself over me, probing me with the tip of his shaft.

He thrust deeply into me, prompting a groan from low in my throat. Alex pulled back, not quite out, and thrust in again. He filled me completely, pushing hard inside my walls.

My Alex, I thought. It was all I could do to think even that small thought as he built an achingly slow rhythm, pulling out until his cockhead was teasing my entrance before plunging deeply inside me, over and over again. He leaned down to lick and nip at my nipples; I grasped his firm rear as he moved. It felt as if my whole body was merging with his, melting under his burning drive, molding to him.

I felt the waves building inside me, the ripples in the

pond, and I climaxed around him as he exploded into me with savage synchronicity.

I was suspended there for a moment, on that fiery high, and then the world came back. It was like waking from a dream, only Alex was slowly withdrawing from me, still there, still warm and real. My fears were forgotten. He gathered me in his lap and unclasped and removed the bunched-up bra so my breasts swung free. He kissed each globe tenderly, and then he held me close. I nestled against him, feeling the chill of the empty house, in spite of the fireplace.

"Sorry about the pantyhose," he said. "I'll buy you a replacement."

"Don't be silly."

"If I destroy it, I replace it," Alex said. "Plus, it'll give me a chance to shop for you in the lingerie department."

I looked up to see his mischievous smile. A funny thought crossed my mind, and I unsuccessfully tried to suppress my giggle.

"What?" he asked.

"It's just that I slept with you after our 'first date.' Again. I had no idea I was such a loose woman."

"Don't think I don't appreciate it," he said with humor, kissing me as I looked up at him. "And don't think of yourself that way. After all, how could you resist my charms?"

I pinched his chest.

"Ow," he said.

"If your parents were here, they'd be horrified, you know. Suppose we did this after the prom or something?"

"I never went to prom," Alex said.

"I went once, and only because I helped with the decorations. You didn't miss much."

"I think my parents would have been thrilled to find me

in any kind of positive social interaction," he said drily, "even
if it meant fucking on their couch."

WE HAD a small job for Thanksgiving dinner: Bring the cranberry sauce. And since I thought cranberries came out of a
can, Alex came to the rescue Thanksgiving morning with a
bag of the real thing.

He'd dropped me off the night before and gone home. I
didn't know what to make of his leaving. I thought he would
stay. He said he didn't have a change of clothes, and he was
tired, and I understood all that on a practical level, but the
separation after our intense joining felt strange. And I
detected a trace of melancholy in him, another reason to
worry. My bed felt doubly cold without him.

He returned, bright and cheerful, late in the morning, in
jeans, a light gray button-up shirt and a charcoal sport jacket,
the very picture of the clean-cut boyfriend. He handed me a
bag of cranberries.

"What do I do with these?"

"This is seriously the easiest thing to make in the world,"
he said with mild exasperation. "Read the bag. Do you have
sugar?"

"Yes." It was one of the things I'd purchased when
stocking my kitchen, but since I rarely baked, I hadn't even
opened the bag.

"Bring a cup of water and a cup of sugar to a boil. Add
cranberries. Boil, then simmer for about ten minutes. *Voila.*
Cranberry sauce."

"But I'll miss all the little ridges in the log from the can," I
teased.

"I'll give you a log with ridges," he said, pressing me against the vintage kitchen table for a heated kiss. When he released me, I was ready to skip the cranberry sauce, but he had other ideas. "Where's the sugar?"

He was right about the recipe. In no time at all, the cranberry sauce was ready, and we poured the hot, garnet mixture into a ceramic bowl I'd made, a pretty one with a blue and burgundy glaze that complemented the color of the sauce.

"Maybe I'll give the bowl to Aunt Kay. Try to get on her good side," I mused.

"If you were on her bad side, she wouldn't have invited you," Alex pointed out.

"But she gets so much pleasure out of preparing a juicy report for my mother, I think she would have asked me anyway."

We were about to find out. At 3 p.m. — they planned an early dinner, at 4 — we were on the doorstep of their modest, 1960s Bohemia Beach house, a few blocks west of A1A and the ocean. Alex looked sharp and sexy, as usual. I wore a loose, silky, sleeveless black-and-white dress with a geometric print, topped with a modest gray cardigan sweater, along with my black sandals. I did love that I was wearing sandals in November. In Ohio, all ten toes would have been lost to frostbite by now.

I held the bowl of cranberry sauce. In one hand, Alex held two bottles of wine, a pinot grigio and Beaujolais Nouveau. With his free hand, he clasped mine and shot me a smile as the door opened.

There was my Uncle Phil, his two tufts of remaining hair, gray-brown, sticking almost straight up on either side of his bald pate. He wore a sweater vest over a short-sleeved white shirt, khakis and threadbare bedroom slippers.

"There's my dear little Sloane," he said, reaching out his arms. I released Alex's hand and gave my uncle a quick hug. "Look out," he whispered in my ear. "She's on a tear. She burned the pumpkin pie, and she's convinced dinner is ruined."

"Doesn't she make three kinds of pies?" I asked as we separated.

"Of course, but you can't have Thanksgiving without pumpkin," he said, ever droll. "And is this your boyfriend?"

I felt my face grow warm. That description still threw me, somehow.

"Yes, this is Alex," I said. "This is my Uncle Phil."

The men exchanged a hearty handshake.

"At least I have a guy to watch football with," my uncle said. "Damien's useless."

"I actually don't watch it much, but I like a good Thanksgiving game," said Alex. I wondered if he spoke with complete honesty, but Uncle Phil didn't seem to care.

"I hope we have good games, but they never are. Always a blowout," my uncle said. "Here, come on in. I'll take the wine. Better deliver the sauce right away to Kay so she can spend twenty minutes rearranging the table."

I saw Alex suppress a smile, and we entered.

Uncle Phil drew Alex toward the living room, and I went to the kitchen, where Aunt Kay and Calista were checking the meat thermometer.

"Almost there," said Cali, dressed in jeans and a pretty pink V-neck sweater, her blond hair pinned up haphazardly on her head.

"Thanks, dear. I can't read that thing without my glasses," said my aunt, who was known always to need glasses while never actually having them.

Aunt Kay wore stretchy lime green pants and a shirt printed with tropical flowers that was mostly obscured by a brown apron with a turkey printed on it. The brown almost matched the dominant color in her cropped waves of high-lighted hair.

"That smells delicious," I said. The aromas of turkey, sweet potatoes, baked goods and butter swirled about the kitchen; this is what a Norman Rockwell painting would smell like, I thought, if it had a scent.

"Sloane!" Cali turned and gave me a hug. "Where's Alex?"

"Uncle Phil's got him."

"Probably for the best at the moment," she whispered into my ear.

"What's that?" asked Aunt Kay, who was now violently mashing a pile of peeled and boiled potatoes in a bowl. "Are you living with that boy?"

"No, Aunt Kay. I still have the carriage house. Thanks for the wardrobe, by the way. It's perfect."

"Well, it was your grandmother's, so you might as well have it," she said. "It's just been sitting in our garage. What's this?" She pointed to the bowl of cranberries, which I'd set on the counter.

"Cranberry sauce. The bowl is for you."

"Where'd you get that?" she asked. "Target?"

I blanched, and Cali grinned.

"I made it," I said.

"It's beautiful," my cousin said, trying to get her mother on board.

"I guess that is kind of pretty," Aunt Kay said, cutting chunks of butter into the hot potato mixture, adding butter-milk and mashing it some more. "Saw something like it the other day, maybe at Target, I'm not sure."

Oh, great. I'm almost as good as something she saw at Target. I felt better when I saw Cali shaking her head, smiling.

I helped them extract and organize the dishes: the mashed potatoes, the sweet potato casserole, a string bean medley ("not that damn thing with the dried-up onions," my aunt declared), dressing, cranberry sauce and crescent rolls, along with, of course, a platter of turkey that my aunt carved from the enormous bird.

Aunt Kay fussed over the table in the dining room, finally getting everything where she wanted it amid the creamy china and crystal — dishes making a rare holiday appearance — and called out, "Dinner's ready!" before vanishing back into the kitchen.

Damien was the first one through the door, having made no change to his usual black attire for the holiday, though his hair seemed to have less product in it than usual. It looked almost calm.

My uncle followed with Alex, and I breathed a small sigh of relief to see him. He was none the worse for wear, and he walked over to me and greeted me with a light kiss. The gesture was territorial, I thought. I was his woman, and let them just try to keep us apart.

It turned out that my aunt had done her best to separate us. She'd made place cards for the oblong table, and mine was set next to Cali's seat, with Damien on the other side next to Alex. Cali noticed the arrangement, too, and was standing next to her designated chair, obviously feeling awkward, when Alex picked up her card and handed it to her.

"Nice to you see you again," he said. "I think this is yours." And he sat next to me with a smile.

"Thanks," Cali replied, amused. "I was looking for that."

She walked around the table and sat next to Damien, who got a wicked grin on his face.

"God, I love Thanksgiving," my dark cousin said, his tone suggesting he wasn't talking about the food.

My aunt entered the room holding four wine glasses and scowled at our rearrangement.

"Did you see my cards sitting there?" she asked.

"Nice calligraphy, mom," Cali said. "Got mine right here."

"Me, too," Damien said, her twin in conspiracy.

"Nice touch," I added with enthusiasm, and my aunt looked confused, as if maybe she hadn't arranged them exactly as she'd planned. Alex just smiled.

My uncle came in with the two bottles of wine Alex had brought, now open, and started filling glasses with each drinker's choice: white or red.

"Where's my glass?" Uncle Phil asked.

"We don't drink wine with turkey," Aunt Kay said, using the royal "we" that meant her and her husband.

"*I* do when someone brings nice wine," Uncle Phil said. "You got another glass?"

My aunt huffed back to the kitchen, returned with a squat, stemless number and set it on the table with a loud *whack*. My uncle filled it to the brim with the Beaujolais.

"Now sit down, Kay, and let's eat," he said, taking the glass and sitting at the far end of the table. My aunt pulled off her apron, lay it over the back of the chair opposite and sat, surveying the feast and her guests.

"Alex, it's so nice to see you. I don't think I've seen you since you graduated from high school with Damien." My aunt's pale blue eyes narrowly took in her exotic visitor.

"Thanks, Mrs. Goode. That was a long time ago."

"So that makes you quite a bit older than Sloane."

"Not really," I interjected. I felt Alex put a hand on my knee, reassuring and ever so subtly sexual.

"Mm-hmm," she said. "Well, Alex, since you're our guest, perhaps you'd do us the honor of saying grace?"

Ah. So she was probing his religion now. Alex looked contemplative for a minute, and then he bowed his head, surprising me. He'd never once shown an interest in religion, or I should say, any one religion; he read widely of many of them, as was obvious from his library, and yet, as far as I knew, he subscribed to none.

"O Lord that lends me life," he said, "Lend me a heart replete with thankfulness."

There was a pause, as if more was expected.

"That's it?" my aunt asked.

"Thank God," Damien said in an unintentional parody of the blessing. "Now we can eat."

"That was short," my uncle agreed with my aunt.

"Shakespeare," Alex said. "It's what came to mind. It goes on, but not in the way you might expect."

"I want to hear the rest of it," my aunt demanded.

"All right." Alex smiled and turned his gaze on me, his gray eyes light and clear. " 'For thou hast given me in this beauteous face A world of earthly blessings to my soul, If sympathy of love unite our thoughts.' "

I knew my face was red now. And there was that word again, *love,* obliquely presented as a prelude to gluttony.

Alex squeezed my knee and picked up his glass of red, taking a long sip.

"That's wonderful," Calista said, raising an eyebrow at me.

"I don't know about that!" Aunt Kay said.

"Works for me. Dig in," said Uncle Phil, oblivious to Shakespeare and the subtleties therein.

Overruled, Aunt Kay began dishing out turkey, and the other dishes made the rounds until our plates were overflowing.

"So how did you meet Sloane?" Aunt Kay asked Alex as everyone began eating.

"At one of my parties."

"Have a lot of parties, do you?"

Alex shook his head, taking a sip of the Beaujolais. "Once in a while."

"They rock," Damien interjected around a mouthful of sweet potato casserole.

"You go to his parties?" Aunt Kay asked her son, sounding shocked.

"Sure," Damien said. "A lot of the artists go."

I addressed Damien, mostly to interrupt my aunt. "Did you submit anything for consideration for the regional show?"

"Of course," Damien said. "Then again, it's probably too strange for Bohemia."

I couldn't help but smile at his brash confidence in his own uniqueness, his sense of superiority.

"I'm sure the jury will appreciate you," I said. "When are we supposed to hear something?"

"December 18th," Alex interjected. He caught my surprised look and shrugged. "That's what I hear."

"Maybe you can put in a good word," Damien said with a diabolical grin. "I'm not above a little friendly influence."

"The jury is untouchable, I'm pretty sure," Alex said, his tone arch.

"You give a lot to the museum, don't you?" Aunt Kay

asked. She was hardly eating. My uncle, on the other hand, was already getting seconds of the turkey and dressing.

"I help them out. I'm on the board," Alex said without elaborating.

"Must be nice to be able to do that," my aunt replied. "You're a lucky young man to have that kind of fortune."

Alex's face shifted; a hard set to his jaw showed she had hit a nerve.

"I don't feel lucky considering how I got the kernel of that fortune," he said, his voice brittle. "All in all, I'd rather have my parents."

"And how did they —?" my aunt blithely began, but I interrupted, seeing the pain in Alex's eyes.

"Cali, what's happening at the newspaper?" I asked as Alex shot me a strained sidelong glance and sipped his wine.

"The end is near," Calista said gloomily. "At least for some of us. They're going to let us know before Christmas who gets laid off, and then the victims will work a couple more weeks, if they want to."

"If you'd just married that nice boy you used to date, you could be in New Jersey by now," Aunt Kay said, as if being in New Jersey was a higher state of being.

"He left for a job," Cali said. "There was no question of me going. I'm fine here." Now she seemed as put out as Alex.

"Just another in a long line of adorable, short-lived boyfriends," Damien observed.

Cali shot him a dirty look and took a bite of her dinner roll.

"You kids just don't seem to be in a hurry to get married," my aunt said. "Do you believe in marriage, Alex?"

I turned toward him to see him swallowing more wine, mulling his answer in vague discomfort.

"Marriage works for some people," he said. His answer bothered me, and I kicked myself for it.

"Are you 'some people'?" my aunt asked with relish.

"I don't know if it works for me. I'm not married," Alex quipped.

"What about gay marriage? Do you believe in that?" my aunt pressed.

"Why not? Love is love, isn't it?"

"*I* don't believe in it," Damien interjected. "I mean, absolutely, we all should have the right to get married, but why would *we* want to copy an institution that heterosexuals have proven to be about as enduring as a piece of chewing gum?"

Cali coughed to cover up a laugh, and Alex's eyes twinkled at my gay cousin's diatribe.

"Oh, Damien, you just haven't met the right girl," my aunt said, her state of denial entrenched as my cousin snorted and took a big gulp of pinot grigio.

I was both amused and mortified. I didn't want to talk about marriage, but at the same time, the idea of a real commitment was something I'd like to know was available to me — to me and Alex — sometime in the elusive and terrifying future.

The rest of the meal passed relatively amicably, as Uncle Phil started reminiscing about turkey hunting as a boy, taking us to dessert, which we survived despite the lack of pumpkin pie.

After a decent interval in which we resorted to our medieval roles — women washing dishes, men watching football — Alex and I made our goodbyes and escaped.

"Sorry about that," I said to Alex as we got into his car. The starlit evening was cool and pleasant and especially quiet on this holiday night.

"Well, at least they didn't grill *you* all night," he said lightly, but his tone was brittle.

"I'm sorry," I said again. "I really thought they might focus on me. I guess you were more interesting."

"A real novelty, apparently," Alex said, steering the Mustang out of the driveway and onto the grid of roads that would take us to the beach. "Mind if we head to my place?"

"A little ocean therapy would be good for me right now," I said.

"And wine therapy. And sex therapy."

"You are all about the therapy," I joked.

"Don't remind me." He smirked. "Do you like having a family?"

I laughed. "Occasionally."

"All in all, I'm glad they're yours."

"You mean you wouldn't want them someday?" *Shit.* I was teasing him, but I hadn't mean to say that, to imply —

"Sure," Alex said carelessly. "Though if your mom is anything like your Aunt Kay, I'd have to skip all the major holidays."

Whoa. He'd answered my unintended question without a moment's hesitation. I decided not to press, but I felt warmer, comforted, imagining an actual future with Alex — though his response had been glib, and I still had no assurances. And I was still too chicken-shit to tell him how I really felt.

"What *would* your mother say if she knew what I was going to do to you tonight?" Alex continued in the same light vein. And I felt a familiar ache, watching his strong profile, feeling my desire grow.

"What are you going to do to me?"

"First, I'm going to — ah, but if I tell you, it won't be a surprise."

"You can tell me," I said eagerly, feeling a tingle through my body, the rising tide of arousal between my legs.

"You know, you came off too lightly at the hands of the Midwestern Inquisition," he said. "And now that I've been scarred by my experience, I feel it's my job to persecute you properly."

I bit back a smile. "So I should expect the Midwestern Inquisition?"

"Worse. The Florida pirate inquisition."

Now I was turned on. Alex as a pirate was too much to bear.

"In costume?"

"I don't think we'll have time for that, lass," he said, pulling into the drive of his building and parking in the garage. "First, give me your panties."

"What?"

"You heard me. Hand them over and don't say anything, or I'll have to punish you, prisoner."

I dutifully pulled off my underwear and handed him the slip of gray fabric. He put it in his jacket pocket, barely containing his smile, and escorted me into the lobby.

I was tingling with excitement and a tiny bit of dread as he followed me closely to the elevator, one hand caressing my buttocks. The doors opened, and an older woman emerged. Alex slipped his hand out from under my dress just in time.

"Alex! Happy Thanksgiving," said the white-haired woman, cheerful in a zip-up sweatshirt, sweatpants and sneakers.

"Thanks, Mona. Did you have a nice one?"

"Just Frank and I. He's asleep, and I'm going to walk off the turkey. And who's this?"

"Sloane, this is my neighbor Mona," Alex said congenially, as if he hadn't just stolen my underwear.

"Nice to meet you," I said as steadily as I could.

"It's nice to see Alex with a friend," she said with an approving smile. "I'll see you later."

"Have a good evening," Alex said as we got on board the elevator. When the door closed, he used his key to tell the car to go to the top, and then he turned to me.

"I told you not to talk," he said, the imperious pirate, though without the accent.

"How could I not talk? I couldn't offend your neighbor."

"There you go again." The elevator stopped at the eighth floor, and the door opened. He guided me into his foyer, and the door closed behind us. "Stop here. Bend over."

My eyes widened. He wasn't kidding. And God, I was wet.

"Grab your ankles," he said, his voice husky.

I did as I was told, dropping my purse on the floor, feeling the stretch of my legs and a slight discomfort. And a breeze as my dress rode up, almost baring me.

He took care of that "almost." He pushed the dress up around my waist, and I felt the cool air on my skin, on my naked sex. I closed my eyes, waiting.

And then he spanked me.

"Unnh." It wasn't quite a moan. Wasn't quite a word. It was my expression of negligible pain, of nascent pleasure, as the sting translated almost immediately into an electric rush of sensation.

"Did you say something?" he asked. I shook my head vigorously.

"Good. Because you already spoke twice. Which means I have to do that again." He spanked me again, harder this time and on the other side, and I bit back a cry.

In a moment, his hands were caressing the sensitive skin, massaging it, and I felt an exotic euphoria. He kissed the hot skin on both sides, then reached between my legs and ran a finger from my clit through my wet slit and all the way back.

"You look so fuckable like this," he whispered. "But I want to get you somewhere more comfortable. Stand up and follow me."

I stood, feeling just the slightest tingle where he'd smacked me, knowing it was part of the game. A game, I had to admit, I very much enjoyed.

I didn't ask where Alex wanted me. I wasn't sure if I was allowed to talk yet. I smiled a tiny smile and then suppressed it. I was his prisoner, after all, and I could be in deep trouble.

He took me into the kitchen first. I stowed my purse, and he told me to sit on a stool by the counter. Then he slipped off my sweater and lifted up my dress, arranging it so my pussy was exposed. He pushed my legs apart and stepped back, regarding me coolly.

"Wait here," he said, disappearing into the wine room. I resisted the urge to pull the dress down around me. I sat open and vulnerable in the large, empty kitchen, fantasizing about how Alex was going to screw me. Damn, but he knew how to push my buttons.

He emerged with a bottle of cabernet, of course, and took his time opening it, looking at me often, his gazes lewd and long, as he poured two glasses. He handed one to me and watched me drink.

"Thirsty?" he asked, taking a healthy swallow from his own glass.

As aroused as I was, I wanted to defy him, to get a reaction out of him. I smirked and downed the whole thing. He raised his eyebrows and took the glass, placing it on the counter with his. And then he moved slowly toward me, putting his hands on my knees. He lowered his face between my legs and kissed and mouthed my bud, prompting me to gasp with the sudden sensation of his heated and skilled tongue on my chilled and sensitive skin. Pleasure radiated from the spot where he tongued me, and I squirmed, wanting to push myself to him, unable to from my perch.

After a moment, he stood with a smile, licking his lips, and downed the rest of his wine. He held out a hand. I stepped off the stool, my knees wobbly, and followed him, eager for more.

Alex led me into the library, in front of the couch, and turned on his fireplace and the sconces.

"I have something for you," he said. "I told you I was going to do a little lingerie shopping for you. The pantyhose for later, and a few other things for now. Take off your dress."

My breath came shallow as I stepped out of the sandals and pulled the dress off over my head. A simple, satin bra in silver-gray was all I wore as he looked at me; he still had my panties.

"I couldn't stop thinking about you in that corset at Halloween," he said in a low voice, his gray eyes dancing in the firelight. He shrugged off his jacket and lay it over the back of the couch, and he started unbuttoning his shirt, revealing the alluring skin underneath. He left the shirt on, open, freed from his jeans, and I got wetter just watching him move around the room with his easy, muscular grace.

"So I got you this," he continued, pulling a garment from a pink shopping bag I recognized as being from The Velvet Glove. I realized he must have gone shopping last night after he'd left me; the store, given its wares, was known for its late hours.

When I saw what was in his hand, I pursed my lips and exhaled, wanting so badly to talk, to admire the corset he'd bought for me. It was deep red satin, embroidered with black roses. Thick black ribbons laced up the back. They were loose. Alex pointed to my gray bra, and I released the clasp in back and let it drop to the floor. My nipples pebbled for him, cool and aroused, as he came up to me, pulled the luxurious red garment gently over my head, eased my breasts into the cups and began drawing the laces taut against my back.

"You need help to put this on — and to take it off. From me and no one else," he said in a steely voice as I felt him draw the corset tight against my belly, which was still over-stuffed from dinner. I couldn't help it. A little chuckle came out.

He paused in his work at the ribbons and looked around at me. I touched the seam on the front of the corset that covered the hooks and eyes, opening it slightly so he could see the fasteners. I saw him try to suppress a smile.

"You'll get my help whether you want it or not," he growled, but there was humor in the sound, and I laughed on the inside at his playfulness. He made me feel safe in my desires; under his control, I was free.

As he resumed his lacing of the ribbons at my back, my anticipation grew. When he finished, my breasts were plumped high in the cups of the garment, and I felt thoroughly sleek and sexy.

Then he came around to my front and popped my breasts out of the cups so they stood at attention above the fabric. I wanted to make a smart-ass remark about the pointlessness of having underwear that didn't cover up anything, but I bit my lip, enjoying the depravity of being half-dressed in front of him, my exposed nipples peaking in the firelight. I watched him as he went to the bag and pulled out a garter belt and stockings.

Alex dressed me. The peculiar intimacy of this act only served to heighten my awareness of him, as his fingers worked their way up my legs, pulling up the silky black stockings; as he hooked the garter belt and buttoned the garters to the legwear. He didn't bother with panties. As he put everything in place, I leaned on his shoulders, and he occasionally ran a finger through my wet crease as he'd done in the foyer, making me shiver.

"Are you cold?" he asked.

I shook my head. He smiled at my close-mouthed answer.

"One more thing," he said, and he reached to a box on the floor and pulled out a pair of black pumps with wicked spike heels and open toes. I gulped when I saw the label. Jimmy Choo. I shook my head.

"What's the problem, prisoner?" Alex said with mock severity. "You don't like the heels?"

I shook my head again, reaching out to caress the black patent leather. I pointed to the label and frowned.

"Ah, you don't like my extravagance. You forget, this isn't a gift for you. This is a gift for me." He grinned and put the shoes on the floor. He held my hand as I stepped into them, immediately gaining a few inches in height. I still looked up to him, but I was closer to his eye level. Now I felt almost tall.

The heels completed my transformation. I felt my sexual power as much as Alex must have — his eyes had that smoky look as he circled me, looking me over.

He stopped in front of me and caressed my breasts, gently pinching each nipple, spurring my soft moan.

"You are so beautiful, Sloane," he whispered, dropping

the act, his voice suffused with emotion. "You can talk. Say whatever you want. I want to hear you when I fuck you."

"Oh, Alex." My voice was breathy. I reached out and touched his cheek as he devoured me with his eyes.

He shot forward and smothered my mouth with his, his tongue hungry as he wrapped an arm around my waist, pulling me in tightly. His other hand continued to play with my breasts, until he slid it down and began circling my throbbing clit with his thumb. As he did so, he pushed a finger between my slick folds, pinching and kneading my tender flesh inside and out until I whimpered under his demanding kiss.

"Now we finish what we started," he said, turning me so I faced the couch. "Bend over and hold on."

I leaned forward, bracing my hands on the back of the couch, moving my butt back and forth, tempting him, wanting him. He made a low noise in his throat, and I looked over my shoulder to see him stepping out of his jeans and briefs, his cock hard and thick and more than ready for me. He dropped his shirt on the floor and advanced toward me, putting a warm hand on my back, steadying, possessive. I groaned at this simple touch, and groaned louder as he used his other hand to work two fingers inside my slit, bringing me to the brink of orgasm.

And then I felt the moist head of his shaft slide into my creamy depths, deep and hard, coming up against my most sensitive spot as he thrust inside me. I could feel his balls slapping me as he drove in deeper, and I moaned with abandon, pushing back against him, teetering on the heels, falling out of the corset, a being of pure sexuality. Somewhere inside me was the burning love I felt for Alex, but even that was subsumed by the conflagration of this desire, this searing need, met again and again by his swelling cock pounding inside me. He reached around, twisting my breasts; he caressed my back and my legs as he moved; he took in every inch of me, this pretty package he'd created. I bent over farther, folding my arms under my lowered head on the soft cushions of the couch, offering myself to him more wantonly. He groaned, grasped my ass, fucked me harder; I turn my head to glimpse him out of the corner of my eye, a magnificent rutting beast in the firelight.

As I came, I knew I cried out loud and long. It was like hearing someone else, a stranger's voice through a thin hotel room wall, as I acknowledged the tremors wracking me in a rolling earthquake of ecstasy. I felt him come with me and reveled in his own unrestrained cries, knowing I did this to him.

I did this to him.

My Alex.

THE NEXT FEW weeks were strange and happy as I returned to class and spent many of my nights with Alex, even going to the Junction Box with him one Friday to hear Ez and the Emeralds. Alex was nervous about the crowd, but he ended up having a good time. Even better, I thought, he was starting to make real friends.

At the school, I worked on Christmas presents instead of an epic art project. I'd be more daring in the winter session, but for now, it felt good to make appealing pieces of pottery that I knew would please the few people on my list. All the while, I waited to hear who would get into the juried exhibition.

For Alex, I worked on an ice bucket for chilling wine, delicately patterned with swords and flourishes. I added raised shields on opposite sides, one featuring a castle, the other a ship — just the thing for a guy who was rediscovering his love of fantasy. The two handles were the crowning touch: snarling, hand-carved dragons. Gary especially admired the piece, and he helped me finish it with some of his texturing tricks. It became a work of art in spite of myself.

Around me, the peculiarities of a Florida Christmas unfolded. Blow-up decorations of sleighs and snow globes, along with excessive light displays, belied insistently green yards and trees and the fact that temperatures hovered around 75 degrees, with dips into the 50s at night. I saw guys wearing Hawaiian shirts splashed with reindeer. Locals dressed up as Santa and gathered to surf in the ocean in front of a massive crowd. And people wore shorts to outdoor holiday events.

I had trouble getting into the spirit, given the warm spell. Still, I harbored romantic notions about Christmas, spurred by memories of its beauty as I was growing up, and I talked Alex into getting an artsy white stick tree we could put in front of his balcony doors.

The eve of my last day in class before the holidays — the night before I was supposed to hear whether I'd been accepted into the regional exhibition — the temperatures finally dropped in the wake of a cold front. We ate Chinese food and strung the tree with white lights while listening to classic Christmas tunes. We drank wine and laughed over memories of our favorite holiday movies. And for my part, I felt almost normal. Comfortable. At home with Alex as we decorated the tree.

For sparkle, we added garlands of silver beads and

flocked silver balls we'd just bought. I found it funny that neither of us had ornaments; Alex wasn't ready to use the ones from his childhood, which were still at his old house. So I added pretty whelk and scallop shells I'd picked up and strung with red ribbon. And then Alex surprised me with a wooden box of a dozen Swarovski crystal snowflakes nestled in blue velvet.

"Where did you get these?" I asked, touching the smooth facets of the cool crystals.

"An antiques shop in town. They had several years' worth. It was too late for me to collect them on my own. I thought you might like them."

"They're gorgeous," I said, kissing him, savoring the sweet heat of his mouth on mine.

He looked on with pleasure as I carefully hung each snowflake on the tree, aware of how much they must have cost. They winked at me in the lights, hinting of an enchanted snowfall in a fairy forest far, far away.

"Let's go out and look at the tree!" I cajoled Alex.

He laughed. "On the balcony?"

"No, the beach!"

He escorted me outside, keeping an arm wrapped tightly around me; our sweaters did little to fend off the descending chill on this crisp, clear night. We walked down almost to the waterline, near low tide, and looked up toward his condo.

With all the lights off except those on the tree, the effect was like a little burst of magic in the darkness. A few other condos also sported glistening trees, but none were as pretty ours. Of course, I was biased.

Ours. I thought about what that meant as I turned to Alex, wrapping my arms around his waist, turning my face up to his. He leaned down and kissed me warmly, tenderly.

"It's almost as pretty as you," he whispered, hugging me tightly.

My blood rushed in my ears, blending with the relentless rhythm of the waves, as I felt his body meld against mine.

"I can't believe how much has happened in the past two months," I murmured into his ear. "And how lucky I am."

"That's my line," he said, pulling back slightly, rubbing a thumb over my bottom lip. He nipped the spot he'd just touched and kissed me again. "Come over tomorrow, and we'll celebrate. And then I thought we might go out of town for Christmas. The Keys. Would you like that?"

"I'd love to go to the Keys!" I exclaimed. "But what are we celebrating?"

His gaze flickered. "I — it's your last day of fall classes, remember?"

"That's right," I said, wondering what he was holding back as he kissed me again.

"Let's go up," Alex said. "I'm cold. And I want to try out the tree."

"Whatever do you mean?"

"Making wild monkey love by Christmas tree light, of course," he said, and I laughed, snuggling in his arm as we turned back to the condo.

School was festive the next day. There were decorations and spirited students wishing one another a happy holiday as they finished up their projects for the session, some taking them home, some making plans to continue their work in January. The more ambitious students were abuzz about who might be chosen for the juried show; the announcement was expected that afternoon, and I heard a list would be posted in the lobby. Every time I walked through, I anxiously looked at the bulletin board. A few students hung out there almost all day, drinking coffee and chatting nervously.

I didn't have that much time to dwell on what might happen. Gary and I were kept busy unloading kilns and organizing all the finished work, a mad rush of pots that, on the whole, looked nicer than they had at the beginning of the session.

"What are your plans for Christmas?" I asked.

"Oh, family stuff and making more pottery. My other work is pretty nonexistent during the holiday week, and I have a key to the school, you know," he grinned. "What about you?"

"Alex and I are talking about going to the Keys," I said. "I've never been."

"It's a special kind of perfect, except for the thousands of tourists that will be crowding the islands over the next two weeks. But I'm sure he can afford a place that keeps out the hoi polloi."

I felt my face get a little warm, hearing Alex talked about that way.

I heard a noise behind us and looked to the door to see Montrose standing there, much as he had when he'd caught me alone here before, wearing black, looking more venomous than usual. I blanched, fighting a sick, cold feeling in my stomach, and I saw Gary observing both of us, his brow furrowing.

"Yes," Montrose said, "must be nice to have such a *resource* at your disposal."

Anger displaced my discomfort. "He's not a *resource*. He's my *boyfriend*."

Montrose waved his hands dismissively, much as he had that night after his drunken advances in the rose garden.

"He's a resource when he serves on the jury for the museum and his *girlfriend* happens to be one of the chosen artists."

"What?" I was confused. Was I one of the chosen artists? And — had Alex been on the jury? My stomach did a slow roll. I hoped he hadn't. Especially if I got into the show. Especially when it had been so important to me to make it on my own.

"Happy holidays," Montrose said, meaning anything but. "Gorski," he nodded at Gary, then vanished again, leaving me stunned and Gary looking pissed.

"What is he talking about?" I asked.

"Let's go see," Gary said quietly, and we paused in our work to walk out to the lobby.

A crowd of students surrounded the bulletin board, where a new sheet of yellow paper was tacked in the center, on top of the news of classes, shows and apartments for rent. A few artists turned away with a clap and an exclamation of joy. Many more looked and left with glum expressions, with "Oh, wells" and promises to their friends that a few drinks would cure their disappointment as happy hour neared.

Gary put a friendly hand on my shoulder as we approached the board, and we worked our way into the loosening knot of students gazing at the list.

I saw Gary's name first, and I felt a flash of happiness for him.

"Way to go," I said. I knew his skills far surpassed mine, and even if he knew it, too, it had to be a thrill to be accepted, to be validated, to be proven worthy while competing against professional artists from all over the state and the Southeast. And he'd done it. So had Damien, I noticed.

"Thanks," Gary said. "We're in this together." Perplexed, I looked at him and saw his wide grin. "See?"

He pointed to the top of the list — it was alphabetical, of course, and my anxious eyes had spun right to the middle. But there I was. *Sloane Abbey, "Monsters of the Deep,"* it read.

I felt a rush of elation. And then a bone-crushing weight descended upon me.

Was Montrose right? Had Alex been on the jury? Was I on the list just because I was his fucking *girlfriend*?

"Do they ever reveal the jury?" I asked, trying and failing to keep my anxiety out of my voice.

Gary's response was soothing. "They generally announce it the same day as the selections. Wait a sec." He reached over and lifted the paper on the board, to the protests of the few students still trying to find their names, to reveal a second page. "Here it is," he said. "Montrose was on it. Interesting. And — "

He didn't have to say any more.

Alphabetical. Top of the list. *Alex Alwend.*

ALTHOUGH I WAS INCLINED to drive straight to Alex's from school, to confront him, to scream at him, to throw large, breakable objects in his direction, I went home first, took a shower and dressed meticulously for what, I tried to reconcile to myself, might be the last time I ever spoke to him.

He had toyed with me, and I had enjoyed it. Had let him possess me, even control me in the name of pleasure. In the name of, I scowled to think of it, *love.*

But a man who would use his influence to promote me without my permission, to undercut all of my work and ambition, was not a man who loved *or* respected me.

Could it really be true? I had to hear it from his own lips.

And I had to be cool, confident, self-possessed, and ready to walk away, to show him what he was about to lose.

I dressed in black — short black dress; a soft, short, thrift-store jacket with a silver faux-fur collar; black tights; black heeled boots. A long necklace of silver loops — not his pearls. Long silver earrings that made a statement. It was an outfit that declared my strength. But I still cried as I tried to put on my eye makeup, and I had to wipe it off and start all over.

I brushed my hair, leaving it long and straight. I stroked my lips with my deepest red lipstick. In the bathroom mirror, I practiced saying "Goodbye."

It made me feel hollow, not powerful. It made me feel lost.

My drive to Bohemia Beach seemed endless as I wended through the neighborhoods full of jolly Christmas lights and to the causeway, which soared over the dark water as if it would take me straight up into the stars. I had been so seduced by this place — not just Alex, but this place. This place full of beauty and magic and, I saw now more than ever, darkness.

I parked in the condo lot, pressed the code and entered the lobby. From inside the elevator, I texted him: "I'm here."

After a few moments, I felt the car move. All of my usual anticipation at this climb to the eighth floor had turned on itself, into something sour and sad, and when the doors opened, I entered the foyer with frost in my heart.

I went through the double doors and entered the living space, remembering the party where I'd met him, the noise and the chaos. Remembering him touching me, the beginning of the most intense experience of my life.

And then, there he was, Alex, coming toward me in jeans

and a black sweater, barefoot, gorgeous, kissing me on the cheek. A twinkle was in his eye.

"You have something to tell me?" He smiled.

I didn't smile back. Worse, I felt those perfidious tears working their way into my eyes again. I blinked them away and allowed a small, cool smile in return.

"I think you already know."

"Maybe you should tell me anyway," he said, taking me by the hand and leading me into the living area, to the couch next to the tree. "By the way, you look incredible. I thought we were staying in? Though I almost have to take you out to show you off now."

"What's to show off?" I settled into the couch. "Just an ordinary girl who will forever be known as someone who couldn't make it on her own."

Alex sat next to me, looking confused. "What are you talking about?"

"The juried show."

"You made it," he said, grinning. "I knew you would. That piece was incredible. And it spoke to me, as you must have realized it would."

I bit back my rising anger. "Spoke to you enough that you insisted I be chosen for the show?"

He looked stunned for a moment, and then a slow realization came over his face.

"No, Sloane," he protested.

"Don't try to deny it. You were on the jury. You never told me."

"It was a secret," he said. "I was honored to be chosen for the job. At least someone thought I had enough sensibility to do it. I wasn't going to jeopardize my position by revealing my role."

"Even to me."

"Especially to you," he said. "What's wrong? You were chosen! It's fantastic!"

"Because of you," I said, my voice cracking. I looked down, trying to hide the anguish seeping through my anger. "I can't do this, Alex. If you couldn't respect me enough to let me achieve this on my own, you'll never respect me."

"Wait a minute." His voice was clipped and tinged with worry, yet brimming with power. He reached over and lifted up my chin.

"Sloane," he said. "I would never do that to you. I recused myself."

"You what?"

"Recused myself. I refused to rate your work. You got in based on the ratings of the other judges."

I looked at him incredulously. "I did?"

"Of course you did."

"Even with Montrose on the jury?"

Alex lifted his eyebrows. "Yes. He actually rated you fairly highly. And the others couldn't say enough about your work, about how delightful and dark it was. How it made you think, told a story, was beautifully executed. And they were right."

"They really liked it?" I felt all of my pent-up emotions spill over, my anger shatter into relief, and another wave of hostility toward Montrose King. "Montrose told me I got in because of you."

"That bastard," Alex said. "I guess he wants revenge for his humiliation. But it makes me sad that you believed him."

"Oh, Alex — I'm — I'm sorry."

"Don't be sorry," he said, brushing a stray hair from my face. "I'm sad because I can't believe you could think so little of yourself. That you aren't worthy, when you are the most extraordinary person I've ever met. Anyone who could pull me out of myself the way you have — I just have to thank you."

I was snuffling, now, in a most unattractive way, and the corner of Alex's mouth turned up, wry and sympathetic.

He got up and disappeared for a moment, then came back with a tissue. I took it gratefully, dabbing my eyes, getting myself under control. Almost.

I had to tell him how I felt.

Alex sat next to me, took the tissue and threw it over his shoulder. He held both my hands, looked into my eyes and spoke.

"I'm so in love with you, Sloane."

I felt my words bunch up in my throat, and the tears that had stopped cranked on again. I let go of his grasp and reached up, holding his face in my hands, and drew him to me. I kissed him, a deep, lingering kiss, feeling the familiar current between us as he responded, passionate, tender.

"I love you, too," I whispered.

"I know."

"What?"

"You talk in your sleep." He smiled. "I love hearing you talk in your sleep."

"But you said — you said I said something about bananas foster."

He chuckled. "You said that, too."

"It was just a dream," I said, unable to prevent myself from kicking at his presumption. "I might've been talking about someone else."

"You used my name. Sometimes I would stay awake just to listen, hoping you would say it again."

"Well, once I dreamed that I was in love with Alan

Rickman in 'Die Hard,' but of course I wasn't. He was so nasty."

"But he had that great piratey accent," said Alex, looking more and more amused.

"I think it was supposed to be German."

"So you don't love me? Is that what you're saying?"

"No," I said. "I mean, *no,* that's not what I'm saying. I love you." My God, I was actually saying it. "I love you so much. I just can't believe you love me."

"What, you don't want to belong to any club that would have you as a member?"

"I always liked that joke. But in a way, it's true. Growing up in my house, I kind of got to learn that no club would have me."

He looked into my eyes with compassion, wrapped me in his arms and engulfed my mouth with his.

When he released me, I felt better. Whole. He loved me. And he believed in me.

"I thought you thought I was some innocent girl," I said, "a fool you would dump overboard once you were done with me."

His eyes narrowed. "Where did you get that idea?"

I lowered my gaze.

"I read one of your stories," I confessed in a whisper.

Alex laughed out loud, a deep, resonant sound, and I looked up in disbelief. He thought it was funny?

"Where'd you read it?" he asked.

"What do you mean? In your office!"

"Oh," he said. "Well, it's not like it was a secret. If it's the one I think, I also posted it on a web site that does critiques. Anyway, you should know better, Sloane. Characters are never truly based on real people, at least not in my stories, though there may be a grain of inspiration there."

"But you had the pirate, and I thought it was you, and then the girl who trusted him — oh, God. I'm so vain, I thought this story was about me. Is that it?"

He laughed again. "There's something to the notion of you as her, I suppose. You trusted me. You brought out the best in me. When I met you, you had a touch of innocence about you. And I take it you didn't read the ending. The pirate and the girl end up falling in love." I felt a mix of foolishness and excitement as he continued. "But you should never assume a fictional character is you. It's like what you say about your sculpture — inspiration mostly comes from within. And Sloane, I want you to know right now, I am never going to dump you overboard."

Warmth and joy suffused me — my mind, my heart, my body.

"I am so happy to hear you say that." I smiled at him, rediscovering my sense of mischief in my happiness. "But I dearly hope you'll dress like a pirate again."

"Come here, wench," he said, his voice playful and intense and aroused.

He crushed me to him, his mouth a sensual messenger from his heart, from his soul, an envoy from the dark place where he'd once lived, telling me he'd returned to the light, that he was mine.

I felt his urgency increase, and he reached down to slip off his jeans, to pull off my shoes and tights and underwear, to push up my dress. He braced himself over me, and I widened my legs for him to slide inside me.

He made love to me there on the couch, looking into my eyes, pushing me back into the cushions as he drove his passion into me under the shimmering lights of the tree, to the thrumming roar of the ocean and the beating of my heart.

ALEX SUGGESTED we throw a New Year's Eve party — more elegant than the party when I'd first met him, he promised, and less crowded — but the word was out. He threw a good party, and the condo was packed with happy people having a good time: artists, musicians, bon vivants, friends and neighbors, and a famous hometown surfer with a small entourage whose presence was slightly puzzling but definitely added excitement to the mix.

I'd dressed up, playing hostess in a little black dress and those black Jimmy Choo's Alex had bought. I wasn't much for teetering heels, but it seemed a shame for only one person to see me in such incredible footwear.

Alex wore black slacks and a gray jacket over a white shirt, complementing my muted palette, but more to the point, he looked elegant and relaxed, talking to people, for once, at home at his own party. He was even just a tiny bit happy from champagne, or at least I thought it was the champagne. I smiled to see him slip through the crowd, chatting as he went.

A jazz trio played classics from the American songbook, and floor space had been opened for couples to dance under a sparkling mirror ball, hung earlier by Jimmy the handyman. I was starting to think the mirror ball might be a fun permanent addition.

Half-hidden colored spotlights added to the festive air. Tables were laden with food, and a server wandered through with canapés. A bartender mixed up cocktails and poured champagne. In the background, the Christmas tree still glowed.

Calista drifted by, looking glum but gorgeous in a form-fitting ice-blue silk dress that set off her eyes and piled-up blond hair.

"Hey, Cali!" I called out. "What's the news in news?"

She turned and gave me a bittersweet smile and a hug.

"Not good. I'm out. One of two photographers laid off, along with a bunch of reporters and editors. Oh, and my date stood me up."

"What? Why didn't you tell me? I mean about your job," I said.

"You weren't around." She glanced over at Alex, who was chatting with Damien and his date, a handsome Latino guy with cafe au lait skin, glowing brown eyes and eyebrows far better maintained than my own. Alex caught my eye and made his way over to us.

"Alex and I went to the Keys," I told my cousin, a little sheepishly. "I'm sorry about your job. You're so good."

" 'Good' doesn't matter anymore in the era of pencil-pushing money men," she said. "Don't worry about it. I told you I've been working on Plan B. I'll step up the portrait shoots I've been doing, try to book some weddings. I'll make it. They're letting me work about a week into January, which will give me one more paycheck, and I get a small severance that'll help."

"The art school is looking for someone to teach portrait photography next session," Alex said. "Want me to put in a word?"

I wanted to hug him. Cali's face brightened. "That would be great!" she said.

"No problem. Expect a call on Monday."

"Thanks!" She moved away with a new lightness to her step.

I kissed Alex's cheek and whispered in his ear: "You are wonderful."

"They really do need an instructor. She'd be perfect," he said. "And I like that making her happy makes you happy." He turned and kissed me on the mouth, sending a delicious warmth rushing through my body. "Mmm, champagne. Want some more?"

I lifted my glass. "I have some."

"That stuff is good, but I'm holding the best for us," he whispered, taking the glass and handing it to the passing server.

He grabbed my hand and led me through the kitchen, past a caterer pulling a tray out of the oven, and to the wine room. I heard him lock the door behind us, and I felt a prickle of excitement, wondering what he was up to.

The room's familiar coolness struck me, along with the memory of the first time I'd met him here, barely three months ago. So much had changed.

Alongside two crystal flutes on the coffee table, the champagne was chilling in the fantastical ice bucket I'd made for him. He loved it, or so he'd told me when he opened it just before we headed for the upscale resort in the Keys. On Christmas Eve, he'd given me pearl and diamond earrings far prettier than my pirate props, but they didn't grab my heart as much as the gift I found in my carriage-house apartment once we got back home: a pottery wheel.

Now, he gestured for me to sit on the couch. He joined me, pulled the towel off the bucket and lifted out the dripping bottle. He slowly worked off the foil and muselet. I noticed it was the same kind of champagne he'd brought to our first picnic at his childhood home.

"This past week has been perfect," he said as he untwisted the wire that held the cork in place.

"For me, too."

The Keys had been magical: a private cottage on a rocky beach with turquoise waters, a hammock and warm, sunny days, most of which we spent inside, enjoying each other.

"I want you to know something," he said, picking up the towel and covering the cork. He worked it with his thumbs, and it opened with a satisfying *pop* and fizz. He turned his gray eyes to me. "I feel like you know me better than anyone. But what you may not know is that after everything that happened, my parents, my wild years, I came back to Bohemia Beach because I felt like I had no other option. It was the only home I knew. I thought maybe I could do some good here with what I had, partly because I thought it might be what my parents would have wanted. But it didn't feel like home again until you came here, until you entered my life. I know this place hasn't been your home, but I hope it will be from now on. With me."

His words left me brimming with empathy and love and uncertainty.

"What are you saying?" I asked.

"I want you to live with me. Live with me here, in Bohemia Beach."

"But —" I thought of my struggles to make it this far, to make it on my own, to prove myself.

"Don't protest too much," Alex said. "Not yet. Do I make you happy?"

"Yes," I said without hesitation. "More than I've ever been."

"I respect you as an individual. As an artist. I won't ever take that from you. I will only ever take what you are willing to give." He smiled with just a trace of seduction, with palpable love.

I let out a slow breath. "My apartment —"

"Would make a great studio. I've mentioned it to Mrs. Doctor —"

"Dr. Doctor."

"Right." He grinned. "We can rewire it for a kiln, no problem. You can work there when you're not at the school. Get away from me whenever you want, though I hope it won't be too often. And you can still work at the school, of course, even if it is with Gary."

I couldn't help but be amused by his joking reference to Gary. "Now I know you're serious."

"Are *you?*" Alex asked. "Can you? Will you?"

He carefully filled the glasses as I closed my eyes, trying to think. But I couldn't. My heart was shouting *yes.*

"It's a big step," I said. "I don't want to feel like I take everything from you."

"I don't want you to think of it that way. You'll be sharing my life. You'd be giving me everything, the best gift a man could ask for. You."

He handed me a glass of the champagne, and I put it to my lips.

"You might want to be careful with that," Alex said. "There's a promise in it."

My eyes opened wide as I peered through the faceted crystal. A ring rested amid the golden bubbles, an unusual ring.

The only way to get to it was to drink. And so I did, almost draining the glass, letting the ring touch my lips. I pulled it out and held it up so the light caught it.

It featured a tiny swirl of gleaming platinum, reminiscent of a hurricane, overlaid with a ship's wheel. At its center was embedded a glittering aquamarine.

Between the points of the wheel, outlined in a delicate platinum rope, were small diamonds.

"My pirate," I whispered.

"The stone is the color of the sea, and your eyes," he said as I admired its sparkling blue-green depths. "Turn it over."

A compass rose was etched into the underside of the ring, with an opening that let the aquamarine shine through.

"To misquote Auden, you are my north, my south, my east and my west," Alex said. "My guide in the storm. With you, I know where I'm headed. This isn't an engagement ring, only because I thought that might freak you out."

"That's true," I said, looking up at him, one corner of my mouth turning up even as I felt my eyes moisten.

He chuckled, but his gaze gleamed with earnestness. "If you will accept this, it's a promise of one. Whenever you're ready. Help me sail my ship. I love you. I need you."

Those last few words were the ones that took my breath away. I knew he loved me. But I didn't really know he needed me. For I knew I both loved and needed him, the way I'd never needed anyone.

I put the glass down and put on the ring — on my right hand, for now. It felt light there, right there. And at that moment, in the light of the stone at its center, I could see a future with Alex, one for which I would risk everything.

When I looked up at him again, his eyes were filled with emotion. I wrapped my arms around his neck, too choked up to know whether I was laughing or crying.

"Yes, Alex," I managed to say, kissing his cheek, his neck, his lips.

I could feel him smile against my mouth as he cupped my neck, sweetly devouring me.

"Yes to moving in?" he whispered between kisses.

"Yes."

"Yes to the future — to thinking about the future?"

"Yes. I always want to say yes to you," I whispered as we paused for breath. "But you'll know it when I say no."

Alex laughed, a sound I longed to hear over and over. He kissed me anew, a kiss as deep as the ocean that even now I could feel vibrating in my bones, becoming a part of me, the way he had become a part of me. I was home.

AFTERWORD

Thanks for reading! Sign up for my newsletter to get fun original content, giveaways, news and cocktail recipes, and I'll send you a free story. I also have a Facebook group where readers can hang out and chat about books and life — please join us in Lucy's Lounge.

MORE ONLINE:
LucyLakestone.com
Facebook.com/LucyLakestone
Twitter.com/LucyLakestone
Bookbub.com/authors/lucy-lakestone
Pinterest.com/lucylakestone/
Amazon
Goodreads
YouTube

ACKNOWLEDGMENTS

Thanks to the members of my talented writers' groups for their feedback, friendship and wine-fueled discussions of books and writing. I'd also like to thank the members of Spacecoast Authors of Romance for their support and inspiration. Thanks to Kathryn Gonzalez for shooting the crazy author photo session at the beach. Lastly, thank you to the tireless elves at Sky Diary Productions and Velvet Petal Press and to editor and friend Holly Martin for her perspicacious reading of the novel.

ABOUT THE AUTHOR

Lucy Lakestone is an award-winning author who lives on Florida's east central coast, among the towns that serve as an inspiration for the hot romances of her Bohemia Beach Series, including *Bohemia Beach, Bohemia Light, Bohemia Blues* (winner of the Golden Quill), *Bohemia Heat, Bohemia Nights* and *Bohemia Bells*. She's been a journalist, photographer, editor and video producer but prefers living in her imagination, where the moon is full and the cocktails are divine. She is also the author of a novel of romantic suspense, *Desire on Deadline*.

BOHEMIA LIGHT

The second BOHEMIA BEACH *novel*

⌾ঞ৹

a wandering surfer meets his match ...

Photographer Calista Goode is fresh from losing her job and barely over losing her latest lackluster boyfriend. So when she's tempted by a flirtation with pro surfer Wyatt Brooks, she figures a little no-strings fun is just what she needs. After all, he's poised to leave Bohemia Beach forever. But a chance kiss leads to a reckless tryst, throwing her life in turmoil. Her life may be in turmoil, but Wyatt faces a crisis, too — a turning point that brings his dangerous desires right to her door. Determined to protect her heart, Cali doesn't count on the overpowering allure of this serious, sexy surfer, who's about to make waves in her life and her art that threaten to wash away her every barricade.

LEARN MORE AT

LucyLakestone.com